Mulberry and Peach

ASIAN VOICES

HUALING NIEH

Mulberry and Peach
Two Women of China

Translated by Jane Parish Yang with Linda Lappin

Beacon Press   Boston

Beacon Press
25 Beacon Street
Boston, Massachusetts 02108

Beacon Press books
are published under the auspices of
the Unitarian Universalist Association of Congregations.

First published as a Beacon Paperback in 1988 by arrangement with
The Women's Press, Ltd.
Printed in the United States of America

95 94 93 92 91 90 89 88   8 7 6 5 4 3 2 1

Library of Congress Cataloging-in-Publication Data
Nieh, Hua-ling, 1926–
    Mulberry and Peach—two women of China.
    (Asian voices)
    Translation of: Sang Ch'ing yü T'ao-hung.
    I. Title.   II. Series.
PL2856.N4S213   1988   895.1'35   87-47881
ISBN 0-8070-7110-2
ISBN 0-8070-7111-0 (pbk.)

Contents

PROLOGUE

The Man from the USA Immigration Service

'I'm not Mulberry. Mulberry is dead!'

'Well, what is your name, then?' asks the man from the Immigration Service.

'Call me anything you like. Ah-chu, Ah-ch'ou, Mei-chuan, Ch'un-hsiang, Ch'iu-hsia, Tung-mei, Hsiu-ying, Ts'ui-fang, Niu-niu, Pao-pao, Pei-pei, Lien-ying, Kuei-fen, Chü-hua. Just call me Peach, OK?' She is dressed only in skin-coloured bikini panties and a peach blouse.

The Immigration agent is standing in her doorway. He is dressed in a dark suit with a black and grey striped tie. He wears sunglasses, although it's an overcast day. The dark lenses disguise the only distinguishing part of his face: eyebrows, eyes, the bridge of his nose. Only the anonymous parts are visible: bald head, sharp chin, high forehead, beak nose, and pencil-thin moustache.

He takes a form out of his briefcase. The form is covered with a cramped script in fountain pen. In the corner is the number: (Alien) number 89–785–462. In the other corner is a woman's photograph. The name Mulberry is written under the photo. One item on the form is checked in red: Application for Permanent Residency.

He points at the woman's photograph. 'This is you in the picture, right? There's a mole under her left eye and her right earlobe has a small notch. You . . .' he says, pointing at Peach, 'have a mole under your eye and there's a notch in your right earlobe.'

Peach laughs. 'Mr Dark, you have a real good imagination. What you see isn't real. What I see is real. You know what I see when I look at you? A tiger with nine human heads.'

'Please don't make jokes,' the agent says. 'May I come in and talk with you?'

'Only on one condition. You can't call me Mulberry.'

The agent comes in, looks around. 'There's no furniture in here.'

3

'The furniture belonged to Mulberry. I don't want anything that belonged to a dead person, so I called the Salvation Army to haul it away. Besides, furniture gets in my way. I like it like this.'

Peach moves aside heaps of clothing, boxes, bottles, newspapers, paints, and pieces of paper and sits down on the floor. She pats the floor beside her, 'Sit down here.'

Things are piled all over the room. There isn't any place for him to sit. He stands in the middle of the room, looking around at the walls on which are scrawled crooked columns of words in English and in Chinese.

A flower but not a flower
I am the flower
Mist yet not mist
I am Everything

When women grow beards
and men bear children
the world will be at peace

Who is afraid of Mao Tse-tung?
Who is afraid of Chiang Kai-shek?
Who is afraid of Virginia Woolf?

Mulberry murdered her father, murdered
her mother murdered her husband
murdered her daughter.

The head is connected to the thighs
Genitals grow out of the neck
normal people

Collins Radio Company
Warning Poster
Safety First
Beyond this point safety glasses must be worn
No running do not touch   Emergency Clinic
In work or play no matter where
no matter when
Safety First

Electric mirror electric comb
electric toothbrush electric brain
electric people
electric fan electric sun electric moon
electric kiss electric sex electric god
electric Virgin Mary electric electric electric
electric genitals.

A woman from Lone Tree
Car accident on a one-way street
Cause unknown
Name unknown

There are also drawings on the wall: A naked figure, beheaded, his two nipples, eyes; his protruding navel, a mouth. In one hand he holds a huge axe and hacks at the sky. With his other hand, he gropes for his head on the ground. To one side is a black mountain with a gaping hole. The head lies beside the hole.

A tall man sits stiffly in an armchair. Leopard's face: golden forehead, golden nose, golden cheekbones, black face, black eyes, white eyebrows. Forehead painted with red, white and black stripes. He bares his chest. His chest is an idol's shrine enclosed by bars. A thousand-handed Buddha sits in the shrine. The hands stretch out through the bars. The Buddha is locked inside.

A gigantic, swollen penis stands like a pillar in the middle of the floor. A butterfly bow has been tied around the glans and the two ends of the ribbon trail to the floor. Rose petals are strewn around it. A tiny Pekinese dog squats beside it, gazing up at a card that dangles from the bow: Happy Deathday Mulberry.

The agent stands in the room, still wearing his sunglasses, pen and notebook in his hands. 'May I copy down the things on the wall?'

'Go ahead. I could care less. If you want to investigate Mulberry, I can give you a lot of information. I know everything about her. Wherever she went, I was always there. What are you after her for, anyway?'

'It's classified. I can't tell you. Can I ask you some questions?'

'If you want to know about me, I won't tell you anything. If you want to know about Mulberry, I'll tell you everything I know.'

'I appreciate your cooperation.' The agent looks over Mulberry's form. 'What is Mulberry's nationality?'

'Chinese.'

5

'Where was she born?'

'Nanking.'

'Date of birth?'

'October 26, 1929.'

'And you,' he says pointing at Peach, 'where were you born?' The dark glasses flash at her. 'Where were you born, what date?'

Peach giggles. 'Mr Dark, don't try to be so smart! You think I'm going to tell you that I was born in Nanking on 26 October 1929 so you can prove I'm Mulberry? Well, you're wrong, Mr Dark. I was born in a valley when heaven split from the earth. The goddess Nüwa plucked a branch of wild flowers and threw it to the earth. Where the flowers fell, people sprang up. That's how I was born. You people were born from your mothers' wombs. I'm a stranger wherever I go, but I'm happy. There are lots of interesting things to see and do. I'm not some spirit or ghost. I don't believe that nonsense. I only believe in what I can smell, touch, hear, see . . . I . . .'

'Excuse me, Mulberry may I . . .'

'Mulberry is dead. Mr Dark, I won't let you call me by a dead woman's name.'

'You two are the same person all right.' His moustache twitches slightly. He pushes his sunglasses back up on his nose.

'You're wrong. Mulberry is Mulberry and Peach is Peach. They're not the same at all. Their thoughts, manners, interests, and even the way they look are completely different. Mulberry, for instance, was afraid of blood, animals, flashing lights. I'm not afraid of those things. Mulberry shut herself up at home, sighing and carrying on. I go everywhere, looking for thrills. Snow, rain, thunder, birds, animals, I love them all. Sometimes Mulberry wanted to die, sometimes she wanted to live. In the end she gave up. I'd never do that. Mulberry was full of illusions; I don't have any. People and things I can't see don't exist as far as I'm concerned. Even if the sky fell and the world turned upside down, I still wouldn't give up.'

'You smoke?' The agent takes out a cigarette.

'Good idea! Mulberry didn't smoke. Let's have a cigarette to celebrate her death.' She lights her cigarette, stretches out on the floor, staring up at the ceiling while she smokes. The window is open; a gust of air blows in. The newspapers on the floor rustle in the breeze. 'Ooh, what a lovely breeze!' She rolls on the floor in the breeze.

The agent looks away and goes to close the window.

'Mr Dark, please don't close the window. Wind should blow, water should flow. You can't stop it.' Peach unbuttons her blouse, exposing her breasts. 'What a nice breeze! Soft as a deer's skin!' The cigarette in her fingers falls to the floor.

'Mulberry, please behave yourself.' He puts the cigarette out with his foot.

'Mulberry . . . is . . . dead. I am Peach.'

'Please button your blouse.'

'Even if I button it, I'm still naked inside.'

'Don't make jokes. I represent the Immigration Service of the Department of Justice and I am here to investigate Mulberry.' He shivers in the breeze. 'OK, Peach, you win. I need your cooperation. Please tell me everything you know about Mulberry.'

'OK, listen.' Peach sprawls on the floor and pillows her head with her arms. She crosses her legs and swings her calf up and down as she talks. She is speaking in Chinese.

The agent can't understand. He paces back and forth. The papers rustle under his feet. He motions for her to stop, but she goes on speaking in Chinese. Gusts of wind are blowing in.

He finally interrupts her. 'Excuse me, may I use your bathroom?' The glasses slide down his nose, revealing his thick eyebrows. His eyes are still hidden.

'Of course.'

When he comes back, Peach is standing by the window, her blouse half-open, her breasts full. She looks out the window and smiles faintly. Her belly is slightly swollen.

The agent from the Immigration Service picks up his briefcase and walks out, without saying goodbye.

PART I

ONE

Peach's First Letter to the Man from the USA Immigration Service

(January 1970)

CHARACTERS

PEACH, one half of the split personality of the woman Mulberry-Peach. She is running away from the US Immigration Service agent while writing him about her wanders across America.
THE MAN FROM THE IMMIGRATION SERVICE, he represents the modern institutionalized threat.

Dear Sir:

I'm wandering around these places shown on the map. If you want to chase me, come on. Anyway, I'm not Mulberry. Sometimes I hitchhike. Sometimes I take a bus. As soon as I get somewhere, I leave. I don't have any particular destination. I'm always on the road. You can meet a lot of interesting people on the road. There is so much to see. One by one, the horizons sink behind me and new ones rise ahead of me.

Right now I'm on Highway 70 heading east. We're going 100 miles an hour. The car is black, painted with large red letters: March Against Death.

I got this ride in St. Louis. I was standing by the road and a car came toward me. I waved. The car stopped. Inside were all kinds of people: white, black, yellow. I couldn't tell the men from the women, they all had such long hair.

Conversation with the driver:

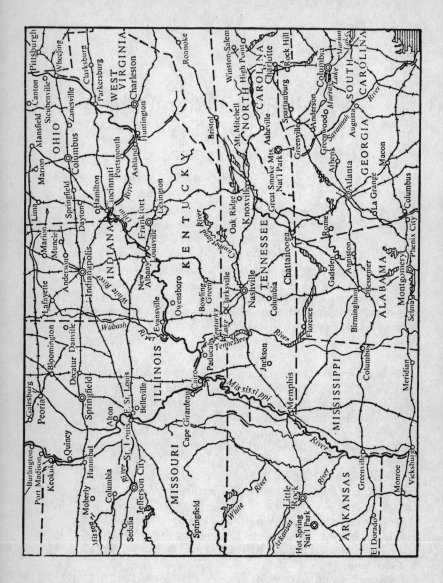

'Hey, you want a ride? Where are you going?'

'I'll go wherever you're going.'

'We're going to Washington to join the March Against Death.'

'I'll come along to watch the excitement!'

'Where are you coming from?'

'The moon.'

'Don't be funny. So you're the moon princess, huh? Why did you come back to earth?'

'I came back to start over. First, I want to have a baby so that human beings won't become extinct.'

'Has the earth changed any since you've been gone?'

'It's weirder, but it's more interesting.'

'OK, Moon Princess, get in!'

Inside the car is a mess strewn with newspapers, paper, coke cans, boxes, cigarette butts. Overcoats, blankets, and sleeping bags are piled on the seats. Eight people are squeezed together on top of these things. Counting me, that makes nine. I don't know where they are from. They are talking about student demonstrations all over the world: Japan, England, France, Czechoslovakia, Poland, Yugoslavia, and the US. They are talking about the dead. They tell me about the March Against Death, a demonstration against the war in Vietnam They tell me that such protests are becoming increasingly desperate and increasingly useless. But they want to show the world that people don't want to die anymore. Tonight in Washington 45,000 people carrying candles and wearing name tags with the names of soldiers killed in Vietnam, will walk single file from Arlington National Cemetery to the foot of Capitol Hill where there will be twelve coffins. The protest will last forty hours. Each person will place his name tag with the dead soldier's name in a coffin.

I tell them I also want to wear a tag. The name of the dead person is Mulberry.

They yawn one by one. It's boring to talk about death. The sun is shining right in our faces. Powdery snow drifts in the sunlight. If they keep on talking like this, I'm going to get out.

Someone in the front seat holds up a poster:

NOTICE
Office of Civil Defense
Washington, D.C.

Instructions: What to do in case of Nuclear Attack
When the First Warning is Sounded
1. Stay away from all windows.
2. Keep hands free of glasses, bottles, cigarettes, etc.
3. Stand away from bars, tables, musical instruments, equipment, and other furniture.
4. Loosen necktie, unbutton coat and any other restrictive clothing.
5. Remove glasses, empty pockets of all sharp objects: pens, pencils, etc.
6. When you see the flash of nuclear explosion, bend over and place your head firmly between your legs.
7. Then kiss your ass goodbye.

You said you wanted me to tell you about Mulberry. Today I'm sending you her diary. I'll be sending you more material about her, piece by piece. Let me tell you, I know every detail of her life. I know her thoughts, feelings, illusions, dreams, and memories. I even know things she didn't know or remember. We can work together on this. But you'll have to remember one thing: I am not Mulberry. She is afraid of you. But I'm not. As long as you don't call me by a dead woman's name, I can give you a lot of information about her.

I am also enclosing her photo album which she bought from a Japanese prisoner after the war, when she was returning from Chungking to her home in Nanking.

Peach
13 January 1970

TWO

Mulberry's Notebook
Chü-t'ang Gorge on the
Yangtze River

(27 July 1945–10 August 1945)

CHARACTERS

MULBERRY, (16 years old), during the Anti-Japanese War, Mulberry is running away from home with her lesbian friend, Lao-shih. Sometime after her parents' marriage, Mulberry's father became impotent as the result of a wound received in a battle between rival Chinese warlords. Later, the mother, who before her marriage had been a prostitute, began an affair with the family butler, and began to abuse her husband and children. As the story opens, Mulberry is running away to Chungking, the wartime capital of China.

LAO-SHIH, (18), a dominating, mannish girl about Mulberry's age. Her father was suffocated in the huge tunnel in which people hid from the continuous Japanese bombing of Chungking in the summer of 1941.

THE OLD MAN, (in his 60s), he represents the traditional type of Chinese. He has been in flight from the Japanese since they occupied Peiping, his home, in 1937.

REFUGEE STUDENT, (in his 20s), he represents the generation growing up during World War II. He is patriotic, aware of his rootless condition. He is rebellious against the old system represented by his father, who had seven wives and forty-six children, and lived in a huge gloomy house in Nanking. His father works for the Japanese. The angry young man reveals the inevitability of the coming revolution.

PEACH-FLOWER WOMAN, (in her 20s), she represents the natural life force, vital, exuberant, sensuous and enduring. It is this spontaneous life force that has enabled the Chinese to survive thousands of years of wars, revolutions

15

and natural disasters. She became the wife of a boy seven years her junior when she herself was a child. She raised the baby husband, and worked hard on the farm. When the husband grew up, he left her and studied in Chungking. The rumour is that he lives with another woman in Chungking. Peach-flower Woman is going there with her baby to look for her husband.

There is no sun. There is no moon. There is no sky. The sky and the water are one, both murky. The river dragon stirs up the water. His hundred hairy legs and clumsy tail swish back and forth, churning the water.

From the window at the inn in Tai-hsi, I can see the mountains across the river, so tall I can't see the top, like a black sword piercing the sky. The sky dies without losing one drop of blood. The gorge suddenly darkens.

A torch flares up along the river. A paddlewheel steamboat, blasted in half by the Japanese, lies stranded in the dark water like a dead cow. Along the river several lamps light up. Near the shore are several old wooden boats. Our boat, crippled while rounding the sandbanks at New Landslide Rapids, is tied up there for repairs.

The village of Tai-hsi is like a delicate chain lying along the cliffs. There is no quay along the river. When you disembark you have to climb up steep narrow steps carved out of the cliff. When I crawled up those steps, I didn't dare look up at the peak, or I might have fallen back into the water, a snack for the dragon.

A torch bobs up the steps. After a while I can see that there is a man on horseback coming up the steps, carrying a torch. The torch flashes under my window and I glimpse a chestnut-coloured horse.

Lao-shih and I ran away together from En-shih to Pa-tung. I am sixteen and she is eighteen. We thought we could get a ship out of Pa-tung right away and be in Chungking in a flash. When we get to Chungking, the war capital, we'll be all right, or at least that's what Lao-shih says. She patted her chest when she said that to show how certain she was. She wears a tight bra and tries to flatten her breasts, but they are as large as two hunks of steamed bread. She said, 'Chungking, it's huge city. The centre of the Resistance! What are you scared about? The hostel for refugee students will take care of our food, housing, school and a job. You can do whatever you want.' We are both from the remote mountains of En-shih and are students at the Provincial High School. Whatever I don't know, she does.

When we got to Pa-tung, we found out that all the steamships have been requisitioned to transport ammunition and troops. Germany has surrendered to the Allies and the Japanese are desperately fighting for their lives. A terrible battle has broken out again in northern Hupeh and western Hunan. There weren't any passenger ships leaving Pa-tung, only a freighter going to Wu-shan, so we took that. When we arrived in Wu-shan, we happened upon an old wooden boat which carried cotton to Feng-chieh, so we took that.

Towering mountains above us, the deep gorge below. Sailing past the Gorge in that old boat was really exciting, but it cracked up on the rocks of New Landslide Rapids and is now at Tai-hsi for repairs.

Lao-shih just went out to find out when the boat will be repaired and when we can sail. A unit of new recruits is camped out in the courtyard of the inn. Tomorrow they'll be sent to the front. I sit by the window and undress, leaving on only a bra and a pair of skimpy panties. The river fog rolls in and caresses me, like damp, cool feathers tickling my body. The river is black and I haven't lit the lamp. I can't see anything in front of me. The few lamps along the river go out one by one. Before me the night is an endless stretch of black cloth, a backdrop for the game I play with my griffin:

> Griffin, griffin, green as oil
> Two horns two wings
> One wing broken
> A beast, yet a bird
> Come creep over the black cloth

And the griffin comes alive in my hand, leaping in the darkness. The wings outstretched, flapping, flapping.

'Hey.'

I turn. Two eyes and a row of white teeth flash at me from the door. I scream.

'No, don't scream. Don't scream. I was just drafted and tomorrow I'm being sent to the front. Let me hide in your room just for tonight.'

I can't stop screaming. My voice is raw. When I finally stop, he is gone, but two eyes and that row of teeth still wink at me in the dark. A whip cracks in the courtyard.

'Sergeant, please, I won't do it again. I won't run away again . . .'

The shadows of the soldiers in the courtyard appear on the paper

17

window. The man hangs upside down, head twitching. Beside him, a man snaps a whip and a crowd of heads looks up.

'Lao-shih,' I pause and stare at the jade griffin in my hand. One of its wings is cracked. 'I don't want to go to Chungking. I want to go home.'

'Chicken. You getting scared?'

'No, it's not that.'

'You can't turn back. You have to go, even if you have to climb the Mountain of Knives. That's all there is to it, you know what I mean. Anyway, you can't go back now. Everyone in En-shih knows you've run away by now. Your mother won't forgive you either. You know when she was drunk, she would beat you for no reason, until you bled. She will kill you if you go back.'

'No. She wouldn't do anything to me. As soon as I ran away, I stopped hating her. And I still have Father. He's always been good to me.'

'Little Berry, don't get mad, but what kind of a man is he, anyway? Can he manage his family? He can't even manage his own wife. He lets her get away with everything while he sits in his study, the old cuckold, meditating. You call that a man? However you look at it, he's not a man.' She starts laughing. 'You said so yourself. Your father wounded his "vital part" during the campaign against the warlords . . .' She is laughing so hard she can't go on.

'Lao-shih, that's not funny.'

'So why can't a daughter talk about her father's genitals?'

'Well, I always felt . . .' I rub the jade griffin.

'You always felt guilty, right?'

'Mm . . . but not about his vital part!' I start laughing. 'I mean this griffin I'm holding. I stole it when I left. Father's probably really upset about it.'

'With all these wars and fighting, jewels aren't worth anything anyway. Besides, it's only a piece of broken jade.'

'This isn't an ordinary piece of jade, Lao-shih. This jade griffin was passed down from my ancestors. Originally jade griffins were placed in front of graves in ancient times to scare away devils. My great-grandfather was an only son, really sickly as a child, and he wore this piece of jade around his neck and lived to be eighty-eight. When he died he ordered that it be given to my grandfather and not used as a burial treasure. My grandfather was also an only son. He wore it his whole life and lived to be seventy-five. Then he gave it to my father who was also an only son. He wore the griffin as a pendant on his watch

18

chain. I'll always remember him wearing a white silk jacket and pants, a gold German watch in one pocket and the jade griffin in the other pocket, and the gold chain in between, swishing against the silk. When he wasn't doing anything, he'd take it from his pocket and caress it and caress it and it would come alive. You know what I thought about when he did that?'

Lao-shih doesn't say anything.

'I would think about what my great-grandfather looked like when he died. Isn't that strange? I never even saw him. I would imagine him wearing a black satin gown, black satin cap, with a ruby red pendant dangling from the tip of the cap, black satin shoes. He would have a squarish head, big ears, long chin, and thick eyebrows, his eyes closed, lying in the ruby red coffin with the jade griffin clasped in his hands.'

'Now your younger brother is the only son. Your father will pass it along to him, and you won't get it.'

'Don't I know it. I wasn't even allowed to touch it. I used to get so upset, I would cry for hours. That was before the war when we still lived in Nanking. Mama took the jade griffin from my father's pocket. She said she should be the one to take care of the family heirloom and that father would only break it sooner or later by playing with it. She had it made into a brooch. I really liked to play with cute things like that when I was a kid, you know? I always wanted to wear the brooch. One day I saw it on Mother's dresser. I reached for it and she slapped me and by accident I knocked it to the floor. One of the wings was chipped and she shut me in the attic.

'It was pitchblack in the attic. I knelt on the floor crying. Then I heard a junk peddler's rattle outside. I stopped crying and got up. I crawled out the window and stood on the roof, looking to see where the rattle was coming from. The peddler passed by right outside our house. I took a broken pot from the windowsill and threw it at him, then went back to the attic. He cursed up and down the street. I knelt on the floor giggling hysterically. Then the door opened.

'Mother stood in the doorway, the dark narrow staircase looming behind her like a huge shadow. She stood motionless, her collar open, revealing a rough red imprint on her neck. She was wearing the jade griffin.

'In my head I recited a poem that my father had taught me. It was like a magic spell to me:

> Child, come back
> Child, come back

Child, why don't you come back?
Why do you come back as a bird?
The bird's sad cries fill the mountains.

It's about a stepmother who is mean to her stepson. Her own son turns into a bird. I thought that Mother was my stepmother and that my little brother was her son. I thought if I said this poem, my little brother would turn into a bird. I decided that one day I would smash the griffin.'

'But now you want to give it back.'

'Mmm.'

'Little Berry, I think it's great you stole it. Your family loses twice: they lost their daughter and their jade. This time your mother might stop and think. Maybe she will change her ways.'

'Has the boat been repaired?'

'Not yet.'

'God. How long are we going to have to wait here?'

Tai-hsi has only one street, a stone-paved road that runs up the cliff. It's lined with tea houses, little restaurants, and shops for groceries, torches, lanterns, tow-lines. Lao-shih and I are eating noodles at one of the restaurants. The owner's wife clicks her tongue when she hears that our boat was crippled at New Landslide Rapids and will be heading for Feng-chieh once it's repaired.

'Just wait. New Landslide Rapids is nothing. Further on there's Yellow Dragon Rapids, Ghost Gate Pass, Hundred Cage Pass, Dragon Spine Rapids, Tiger Whisker Rapids, Black Rock Breakers and Whirlpool Heap. Some are shallow bars, some are flooded. A shallow bar is dangerous when the water is low, a flooded bar is dangerous when the water is high. If you make it past the shallow bar, you won't make it past the flooded one. If you get past the flooded one, you'll get stuck on the shallow one . . .'

Lao-shih drags me out of the restaurant.

'Little Berry, I know if you hear any more of that kind of talk, you won't want to go on to Chungking.'

'I really don't want to get back on that boat. I want to go home!'

Lao-shih sighs. 'Little Berry, if that's how you feel, why did you ever decide to come in the first place?'

'I didn't know it was going to be like this.'

'All right. Go on back. I'll go to Chungking all by myself.' She turns away and takes off, climbing up the stone-paved path.

20

I have to follow. We get to the end of the path and stop. Before us is a suspension bridge. Beyond it are mountains piled on mountains, below, the valley. There's a stream in the valley and the waters are roaring. Even from this high on the cliff, we can hear the sound of water breaking on the rocks. Six or seven naked boys are playing in the stream below, hopping around on the rocks, skipping stones in the water, swimming, fishing. One of them sits on a rock, playing a folk song about the wanderer, Su Wu, on his flute. There is a heavy fog. The mountains on the other shore are wrapped in mist and all that is visible is a black peak stabbing the sky.

'What do you say? Shall we cross the bridge?' Someone comes up behind us.

It's the young man who boarded with us at Wu-shan. We nicknamed him Refugee Student. He's just escaped from the area occupied by the Japanese. When he gets to Chungking, he wants to join the army and fight the Japanese. He is barechested, showing off his sun-tanned muscular chest. This is the first time we've ever spoken. But I dreamed about him. I dreamed I had a baby and he was the father. When I woke up my nipples itched. A baby sucking at my nipples would probably make them itch like that, itch so much that I'd want someone to bite them. I had another dream about him. It was by the river. A torch was lit, lighting the way for a bridal sedan to be carried up the narrow steps. The sedan stopped under my window. I ran out and lifted up the curtain and he was sitting inside. I told that dream to Lao-shih. She burst out laughing and then suddenly stopped. She said that if you dream of someone riding in a sedan chair, that person will die. A sedan chair symbolises a coffin. I said, damn it, we shouldn't go on the ship with him through the dangerous Chü-t'ang Gorge if he is going to die!

'I was in the tea house drinking tea and I saw you two looking at the bridge,' he says.

'So you've got your eye on us,' says Lao-shih, shoving her hands in the pockets of her black pants and tossing her short hair defiantly. 'Just what do you want, anyway?'

'Hey, I was just trying to be nice. I came over intending to help you two young ladies across this rickety worn-out bridge. Look at it, a few iron chains holding up some rotting planks. I just crossed it myself a while ago. It's really dangerous. When you get to the middle, the planks creak and split apart. The waters roar below you and you're lost if you fall in.'

'That's if you're stupid enough to try it.'

'Miss Shih, may I ask what it is about me that offends you?' Refugee Student laughs.

'I'm sorry . . . and my name is Lao-shih.'

'OK, Lao-shih? Let's be friends.'

'How about me?' I say.

'Oh, you!' He smiles at me. 'But I still don't know your name. Lao-shih calls you Little Berry, kind of a weird name if you ask me . . .'

'I don't want you to call me that, either. She's the only person in the whole world who can call me that. Just call me Mulberry.'

'OK, Lao-shih and Mulberry. You've got to cross this bridge at least once. I just crossed it. It's a different experience for everyone. I wanted to see what it felt like to be dangling on a primitive bridge above dangerous water.'

'Well, what's it like?'

'You're suspended there, unable to touch the sky above you or the earth below you, pitch-black mountains all around you and crashing water underneath. You're completely cut off from the world, as if you've been dangling there since creation. And you ask yourself: Where am I? Who am I? You really want to know. And you'd be willing to die to find out.' He takes a stick and draws two mountain peaks in the dust and joins them with two long thin lines.

A burst of flames shoots up towards us from the valley.

'Bravo.' The boys in the valley clap their hands.

'Hey . . .' yells Refugee Student, 'if someone gets killed you'll pay.'

Lao-shih tugs at his arm telling him that the innkeeper told her never to provoke that bunch of kids. There are eleven of them altogether, thirteen or fourteen years old at the most. They live in the forest on the other side of the bridge. No one knows where they come from, only that they are all war orphans and they live by begging along the Yangtze River. They travel awhile, then rest awhile before going on again. They want to go to Chungking to join the Resistance and save the country from the Japanese. They'll kill without batting an eye. They killed a man in Pa-tung. The ferry across the river wasn't running and there was no bridge, so the boys ferried people across. Someone on the boat offended them. They drugged him with some narcotic incense. They dragged him into the forest, cut open his stomach and hid opium inside it. Then they put him in a coffin and pretending they were a funeral procession, they smuggled opium to Wu-shan.

The boys are still laughing and cursing and yelling down the river. The one with the flute climbs up the mountain. His naked body is covered only with a piece of printed cloth frayed into strips. A whistle

22

on a red string dangles on his chest. He leaps onto the bridge, but instead of walking across it, he grabs the iron chains and swings across from chain to chain with the flute clenched in his teeth. He swings to the middle of the bridge, one hand gripping the chain. With his other hand he takes the flute from between his teeth and trills a long signal to the kids in the valley below.

He shouts, 'Hey, you sons of bitches. How about a party tonight?'

'We'll be there in a minute. Let's catch some fish and have a feast.'

He grips the chain and swings on. The frayed cloth flutters as he moves.

The boys scramble up the mountain. One by one they leap onto the bridge and swing across to the other side. They're naked as well, except for the rags around their waists. It's almost dark. The fog is rolling in. They swing on and on, disappearing into the fog.

'Hey, you guys, swing across.' Their voices call to us through the fog.

'OK, here I come,' Refugee Student jumps onto the bridge and swings across.

'Come on!' says Lao-shih tossing her head and walking out onto the bridge. 'We can't let them think we're chicken.'

I go with her onto the bridge. The roar of the water gets louder. The bridge sways violently. I grip the railing and wait for it to stop swinging.

Dangling from the chain, Refugee Student turns and yells: 'Don't stop. Come on. There's no way to stop it. The faster it sways, the faster you have to walk. Try to walk in time to the swaying.' I grip the railing and move forward. I sway the bridge and the bridge sways me. I walk faster. The mountain, the water, the naked boys, Refugee Student, all fuse together in my vision. I want to stop but I can't and I start to run to the other side while the bridge sways and swings.

Finally our boat is repaired. Lao-shih and I climb aboard singing 'On the Sunghua River', a song about the lost homeland. Twelve oarsmen pull at the oars; the captain at the rudder. There are six passengers on board: an old man, a woman in a peach-flowered dress with her baby, Lao-shih, me, and that crazy refugee student.

We get through Tiger Whisker Rapids.

Rocks jut up from Whirlpool Heap. Black Rock Breakers is a sinking whirlpool. We get through it.

Our old wooden boat is heading upstream in the gorge. To one side is White Salt Mountain. To the other, Red Promontory Peak. From both sides the mountains thrust upward towards the sky as if they were trying to meet, leaving only a narrow ribbon of blue sky above us. The noon sun dazzles an instant overhead, then disappears. The white light glistens on the cliffs. It's as if you could take a penknife and scrape off the salt. The river mist is white as salt. I stick out my tongue to lick it, but don't taste or touch anything. The water plunges down from heaven, the boat struggles up the water slope, climbing a hill of water. A mountain looms before us, blocking the way, but after a turn to the left and a turn to the right, the river suddenly widens.

The captain says that every June when the flood tides come you can't go upstream in this part of the river. Fortunately for us, the June tides haven't come yet. Clouds move south, water floods the ponds; clouds move north, good sun for wheat. Now the clouds are moving to the north. Rocks stick out from the river like bones.

We reach the City of the White Emperor. From here it's only three miles to our destination, Feng-chieh.

The twelve oarsmen tug at the oars. Their gasps are almost chants, ai-ho, ai-ho. Black sweat streams down their bodies, soaking their skin, plastering their white trousers to their thighs. Their calves bulge like drumsticks.

The captain yells from the bow. 'Everyone, please be careful. Please stay inside the cabin. We're almost to Yellow Dragon Rapids. Don't stand up. Don't move around.'

Some men are struggling to tow our boat through the rapids, filing along the cliff and through the water near shore, the tow-line thrown over their shoulders padded with cloth, hands gripping the rope at their chest, their bodies bending lower and lower, grunting a singsong, hai-yo hai-yo as they pull. Their chant rises and falls with the ai-ho ai-ho of our crew. The whole mountain gorge echoes as if it were trying to help them pull the boat up the rapids. It's useless. Suddenly white foam sprays the rocks and a white wave crashes down on the boat. The tow-line pullers and the oarsmen stop singing. Everyone stares at the water. The men use all their strength to pull the tow-line, curving their bodies, bending their legs, heads looking up at the sky. Pulling and pulling, the men are pinned to the cliff, the boat is pinned to the rocks, twisting in the eddies. The rope lashed to the mast groans.

The captain starts beating a drum.

It's useless. The men are stooped over, legs bent, looking up at the

24

sky. The boat whirls around on the rocks. One big wave passes by, another one rushes forward. The boat is stuck there, twisting and turning. The drum beats faster; it's as if the beating of the drum is turning the boat.

The tow-line snaps. The men on the cliff curse the water.

Our boat lurches along the crest of a wave, bobbing up and down, then lunges downstream like a wild horse set loose.

There's a crash. The boat stops.

The drum stops. The cursing stops.

We're stranded on the rocks.

First Day Aground.

Two rows of rocks rise out of the water, like a set of bared teeth, black and white. Our boat is aground in the gash between the two rows of teeth. Whirlpools surround the rocks. From the boat we toss a chopstick into the whirlpool and in a second the chopstick is swallowed up. Beyond the whirlpools, the river rushes by. One after another, boats glide by heading downstream, turn at the foot of the cliffs and disappear.

The tow-line pullers haul other boats up the rapids. They struggle through it. The tow-line pullers sit by a small shrine on the cliff and smoke their pipes.

'Fuck it! Why couldn't we get through the rocks? All the other boats made it.' Refugee Student stands at the bow waving at the men on the cliff. 'Hey . . .'

A wave billows between the boat and the cliff.

'Help.'

No response.

The oarsmen squatting in the bow stare at him.

'Hey. All you passengers in the hold, come out.' He yells to the cabin. 'We can't stay stranded here waiting to die! Come on out here and let's decide what to do.'

Peach-flower Woman comes out of the cabin holding her child. Lao-shih and I call her Peach-flower Woman because when she boarded the boat that day, she was wearing a flowered blouse, open at the collar, some buttons undone, as if she were about to take off her clothes at any moment.

The old man follows her out.

As Lao-shih and I scurry out of the cabin, Refugee Student claps his hands. 'Great. Everybody's here. We must shout together at the shore. The water is too loud.'

The old man coughs and spits out a thick wad of phlegm into the river. 'Please excuse me. I can only help by mouthing the words. I can't shout.'

'Something wrong with your lungs?' asks Refugee Student.

The old man's moustache twitches. 'Nonsense. I've been coughing and spitting like this for over twenty years. No one's ever dared suggest that I have TB.' He forces up another wad of phlegm and spits it into the river.

'If we're going to yell, let's yell,' I start shouting at the tow-line pullers on the bank. 'Hey!'

Lao-shih jumps up and yells along with me. 'Hey!'

There's no response. Lao-shih picks up a broken bowl from the deck and hurls it at the bank, shouting: 'You sons of bitches. Are you deaf?'

The bowl smashes on the rocks.

Peach-flower Woman sits on the deck, nursing her child. The baby sucks on one breast, patting the other with its hand in rhythm with its sucking, as if keeping time for itself, pressing the milk out. Drops of milk dribble onto the baby's plump arm. Peach-flower Woman lets her milk dribble out. With a laugh she says, 'Us country folk really know how to yell. That's what I'm best at. Hey – yo –'

The tow-line pullers on the bank turn around and stare at our boat.

'Go on singing. Sing. Don't stop now!' The old man waves to Peach-flower Woman. 'You sound like you're singing when you shout! If you don't sing, they'll ignore us.'

'Hey – yo –'

'Hey . . . Yo . . .' The mountains echo.

'Send – bamboo – raft –' shouts Refugee Student. Peach-flower Woman, the old man, Lao-shih and I all join in. 'Send – bamboo – raft –'

'Send . . . Bamboo . . . Raft.' The mountains mock our cry.

The tow-line pullers wave at us and shake their heads.

'Na – yi – na – ya –'

'Na . . . Yi . . . Na . . . Ya . . .'

We point to the bamboo on the mountains. 'Cut – bamboo –'

'Cut . . . Bamboo . . .'

They wave again and shake their heads.

'Na – yi – na – ya –'

'Na . . . Yi . . . Na . . . Ya . . .'

'Cut – bamboo –'

'Cut . . . Bamboo . . .'

They wave again and shake their heads.

'Na – yi – na – ya –'

'Na . . . Yi . . . Na . . . Ya . . .'

'Cut – bamboo – make – raft –'

'Cut . . . Bamboo . . . Make . . . Raft . . .'

The men on the cliff stop paying attention to us. The oarsmen squat on the deck, eating.

The captain finally speaks. 'What good will a raft do? There are rocks all around here. A raft can't cross.'

'How come our boat landed here?'

'We're lucky,' says the captain.

'If you're in a great disaster and you don't die, you're sure to have a good fortune later!' says the old man. 'Let's sing to the bank again!'

'Ho – hey – yo –'

'Ho . . . Hey . . . Yo . . .'

'Tell – the – authorities –'

'Tell . . . The . . . Authorities . . .'

Two of the tow-line pullers start climbing the mountain path.

'Good,' says the old man, 'those two will go tell somebody. Go on singing.'

'You sure know how to give orders! But you don't make a sound,' says Refugee Student.

'Forget it,' Lao-shih says, 'here we are fighting for our lives. Let's not fight among ourselves.'

'Hey – you – there – hey –'

'Hey . . . You . . . There . . . Hey . . .'

'Send – life – boats –'

'Send . . . Life . . . Boats . . .'

The two men on the path stop and turn to look at us.

'Good,' says the old man, 'they'll do it.'

'Na – na – hey – yo –'

'Na . . . Na . . . Hey . . . Yo . . .'

'Send – life – boats –'

'Send . . . Life . . . Boats . . .'

The two men on the path turn again and proceed up the mountain. Two others stand up.

'I've been steering boats in these gorges my whole life. I've only seen capsized boats, never iife-boats.' The captain puffs away on his pipe.

A boat approaches us, riding the crest of a wave.

'Na – na – hey – yo –'

'Na . . . Na . . . Hey . . . Yo . . .'

'Help! – help! –'

'Help! . . . Help! . . .'

The boat ploughs over another large wave, wavers on the crest and glides down.

'There's an air raid alert at Feng-chieh,' someone shouts to us from the boat as it passes, turns a curve, and disappears.

A paddlewheel steamboat comes downstream.

'Hey, I have an idea!' says Refugee Student as he runs into the cabin.

He comes back out carrying the peach-flower blouse. He stands in the doorway of the cabin, the collar of the blouse tucked under his arm; he stretches out a sleeve and playfully tickles the arm hole as the blouse billows in the breeze.

'You imp,' laughs Peach-flower Woman. 'You're tickling me. You make me itch all over.'

Refugee Student waves the blouse in the air. 'I'm going to use this blouse as a flag. Come on, everyone, sing! The steamboat will see it in the distance and hear our song. Come on. Sing: "Rise up, you who will not be slaves." '

'No, no, not that Communist song. I don't know these new songs,' says the old man.

'Well, let's sing an old one, then. "Flower Drum Song",' I say.

'OK!' Lao-shih races over to pick up the drumsticks and pounds several times on the big drum.

We sing in unison.

> A gong in my left hand, a drum in my right
> Sing to the drumbeat, chant to the gong.
> I don't know other songs to sing
> Only the flower drum song.
> Sing now! Sing. Yi – hu – ya – ya – hey –

Refugee Student waves the blouse. The old man taps chopsticks on a metal basin. I beat two chopsticks together. Lao-shih beats the drum. Peach-flower Woman holds her child as she sings and sways back and forth.

The steamboat glides by.

We stop singing and begin shouting. 'We're stranded. Help! Save us! We're stranded! Help!'

The people on the boat lean against the railing and stare at us. Two or three people wave. The boat disappears.

The water gurgles on the rocks.

'It doesn't do any good to sing!' The captain is still puffing on his pipe. 'Even a paddlewheel wouldn't dare cross here. There's only one thing left to do. The oarsmen will divide into two shifts, and day and night take turns watching the level of the water. We have to be ready to push off at any moment. As soon as the water rises over the rocks and the boat floats up, the man at the rudder will hold it steady and the boat will float down with the current. If the water rises and there's no one at the rudder, the boat may be thrown against those big rocks and that'll be the end of us.'

Lumber planks, baskets, basins, and trunks drift down towards us with the current.

'There must be another ship capsized upstream on the rocks.' The captain looks at the black rock teeth jutting out of the water. 'If it rains, we'll make it. When it rains, the water will rise and when the water rises, we'll be saved.'

Someone has lit a bonfire onshore.

The sky is getting dark.

The Second Day Aground.

The sun glistens on the rock teeth. The water churns, boiling around the rocks.

'It's so dry, even the bamboo awning creaks,' an oarsman says.

Our cabin is beneath the awning. It has a low, curved roof and two rows of hard wooden bunks, really planks, on each side. The oarsmen occupy the half at the bow. That half is always empty; they are on deck day and night. The passengers occupy the half in the stern. Our days and nights are spent on these wooden planks. The old man and Refugee Student are on one side. Lao-shih, Peach-flower Woman and I are on the other side. 'The Boys' Dormitory' and 'The Girls' Dormitory' are separated by a narrow aisle. The old man has been complaining that we are brushing up against each other in the cabin and goes around complaining that 'men and women shouldn't mix.' So he has ordered that men can't go bare-chested and women can't wear clothing open at the neck or low in the back. His own coarse cotton jacket is always snugly buttoned. Refugee Student doesn't pay any attention to him and goes around naked from the waist up. Peach-flower Woman doesn't pay any attention either. She always has her lapels flung open, revealing the top of her smooth chest. The old man puffs hard on his water pipe, although there's no tobacco in it, and makes it gurgle. 'Young people nowadays!'

The old man sits in the cabin doorway all day long, holding his water pipe, looking up towards the small shrine on the shore and occasionally puffing a few empty mouthfuls on his pipe. Refugee Student paces up and down the aisle which is only large enough for one person to pass.

Lao-shih, Peach-flower Woman and I sit in the 'Girls' Dormitory' and stare at the water around us.

'Hey, you've been going back and forth a long time. Have you got to a hundred yet?' asks Lao-shih.

'Ninety-seven, ninety-eight, ninety-nine, one hundred. OK, Lao-shih, it's your turn.'

Lao-shih paces back and forth in the aisle.

Silence.

'. . . Ninety-five, ninety-six, ninety-seven, ninety-eight, ninety-nine, one hundred. OK, I'm done. Little Berry, your turn.'

I walk up and down the aisle.

Silence.

'Ninety-three, ninety-four, ninety-five, ninety-six, ninety-seven, ninety-eight, ninety-nine, one hundred. OK, Peach-flower Lady, your turn.'

She paces up and down with the baby in her arms.

Silence.

The old man begins murmuring, 'Rise, rise, rise, rise.'

'Is the water rising? Really?' Lao-shih and I leap down from the bunks and run to the doorway, jostling each other as we look.

'Who said it's rising?' The old man taps the bowl of his pipe.

'Didn't you just say it's rising?'

'What are you all excited about? Would I be here if the water was rising? I said rise, rise because it's not rising. This morning that little shrine was right next to the water, about to be flooded. But look, it's still safe and dry by the edge of the water. July is the month that waters rise in the Chü-t'ang Gorge. It's now mid-July and the waters haven't risen. So here we are stuck in this Hundred Cage Pass.'

'Hey, I've already counted to a hundred and five,' laughs Peach-flower Woman.

'You're done then. It's my turn again.' Refugee Student jumps down from his plank and starts pacing in the aisle again. 'Hundred Cage Pass! The name itself is enough to depress you! Hey, Captain,' he yells, 'how far is this Hundred Cage Pass from the City of the White Emperor?'

'What is Hundred Cage Pass?'

'What's this place called, then?'

30

'This place is near Yellow Dragon Rapids. It doesn't have a name. Call it whatever you like!'

'Call it Teeth Pass, then,' he mutters to himself. He calls out again. 'Captain, how far is this place from the City of the White Emperor?'

'Only a couple of miles. Beyond that are Iron Lock Pass, Dragon Spine Rapids, and Fish Belly Beach.'

'Captain, can we see the City of the White Emperor from here?' the old man asks.

'No, Red Promontory Peak is in the way.'

'If only we could see the City of the White Emperor, it would be all right.'

Refugee Student laughs. 'Old man, what good would it do to see it? We'd still be stranded here between these two rows of teeth.'

'If we could see it, we could see signs of human life.'

'We've seen people since we ran aground. The tow-line pullers, the people on the boats, the people on the paddlewheel, but none of them could save us.'

'I've been sitting here all day. I haven't even seen the shadow of a ghost on the bank.'

Lao-shih shouts from the door. 'There's another boat coming.'

The five of us rush to the bow.

The people on that boat wave at us and shout something, but the sound of the water breaking on the rocks is too loud and we can't understand what they're saying.

'A lot of . . .?'

'On the way?'

'It must be that a lot of rescue boats are on the way.'

'Yeah, a lot of rescue boats are coming!'

The boat glides away.

'A lot of rescue boats are coming?' says the captain. 'A lot of Japanese bombers are coming.'

We scurry back into the cabin.

In the distance we hear faint thunder.

'That's not aircraft, that's thunder.'

'Right, it's thunder. It's going to rain.'

'When it rains the water will rise.'

The thunder approaches. Then we hear the anti-aircraft guns and machine guns. Bullets pock the water spitting spray in all directions. The Japanese bombers are overhead. Lao-shih hides under her quilt on the bunk and calls out to me. 'Little Berry, Little Berry, hurry up and get under the covers.'

31

Suddenly Refugee Student shoves me to the floor and sprawls on top of me.

A minute ago, we were standing in the aisle. Now our bodies are pressing against each other. He is bare-chested and I can smell the odour of his armpits. Lao-shih's armpits smell the same way, that smell of flesh mixed with sweat, but smelling it on his body makes my heart pound. I can even feel the hair under his arms. No wonder Mother likes hairy men; I heard her say that once when I was walking by her door. The thick black hair (it must be black) under his arms tickles me. I'm not even scared of the Japanese bombers anymore.

The bombers pass into the distance.

We get up off the floor. Lao-shih sits on the bunk and glares at us.

'The boat that just passed us has capsized at the bend in the river,' shouts the captain from the bow.

'What about the people?' asks Refugee Student.

'They're all dead! Some drowned, some were killed by the Japanese machine gun fire.'

'I wish everybody in the world were dead,' says Lao-shih, still glaring at Refugee Student.

I go back to the 'Girls' Dormitory'. Lao-shih strains to scratch her back.

'I'll scratch it for you!' I stick my hand up under her blouse and scratch her back.

'That's good, just a little bit higher, near the armpit.' I scratch the part between her armpit and her back. She giggles. 'It tickles! Not so hard. It tickles.' She has only a wisp of hair under her arm.

Refugee Student is pacing up and down in the aisle. He raises his head. 'Bombers overhead, the Gorge below. So many boats capsized. So many people dead. Nobody cares if the boats capsize, or if people die. They are playing a game with human lives!'

'May I ask a question?' says the old man. 'Who's playing a game with human lives?'

Refugee Student, taken aback, says, 'Who? The government. Who else?'

'These gorges have been dangerous for thousands of years. What can the government do about it?'

'We're in the twentieth century now! Sir, have you heard of the invention of the helicopter? Just one helicopter could rescue the whole lot of us. A place like the Gorges should have a Gorges Rescue Station. As soon as we get to Chungking, we should all sign a petition of protest and put it in the newspapers. We have a right to protest. We're victims of the Gorges!'

The Peach-flower Woman laughs on her bunk. 'Sign our names to a petition? I can't even write my own name.'

'I'll write it for you!' Lao-shih eyes me. I take my hand out of her blouse.

The old man sits on his bunk, rocking back and forth. 'It's a great virtue for a woman to be without talent. A woman is . . .' he is seized with a coughing fit and gasps for breath.

Lao-shih mutters. 'Serves him right.'

Refugee Student looks at the old man and shakes his head. He turns to Peach-flower Woman. 'I'll write your name down on a piece of paper. If you copy it every day, by the time we get to Chungking, you'll have learned how to write it.'

'Forget it! Forget it! Too much trouble.' Peach-flower Woman waves her hand. 'I'll just make a fingerprint and when we get to Chungking, my man can write my name for me!'

'When we get to Chungking, I'm going to turn somersaults in the mud!' says Lao-shih.

'When we get there, I'm going to walk around the city for three days and three nights,' I say.

'When we get to Chungking, I'm going to go running in the mountains for three days and three nights!' says Refugee Student.

'When we get to Chungking, I'm going to play mahjong for three days and three nights!' says the old man.

'Hey, look at that big fish!' Peach-flower Woman points at a big fish which has just leapt out of the river onto the deck.

'A good omen! A white fish leaps into the boat!' The old man shouts, 'We'll get out of here OK.'

The five of us turn to look at the shrine on the bank.

The water still hasn't risen; the shrine is still dry.

'There's a shrine but nobody offers incense. It would be better if we tore it down,' says Refugee Student.

'You ought to be struck down by lightning for saying such a thing!' The old man's moustache twitches. 'And the fish, where's the fish?'

'The oarsmen just put it in a bucket. We can kill it tomorrow and have fresh fish to eat.'

'It must not be eaten. It must not be eaten. That fish must not be eaten.' The old man walks to the bow of the boat, scoops up the fish with hands, kneels at the side of the boat and spreads his hands open like a mussel shell.

The fish slides into the river with a splash, flicks its tail and disappears.

The old man is still kneeling by the side, his two hands spread open like a mussel shell; palms uplifted as if in prayer.

'Dinner time!' yells the captain. 'I'm sorry, but from now on, we're going to have to ration the rice. Each person gets one bowl of rice per meal!'

The two rows of teeth in the river open wider. Even the rocks are hungry!

'One bowl of rice will hardly fill the gaps between my teeth,' says Refugee Student, throwing down his chopsticks. 'I escaped from the Japanese-occupied area, didn't get killed by the Japanese, didn't get hit by bullets or shrapnel, and now I have to starve to death, stranded on this pile of rocks? This is the biggest farce in the world.'

'You can say that again,' I say to myself.

Lao-shih sits down beside me on the bunk. 'Little Berry, I should have let you go back home.'

'Even if I could go back now, I wouldn't do it. I want to go on to Chungking.'

'Why?'

'After going through all this, what is there to be afraid of? Now, I know what I did wrong. This disaster is my own doing. I've been thinking of all the bad things I did to people.'

'I have, too,' says Lao-shih. 'Once my father beat me. When he turned to leave, I clenched my teeth and said, I can't wait until you die.'

'I cursed my father, mother, and brother that way, too. I can't wait until you die,' I say.

'This is the biggest farce in the world,' says Refugee Student as he paces up and down the aisle. 'The first thing I'm going to do when we get to Chungking is call a press conference and expose the serious problems of the Gorges. All of you, please leave your addresses so I can contact you.'

'Leave it for whom?' asks the Peach-flower Woman. She is sitting on the bunk, one breast uncovered. The baby plays with her breast for a while, then grabs it to suck awhile.

We stare at each other. For the first time I ask myself: Will I make it alive to Chungking? If I live, I swear, I'll change my ways.

'Maybe we're all going to die,' says Lao-shih softly.

'Hah,' coughs the old man, turning his head aside, as if one cough could erase what Lao-shih has said. 'Children talk nonsense. All right. Let's do exchange addresses. When we get to Chungking, I invite you all to a banquet and we'll have the best shark fin money can buy.'

'If you want my address, then you've really got me there!' laughs Peach-flower Woman. 'When we get to Chungking, I won't have an address until I've found my man!'

'Don't you have his address?'

'No.'

'Didn't he write you?'

'He wrote his mother.'

'Are you married to him?'

'Yes, I'm his wife. When I went to his house, I was really young. He's seven years younger than I am. I raised him. He went to Chungking to study. I stayed at home taking care of his mother, raising his son, working in the fields, weaving, picking tea leaves, gathering firewood. I can take anything, even his mother's cursing, as long as he's around. But someone came back from Chungking and said he had another woman. I can't stand that. I told his mother I wanted to go to Chungking. She wouldn't allow me to go. She wouldn't even let me go out on the street. So I just picked up my baby, got together a few clothes, and took off. All I know is that he is studying at Chang-shou, Szechuan. When I get there I'm going to look for him. When I find him and if he's faithful, we're man and wife forever. But if he isn't, then he'll go his way, and I'll go mine.'

'Is the boy his?' asks the old man.

'Well, if he isn't my husband's, he certainly isn't yours, either.' She laughs, and lifts the baby up to the old man. 'Baby, say grandpa, say grandpa.'

'Grandpa!' The old man pulls at his greying beard with two fingers. 'I'm not that old yet!' He coughs and turns to Refugee Student. 'If it's an address you want, that's hard for me to produce as well. In June 1937, I left Peking, my home, and went to visit friends in Shanghai. July 7, 1937, the war broke out, and by the 28th, Peking had fallen. So these past few years, I've been fleeing east and west with my friends. When will this war end? I couldn't stay with my friends forever, so I left them. I intend to do a little business between Chungking and Pa-tung. I don't know where I'll live when I get to Chungking.'

'My address is the air raid shelter in Chungking,' says Lao-shih coldly.

'You're kidding!' says Refugee Student.

'She's not kidding,' I interrupt. 'Her mother died when she was young. She escaped with her father from the Japanese-occupied area. She went to En-shih to study at the National High School; he went to

Chungking on business. In 1941, the Japanese bombed Chungking and more than ten thousand people suffocated in the air raid shelter. Her father was one of them.'

'That's right. The famous air raid shelter suffocation tragedy!' The old man talks as if Lao-shih's father became famous because of that.

Refugee Student looks at me.

'I don't have an address either! My home is in En-shih. I ran away.'

'No place like home.' The old man takes a gold pocket watch out of the pocket of his jacket and looks at the time. He replaces it in his pocket, and suddenly I remember the jade griffin on my father's watch chain and think of great-grandfather, clutching the jade in his hands as he lay in the coffin. The old man stares at me. 'I have a daughter about your age. After I left Peking my wife died. Right now I don't even know if my own daughter is dead or alive. Everyone has roots. The past is part of your roots, and your family, and your parents. But in this war, all our roots have been yanked out of the ground. You are lucky you still have a home, and roots. You must go back! I'm going to inform your father, tell him to come get you and take you home.'

'You don't know my family's address!' I sit on the bunk, one hand propping up my chin and smile at him.

The old man begins to cough again, and points his finger at me. 'You young people nowadays. You young people.'

'You sound like my father,' laughs Refugee Student. 'My father had seven wives. My mother was his legal wife. Father treated his seven wives equally: all under martial law. He calls them Number Two, Number Three, Number Four, . . . according to whoever entered the household first. Number Two was once one of our maids. She is five years younger than Number Seven. They got thirty dollars spending money per month and, every spring, summer, fall and winter, some new clothes. Once a month they all went to a hotel to have a bath and play mahjong. The seven women plus himself made exactly two tables. He took turns spending the night in their seven bedrooms, each woman one night, which made exactly one week. They had more than forty children; he himself can't keep straight which child belongs to which woman. The seven women called each other Sister, in such a friendly way, never squabbling among themselves, because they were all united against that man. Their seven bedrooms were all next to one another, dark and gloomy, shaded by tall trees on all sides. When the Japanese bombed Nanking, a bomb fell right in the middle of the house, and blasted out a crater as big as a courtyard. When the bomb hit, it was the first time those rooms were exposed to sunlight. My mother was killed in that bombing. The six women cried. My father didn't even shed a single tear. When the Japanese occupied the area my father collaborated. I called him a traitor and he cursed me as an ungrateful son. Actually, I don't have an address myself.'

We hear muffled thunder in the distance. It might rain. We look at each other, our faces brighten.

Third Day Aground.

'There's thunder but no rain. The Dragon King has locked the Dragon Gate,' says the captain. 'From now on each person gets only one glass of fresh water a day. We only have two small pieces of alum left to purify the water.'

Fourth Day Aground.

Rain. Rain. Rain. We talk about rain, dream about rain, pray for rain. When it rains, the water will rise and the boat will float out from the gash between the teeth.

'I'm so thirsty.'

When people say they're thirsty it makes me even thirstier. Here at the bottom of the gorge, the sun blazes overhead for a few minutes, yet we're still so thirsty. No wonder the legendary hunter tried to end the drought by shooting down nine of the ten suns.

The old man proposes to divine by the ancient method of sandwriting.

Refugee Student says he doesn't believe in that kind of nonsense.

Peach-flower Woman says divining is a lot of fun: a T-shaped frame is placed in a box of sand. Two people hold the ends of the frame. If you think about the spirit of some dead person, that spirit will come. The frame will write words all by itself in the sand, tell people's fortunes, write prescriptions, resolve grudges, reward favours, even write poems. When the spirit leaves, the frame stops moving.

Lao-shih and I are very excited about the sandwriting and fight over who gets to hold the frame and write for the ghost. The old man says he must be the one to hold the frame because only sincere people can summon spirits.

Instead of sand, we use ashes from the cooking fire and put them in a basin. Then we tie the two fire sticks together and make a T shape. The old man and I hold the ends of the stick. He closes his eyes and works his mouth up and down. The stick moves faster and faster. My hands move with the stick. These are the words written in the ashes:

DEEDS RENOWNED IN THREE-KINGDOMS FAME ACHIEVED FOR EIGHTFOLD ARRAY

'That's his poem!' The old man slaps his thigh and shouts. 'It's the poet Tu Fu. I was silently reciting Tu Fu and he came. Tu Fu spent three years in this area and wrote three hundred and sixty-one poems here. Every plant and tree in this region became part of his poetry. I knew Tu Fu would come if I called him.' Then he addressed the ashes: 'Mr Tu, you were devoted to your emperor and cared about the fate of the country. You were talented, but had no opportunity to serve your country. You rushed here and there in your travels. Our fate is not unlike your own. Today all of us here on the boat wish to consult you. Is it auspicious or inauspicious that we are stranded on these rocks?'

MORE INAUSPICIOUS THAN AUSPICIOUS

'Will we get out?'

CANNOT TELL

'Are we going to die?'

CANNOT TELL

'Whether we live or die, how much longer are we going to be stranded here?'

TENTH MONTH TENTH DAY

'Horrible, we'll be stranded here until the Double Tenth Festival. When will it rain?'

NO RAIN

The stick stops moving in the basin.
'Tu Fu has gone. Tu Fu was a poet. What does he know? This time let's summon a military man. We're stranded here in this historically famous strategic pass. We should only believe the words of a military man.' The old man shuts his eyes again and works his mouth up and down. We hold the stick and draw in the ashes.

DEVOTED SLAVE TO THE COUNTRY
ONLY DEATH STOPS MY DEVOTION

'Good. Chu-ko Liang has come. I knew his heroic spirit would be here in the Chü-t'ang region. Not too far from here, Chu-ko Liang demonstrated his military strategy, the Design of the Eightfold Array.' The old man concentrates on the ashes. 'Mr. Chu-ko, you were a hero. Your one desire was to recover the central part of China for the ruler of the Han people. Today China is also a country of three kingdoms: The National government in Chungking, the Communist government in Yenan, and the Japanese puppet government in Nanking. All of us here on the boat are going to Chungking; we are going there because we are concerned about the country. Now, instead, here we all are stranded in this rapids in a place not far from the Eightfold Array. Is it inauspicious or auspicious?'

VERY AUSPICIOUS

'Good, we won't die stranded here?'

NO

'Good! Can we reach Chungking?'

YES

'How long are we going to be stranded here?'

ONE DAY

'How will we get out of this place alive?'

HEAVEN HELPS THE LUCKY PERSON

'When will it rain?'

ONE DAY

'Mr. Chu-ko, when we get to Chungking, we will all go on foot to your temple and offer incense to you.'
The sticks stop moving.

The old man stares at the ashes. After a long time, he returns from his reverie. 'We're stranded in the midst of history! The City of the White Emperor, the Labyrinth of Stone called the Eightfold Array, Thundering Drum Terrace, Meng-liang Ladder, Iron Lock Pass. All around us are landmarks left by the great heroes and geniuses of China. Do you know what Iron Lock Pass was? Iron Lock Pass had seven chains more than two thousand feet long crossing the river. Emperors and bandits in the past used those iron chains to close off the river and lock in the Szechuan Province. The Yangtze River has been flowing for thousands of years, and these things are still here. This country of ours is too old, too old.'

'Sir, this is not the time to become intoxicated by our thousands of years of history!' says Refugee Student. 'We want to get out of here alive.'

'I'm sure it will rain tomorrow. When it rains, the waters will rise.'

'Do you really believe in sandwriting?' I ask. 'Was it you writing with the sticks or was it really Tu Fu and Chu-ko?'

'You young people these days!' He strokes his beard. 'Here I am, an old man, would I try to deceive you?' He pauses. 'I really believe that heaven cares about us and answers prayers. Let me tell you a story from the *Chronicle of Devoted Sons*. There was a man called Yü Tzu-yü who was accompanying his father's coffin through the Chü-t'ang Gorge. In June the waters rose and the boat which was supposed to carry the coffin couldn't sail. Yü Tzu-yü burned incense and prayed to the Dragon King to make the waters recede. And the waters receded. After Yü Tzu-yü escorted the coffin through Chü-t'ang Gorge, the waters rose again.'

'Who's the devoted son aboard this boat?' asks Peach-flower Woman with a laugh.

No one answers.

'How long have we been stranded here?'

'Has it been five days?'

'No, seven.'

'Six days.'

'Well, anyway, it's been a long, long time.'

'The moon has risen.'

'Ummm.'

'What time is it?'

'If the moon is overhead, it must be midnight. Do you have a watch?'

'Yes. It's stopped. I forgot to wind it. Who else has a watch?'

'I do, but I can't see what time it is. It's too dark.'

'It's so quiet. Only the sound of water on the rocks.'

'Is everyone asleep?'

'No.'

'No.'

'Then why don't you say something?'

'I'm so hungry and thirsty.'

'There went a big wave.'

'How can you tell? You can't see them from here.'

'I can hear them. It's very quiet, then suddenly there's a loud splash and then everything's quiet again.'

'Can you hear anything else?'

'No.'

'Are they still fighting?'

'Who?'

'Those people on the bank.'

'Oh, they won't come down here to fight. Mountains on both sides, water below, sky above.'

'Hey, everyone, say something. OK? If nobody speaks, it's like you're all dead.'

'What shall we say?'

'Anything.'

'When it's quiet like this and nobody is speaking, it's really scary. But when you talk it's also scary, like a ghost talking.'

'Well, I'll play my flute, then.'

'Good idea. I'll tell a story while you play the flute.'

'I'm going to play "The Woman and the Great Wall".'

'It was a moonlit night. Quiet like this. He woke up smelling gunpowder . . .'

'Who is "he".'

'The "he" in the story. He woke up smelling gunpowder. There were ashes everywhere. Even the moon was the colour of ash. When he woke up, he was lying under a large tree on a mountainside. The slope faced the Chialing River. Thick black columns of smoke arose from Chungking on the opposite bank. Reflected in the waters of the river, the black pillars of smoke looked like they were propping up the sky. Between the columns of smoke everything was grey as lead, as if all the ashes in Chungking had been stirred up.

'He stood up, shaking ashes and dust off his clothes. He had just woken up. He had been hiding in the air raid shelter dug into the mountain for seven days and nights. The Japanese bombers had come squadron after squadron, bombing Chungking for more than one hundred fifty hours. More than two hundred people had hid in the shelter. Eating, drinking, defecating, urinating, all inside the shelter. He couldn't stand it anymore and had gone outside. Another squadron of bombers appeared, and he didn't have time to run back to the shelter. He heard an ear-splitting crash and sand scattered in all directions. When he awoke, he saw someone digging at the entrance of the shelter. A bomb had destroyed the shelter. He took to his heels, afraid he might be dragged back by the dead inside the shelter. He ran and ran. He didn't know where he was running to. Only by running could he be safe. Suddenly he heard a voice calling out, "Let me go, let me go!" '

'Hey, keep on playing the flute, don't stop.'

'You want me to keep on playing the same song over and over?'

'Yeah. Go on with the story.'

'All right. The voice kept repeating. "Let me go. Let me go." He stopped, looked all around. There was no one in sight, only some graves. There weren't even any tombstones. He walked to the right. The voice came from the left. He walked to the left. Then the voice came from the right. He walked straight ahead. The voice was behind him. He turned and walked back. The voice was silent. He couldn't keep walking in the opposite direction. That direction would take him back to the shelter that was full of dead bodies. He had to keep going forwards. He heard the voice again. "Let me go, let me go." The voice seemed to come from under his feet. He stopped. It was coming from the right. He walked to the right and the voice got louder. He saw an empty grave. The coffin had probably been removed recently. A woman was lying in the grave, her head sticking out of the grave, her eyes closed, repeatedly mumbling, "Let me go." He dragged her out of the pit. Then he recognised that she had been among the people hiding in the shelter. He couldn't tell if she was the ghost of someone killed in an explosion, or a living person who had escaped the bombing. He had a canteen with him. He poured some water down her throat. She regained consciousness. He asked her how she got out of the shelter and into the grave. She stared at him, as if she hadn't heard. She said, "Tzu-jao, can't you run faster than that?" He told her his name was Po-fu. The woman said, "Don't try to fool me. Has the soldier gone?" He said, "The bombers have gone." She became impatient and repeated over and over, "I mean the Japanese soldier who tried to rape me. Has he gone?" The man said, "There are no Japanese soldiers in Chungking." '

42

'The flute sounds especially nice tonight. That poor lonely woman looking for her husband and crying at the Great Wall. What about the woman?'

'Which woman? The woman at the Great Wall or the woman in the grave?'

'The one in the grave. Hurry up and tell us the rest of the story. It's like a modern-day Gothic.'

'OK. The woman sat down, beating the ground with her fist over and over. "This isn't Chungking. This is Nanking. We've just gotten married. The Japanese have just invaded the city." The man groped for his watch in his pocket, struck a match, and showed her the name Po-fu engraved on the watch. The woman said, "Don't try to fool me, Tzu-jao! This is a matter of life and death. Run quick. The Japanese are combing Nanking for Chinese soldiers. They think that anyone with calluses on his hands is a soldier: rickshaw pullers, carpenters, coolies. Yesterday in one day they took away one thousand three hundred people. The dogs in Nanking are getting fat, there are so many corpses to feed on." The woman looked around and asked, "Has the soldier gone?" He could only reply, "Yes, he's gone." The woman pointed to the river. "It was on that road through the bamboo thicket. I was walking in front. He was walking behind me. You know, Tzu-jao, we have been married more than a week and you still haven't been able to touch me. You called me a stone girl." '

'What do you mean, "stone girl"?'

'Stone girl. It means a girl who can't have sex.'

'Go on, you're just getting to the best part.'

'The woman kept on talking like that. She said, "It happened on that road through the bamboo thicket. I was walking in front. He was walking behind me. In full daylight, he stripped off his clothes as he followed me, throwing his uniform, boots, pants, underwear down at the side of the road. He stripped naked, leaving only his bayonet hanging by his side. When he was wearing his uniform, he seemed so much taller. Naked he looked shorter, even shorter than I am. He ripped off my clothes. He tossed me about like a doll. He threw down his bayonet. Just then, Tzu-jao, you came running up. Don't you remember? You ran out of Nanking, but you came back into the city. That Japanese was a head shorter than you. When he saw you, he jumped on your back, two hands gripping your neck. He was biting the back of your neck with his teeth. You reached back and grabbed his penis. You couldn't hold onto it. It was too small. As last you got it. You pulled it back and forth with all your strength. He screamed.

43

Some people from the International Relief Committee came running up. The head of the committee was a German. He ordered the Japanese soldier to leave. But the soldier kept biting your neck. You wouldn't let go of his penis. Finally the German put out his arm and the Japanese saw his Nazi insignia. He slipped off your back and ran. He didn't even pick up his clothes or his bayonet."'

'What a good story. Then what happened to her?'

'When? After the rape incident in Nanking? Or after the bombing in Chungking?'

'After the bombing.'

'Her husband and son were looking for her. Just before the bombers hit, her two-year-old son started crying in the shelter. The people in the shelter cursed him and wanted to beat him to death. The father had to take the child outside. The mother was too anxious to stay in the shelter. She went outside to look for her husband and son. Then the bombers hit and bombed the shelter. After the bombing was over, she didn't know how she got into the grave. She didn't remember anything. She thought she was in Nanking and was reliving the past. Her husband had gone with their child to the police station to look at the list of the dead. I took her to the police station. She was still suffering from shell-shock and didn't recognise her husband and child. She said she had just gotten married and didn't have any children. She still believed she was in Nanking and was reliving the slaughter. When I saw that she was reunited with her husband and child, I left.'

'You? Are you telling us a story, or is that something that really happened to you?'

'It really happened to me. We've been stranded here so long that it seems like a story from a former life,' says the old man.

Refugee Student is still playing 'The Great Wall' on his flute.

> With the New Year comes the spring
> Every house lights red lanterns
> Other husbands go home to their families
> My husband builds the Great Wall

A big wave passes with a crash. Then it's quiet. Another crash, then it's quiet. Human heads are bobbing in the water, their eyes wide open and staring at the sky. Everything is silent.

A large eagle flies overhead. It circles the heads and flaps its huge black wings. It is beautiful. It is dancing.

Suddenly the old man and Lao-shih are sitting on the eagle's wings,

44

each sitting on one side, like on a seesaw. The eagle wheels in the air. They wave at me.

Refugee Student suddenly appears, riding on the eagle's back. He begins to play his flute to the rhythm of the eagle's dance.

The eagle carries them off down the river.

The human heads float downstream.

I call to the eagle, begging them to stop. I want to fly away on the eagle, too.

Peach-flower Woman, her breasts exposed, appears, riding the crest of a wave. She waves at me. She wants me to join her on the waves.

The sound of the flute gets louder.

I wake up. The flute is coming from the stern. Lao-shih, the old man, and Peach-flower Woman are all asleep. Peach-flower Woman hugs her child to her bare breasts.

I sit up.

The sound of the flute suddenly stops.

I go out of the cabin and walk around the bales of cotton which are piled in the stern.

Refugee Student, bare-chested, is lying on the deck.

The gorge is black. He reaches up to me. I lie down on top of him. We don't say anything.

My virgin blood trickles down his legs. He wipes it off with spit.

The Sixth Day Aground.

There is shouting on the river.

We run out. A ship tilts down over the crest of a wave. It spins around in the whirlpool. The people on the ship scream, women and children cry as it spins faster and faster, like a top.

White foam bubbles around the lip of the whirlpool. The foam churns up into a wall of water, separating us from the spinning ship. Then the wall collapses with a roar. The ship splits open like a watermelon. Everyone on board is tossed into the water.

Another huge wave rolls by. Everyone in the water has disappeared.

Silence.

The river rushes on. The sun dazzles overhead.

The beating of the drum begins.

Refugee Student, his shirt off, thick black hair bristling in his armpits and above his lip, is pounding on the drum, every muscle straining, teeth clenched. He raises the drumsticks over his head and pounds on the drum with all his strength. He isn't beating the drum. He is beating the mountains, the heavens, the waters.

The mountains, the heavens, the waters explode with each beat.

'Don't stop, don't stop. A victory song,' shouts the old man.

A crow flies toward our boat.

Refugee Student throws down the drumsticks and glares at the crow.

'Black crow overhead, that means if disaster doesn't strike misfortune will,' Peach-flower Woman says as she holds her child.

I pick up an empty bottle and throw it at the crow. 'I'll kill you, you stupid bird.' The bottle shatters on a rock.

Lao-shih picks up a bowl and hurls it at the crow. 'You bastard. Get out of here!' The bowl shatters on a rock.

The crow circles overhead.

The old man shakes his fist at the crow. His face turns purple. 'You think you can scare us, don't you? You think I'll just die stranded here, do you? When the warlords were fighting, I didn't die. When the Japanese were fighting, I didn't die. Do you think I'm going to die now, on this pile of rocks? Hah!' He spits at the crow.

'Goddam motherfucker,' shouts Refugee Student, leaping at the crow. 'You can't scare me. Just wait and see. I won't die. I'll survive and I'll raise hell, that'll show you. Mountains, waters, animals, crows. Can you destroy the human race? You can destroy a man's body, but you can't destroy his spirit. Ships capsize, people drown, mountains are still mountains and water is still water. Millions of people are being born, millions of people have survived these rapids. The world belongs to the young. Don't you know that, you bastard? People won't die out. Don't you know that? They won't die out.'

The old man claps his hands. 'Attention, please. Everybody. This is a matter of life and death. I have something to say that I can't hold back any longer. I think the captain has been playing a game with our lives. This gorge is even more dangerous than Hundred Cage Pass. Of course he knows this danger. He's been sailing these gorges all his life. This boat should only carry freight; they shouldn't allow passengers. He certainly shouldn't take our money before we arrive safely at our destination. The ticket for this old wooden boat costs as much as a paddlewheel. But since he has taken passengers and taken our money, he is responsible. First, he ought to ensure our safety; next, he ought to take care of feeding us. When we cracked up on New Landslide Rapids, we were delayed four days in Tai-hsi. We trusted the captain. We didn't ask him to return our money. We got back on the boat. Then the tow-line broke at Yellow Dragon Rapids. We've been stranded here since then. The Yangtze River, several thousand miles long, is the greatest river in Asia, and we have to ration drinking water. What a joke. From that day on, he took no emergency measures. Not only that, but when we were screaming for help at the top of our lungs, he made sarcastic remarks. The captain and the crew know how to handle boats. In case anything happens, they'll know what to do and how to escape. We don't know what to do. The passengers and the crew make thirteen people, but there are only six of us, and we are all either too old or women and children. We're outnumbered and we can't fight them. And so, I want to stand up and be counted and speak out for justice. I represent the six passengers, including the baby, and I demand that the captain do something.'

The oarsmen and the passengers are silent.

The captain, squatting on deck, blank expression, sucks the empty pipe in his mouth. 'You people just don't understand the difficulties in sailing these Gorges. We boatmen make our living by relying on the water and the sky. If it doesn't rain, the water won't rise and there's nothing we can do about it. Whether it's sailing the river or riding a horse, there's always danger involved. There's a slippery stone slab in front of everyone's door. No one can guarantee you won't slip on it and crack your skull. For human beings there is life and death, for things there is damage and destruction. It all depends on the will of Heaven. If you want someone to die, the person won't die. But if Heaven commands it, he will die. All I can do now is ask that you passengers calm down and wait patiently a while longer.'

'God, wait for how long?'

'If we have to wait, we at least ought to have food to eat and water to drink!'

'There's plenty of water in the river, and plenty of fish.' says the captain. 'If there's no more firewood, then eat raw fish. If there's no more alum, then drink muddy water. We boatmen can live like that. Can't you?' He sucks hard on his pipe. 'When our tobacco is gone, we smoke the dregs; when that's gone, we smoke the residue.' He reaches down and strikes the drum. 'Those who can't eat raw fish can chew the leather on this drum.'

Refugee Student spits at the captain. 'I'll chew on you.'

The captain throws his head back and laughs. 'Go ahead and chew. Go ahead and slice me up. Kill me. What good will that do? When the water rises and the ship floats up, you will need someone at the rudder.'

'Dice!' I yell as I cross the aisle into the 'Boys' Dormitory'. The old man is sitting on his bunk, rolling three cubes of dice around in his hand. I snatch them away and cast them on the bunk. 'Come on, let's gamble. Everybody, come here.'

'Just what I was thinking!' As soon as the old man gets excited, he starts coughing. 'You should live each day as it comes. I still have four bottles of liquor in my suitcase. I was going to give it to friends in Chungking. To hell with them, let's drink now.' He opens a bottle, gulps down a few swallows and strips off his coarse cotton jacket. He bares his chest. A few hairs stick out of his armpits.

The five of us crowd together in a circle. Lao-shih has ignored me all day. I want to sit next to her on the bunk, but I also want to sit beside Refugee Student. In the end I squeeze in between them. We pass the bottle around the circle. I've never drunk liquor before. I gulp down several swallows in one breath. My face burns. My heart pounds. My left hand rests on Lao-shih's shoulder and my right on Refugee Student's shoulder.

We put the dice in a porcelain bowl in the middle of the circle.

I raise my hand and shout, 'I'll be the dealer!'

'I'll be the dealer.'

'I'll be the dealer.'

'I'll be the dealer.'

'I'll be the dealer.'

'Let's decide by the finger-guessing game. Two people play; the winner gets a drink; then plays the next person. The last one to win gets to be dealer!'

'Let's begin. Two sweethearts!'

'Four season's wealth!'

'Six in a row!'

'Lucky seven!'

'Pair of treasures!'

'Four season's wealth!'

'Three sworn brothers.'

'Pair of treasures!'

'Eight immortals!'

'Six in a row!'

'One tall peak!'

'Four season's wealth!'

'Lucky seven!'

'All accounted for!'

'Three sworn brothers!'

'Six in a row!'

'Pair of treasures!'

'Eight immortals!'

'Lucky seven!'

'I win, I win,' yells Peach-flower Woman. 'I'm the dealer. Place your bets.'

'OK. Fifty dollars!'

'Sixty!'

'Seventy!'

'Eighty!'

'Another seventy!'

'Another eighty!'

Peach-flower Woman laughs. 'You just bet more and more. I haven't got that kind of money. If I win, I get to be the dealer again. If I lose, I'll give up. I get first crack at this!' She grabs the dice and throws them into the bowl with a flourish.

They spin in the bowl.

I take a drink. I see several dice spinning crazily in the bowl.

'Five points! The dealer has got five points!'

'I only want six points, not a single point more!' The old man cups the dice in his hands, blows on them, and then his hands open slowly like a mussel shell opening.

The dice spin in the bowl.

He bends over, glaring at the dice and yelling, 'Six points, six points! Six points! Six points . . . oh, three points.' He lifts Peach-flower Woman's hand and sticks the bottle in it. She takes a drink. She's still holding the bottle and he lifts her hand and puts the bottle in his mouth. He pulls her toward him with his free arm and presses her face against his naked chest. He strokes her face. He finishes off the liquor with one gulp and sucks on the empty bottle like a baby.

'Sir, men and women should not mix. The booze is all gone. I don't have anything for you either. You are supposed to be respectable. You shouldn't touch a woman's body like this,' laughs Peach-flower Woman as she struggles out of his embrace and straightens up. Her chignon comes undone and hair straggles across her chest. The buttons of her blouse pop open, exposing most of her breasts.

The dice click as they spin.

'Six points! Six points! Six points! I only want six points!' Lao-shih yells, rolling on the bunk.

I roll next to her, turn over and climb on her back, as if riding a horse, bumping up and down as if keeping time. I yell with her: 'Six points! Six points! Six points! Six points! Six points! If you keep on ignoring me, I won't let you go. Six points! Six points!'

She suddenly stops yelling, yanks me off and rolls over on the bunk and grabs me. Our faces press together, legs curl round each other, rolling this way and that. She mumbles. 'If you ignore me, I won't let you go. If you ignore me, I won't let you go.'

'Four points,' yells Peach-flower Woman. 'You got four points, Lao-shih! OK, Mulberry, it's your turn.'

I struggle out of Lao-shih's embrace, roll over to the circle and stuff the dice in my mouth. I spit them out into the bowl. 'Six points, come on, six points! Six points! Six points!' Refugee Student is sprawled beside me on the bunk. I pound on his hip with my fist. 'Six points! Six, six, six, six points. How many? How many did I get?'

'Five points. The dealer also got five. The dealer wins!' Another bottle of liquor is passed around.

Refugee Student sits up, grasps the dice with his toes and tosses them into the bowl. He looks at me and begins singing in a flirtatious way. The dice, as if minding their own business, clatter in the bowl.

> Wind blows through the window
> My body is cool
> The willow tree whistles in the wind
> Lovers behind the gauze curtain
> I have a husband, but we're not in love
> Ai-ya-ya-erh-oh!
> Ai-ya-ya-erh-oh!

'Too bad, you lose. You only got three points.' Peach-flower Woman smiles at Refugee Student. With one sweep she rakes in the money.

She beat all of us.

We place larger and larger bets. In the end, we take out all our money and valuables and place them down. Lao-shih and I share our money. We have only two hundred dollars left in our purse. I put down the two hundred dollars. She puts down the purse. The old man bets his gold watch. Refugee Student bets his flute.

We lose again. Refugee Student wins twenty dollars, the price of the flute. He proposes that we change dealers. The three losers all agree. Of course, he gets to be the dealer. In any case, since he's won once already, he's probably the only one who can beat Peach-flower Woman. But the three of us losers don't have anything else to bet.

'I have an idea,' says Refugee Student. 'We play only one more game. This time it will be a game of life or death. Everyone take out his most prized possession. If you don't have anything, then bet yourself. I'm the dealer. If I win, I'll take things, if there are any. If not, I'll take people!'

'And what if you lose?'

'All I've got is myself, you can do what you want with my body, cut it in two, chop it up, lick it, kiss it, fuck it.'

'Good Heavens!' laughs Peach-flower Woman, as she looks at her baby asleep on the bunk. 'My most valuable possession is my son.'

Refugee Student leans over to her and says in a low voice, which everyone can overhear: 'Your most valuable possession is your body.'

The old man chuckles. 'What you say sounds reasonable. I'll bet my house in Peking. If you win, you can go back and take possession. I hope to retire there once the war is over.'

'I'll bet my family heirloom!' I yell as I step over to the 'Girls' Dormitory' and fish out the jade griffin from the little leather case by my pillow and return to the 'Boys' Dormitory'. 'Hey, everybody, this is my family heirloom.'

The old man's eyes suddenly light up. He tries to take it out of my hand. Refugee Student snatches it first and holds out his hand, staring at me. 'Are you going to bet this piece of junk?'

'Yeah.'

'I'd rather have you! A sixteen-year-old virgin!'

Lao-shih jerks me behind her and thrusts out her chest. 'Hey, Refugee Student, I'll make a deal with you. I'll bet this person here! If I win, you get out of my way! If you win, I'll get out of your way. You know what you did.'

'What did I do?'

'Mulberry, did you hear what he just said.'

'I heard. So what did *I* do?'

'Did you hear what she said, Miss Shih?' Refugee Student says. 'Two negatives make a positive. They cancel each other out. OK, everybody, back to your places. I won't steal your precious treasure. So what are you going to bet? Speak up!'

'I don't have anything. I have only myself.'

'OK, if I win, I'll know what to do to you,' Refugee Student leans over to Lao-shih and stares greedily into her eyes.

'Drink up! Come on and drink. It's the last half bottle.' The old man raises the bottle to his lips.

We pass the bottle around. The liquor is gone. The dice click.

We shout.

'One, two, three.'

'One, two, three.'

'Four, five, six.'

'Four, five, six.'

'One, two, three.'

'One point!'

'OK, it's one point.'

'Come on, be good, be good, another one!'

'Be good, be good, don't listen to him. Let's have a two.'

'OK, four points, great, the dealer got only four points.'

The dice click again.

'Five points! Five points! Five points. Hey, you little beauties, did you hear me, I only want one more point than that bastard. Keep my house in Peking for myself. Five points. Five points, please, five points . . . Ah! You fuckin' dice, you did it, you did it! Five points!'

The dice click again.

'Five points, five points, five points, I don't want any more, don't want any less, just give me five points. Good Heavens, let me win just this once in my life. Just this once. Only five points, only five points. Have they stopped? How many did I get? Six points, six points, thank Heavens.'

Everything is floating in front of my eyes. I feel the boat floating underfoot, everyone, everything is floating. The jade griffin is floating. It's my turn, they tell me. I grab the dice and throw them in the bowl. I get a six. They tell me I only picked up two dice and want me to throw again. Lao-shih stuffs the cubes in my hand. I can't hold on to them, they slip from my hand into the bowl. I hear Lao-shih moaning, 'It's over, it's over.'

Dealer, Refugee Student:	Four points
Old man:	Five points
Lao-shih:	Six points
Mulberry:	Three points
Peach-flower Woman:	Four points

'Dealer, I beat you by one point!' says the old man. 'You little punk, I want you to kneel before me and bow three times and kowtow nine times. Nine loud thumps of your head.'

Refugee Student kneels down on the bunk.

'No, no,' says the old man, crossing his legs on the bunk like a bodhisattva statuette. 'Haven't you ever seen your old man pray to his ancestor? Did he ever kneel on a bunk and kowtow to his ancestors that way? Humph. You have to kneel properly on the floor. Knock your head against the floor so I can hear it!'

Refugee Student jumps down from the bunk into the aisle and bends down.

'Hey, you punk, just slow down a little. Have you ever seen anyone kowtowing half-naked? Go put your clothes on!'

Refugee Student grinds his teeth.

Lao-shih, Peach-flower Woman and I burst into laughter.

He puts on his shirt, squeezes down in the narrow aisle between the two rows of bunks.

The old man sits erect on the bunk, strokes his beard and raises his voice like a master of ceremonies, 'First kowtow, second kowtow, third kowtow.'

Refugee Student stands up, bends and bows with uplifted hands, then kneels back down. 'Fourth kowtow, fifth kowtow, sixth kowtow!' He gets up again and bows and kneels back down. 'Seventh kowtow, eighth kowtow, ninth kowtow. Ceremony finished.'

Refugee Student scrambles to his feet and points at me. 'I beat you by one point. It's time to settle with you.'

'That's easy. You won, take the jade griffin.' I pick it up and give it to him.

He doesn't take it and just looks at me. 'What would I do with that? I'm a wanderer. All I want is a pair of grass sandals, a bag of dried food, and a flute. This jade griffin is nothing but a burden. Anyway,' his voice becomes oddly tender, 'I owe you something. I'll repay you by giving back your jade griffin.'

'You don't owe me anything. You said yourself, "two negatives make a positive." I don't owe you anything either.' As I'm talking, I try to put the jade griffin in his hand. I'm sure I'm holding it securely, but when I raise my hand, it slips through my fingers and falls. I let out a cry.

The griffin breaks in two on the floor.

The old man picks up the two halves and fits them together. It looks as if they're still one piece.

'All right, we'll do it this way. You take one half, I'll take the other,' Refugee Student says and stuffs one half into my hand.

'OK, problem solved,' Lao-shih rubs her palms together and noisily grinds her teeth. 'Now, I get to settle with the dealer. I'm the real winner; I beat the dealer by two points. I only wanted the satisfaction of beating you. I won't cut you in two or chop you up. I won't chew on you. I only want you to dress up like a girl and sing the Flower Drum Song.'

'Good idea.' I also want to get even with him. I toss my half of the jade griffin into the opposite bunk.

The three of us, Lao-shih, Peach-flower Woman and myself, strip off his clothes, leaving only his underpants. I remember when he lay naked on the deck, his weight on my body, head hanging over my shoulder, my thighs wet and sticky. I'm still a little sore there. I couldn't stop caressing his body, like a rock in the sun, so smooth, warm, hard. So a man's body was that nice. I wished I could stroke him forever, but when he used all his strength to push into my body, it hurt. How could Peach-flower Woman sleep with her man every night? And even have a baby? I don't see how she could bear the pain.

We dress him in Peach-flower Woman's clothes. He wears the peach flower blouse, blue print pants, a turban of a blue-flowered print wound around his head, two red spots painted on his cheeks, his masculine eyebrows thick and black.

He daintily folds his muscular hands and curtsies. He picks up Peach-flower Woman's red handkerchief and dances with it like a woman, twisting, turning and singing.

> You say life is hard
> My life is hard
> Looking for a good husband all my life
> Other girls marry rich men
> My husband can only play the flower drum.

The old man, sitting on the bunk, laughs until he has a coughing fit. Lao-shih, Peach-flower Woman and I roll with laughter on the bunk.

Suddenly Refugee Student leaps on the bunk and jumps on Lao-shih. 'If you ignore me, I won't let you go! I'm your girl. You have to give me a kiss!' He presses his mouth to hers and strokes all over her body. Lao-shih begins choking and can't speak.

I tackle him to save Lao-shih. 'Good, I've got you both!' He turns over and grabs us both, one on each side, arms locked around our necks, holding us down. 'You come here, too,' he says to Peach-flower Woman. 'I can put you on my chest.' Lao-shih and I beat on his chest with our fists.

He suddenly lets go and rolls over to Peach-flower Woman. He stretches up his hands to her, fingers curled like claws and moves closer and closer to her, saying, 'Now, I am going to settle with you!'

She laughs, her blouse still unbuttoned, straggling hair on her breasts. 'What do you want? Take all the money I've won?'

'Me? I want you!'

She points a finger at him. 'Let me ask you, are you man enough to deal with me?'

'If he isn't, I am,' chuckles the old man.

Refugee Student doesn't say anything. He rips open her blouse and jumps on her, grabs one of her breasts and begins to suck on it. The old man jumps over and grabs her other breast.

She laughs, her full breasts shaking. 'Do anything you want with my poor old body. Just don't take away my baby's food. My milk is almost gone!'

The baby on the bunk starts to cry.

She shoves them aside and goes to pick up the baby.

'I have an idea. I still have two cigarettes. Be my guest.' Refugee Student gropes in his pocket and pulls out two cigarettes – The Dog with a Human Head brand – and steps over to Peach-flower Woman.

She is lying on the bunk nursing her child. Refugee Student lights a cigarette, grabs Peach-flower Woman's right foot and sticks it between her toes. He presses his face against her sole and smokes, his two hands holding her foot.

The old man does the same with her left foot.

She lies flat on her back, her limbs flung out as the child clutches her breast and sucks loudly and the two men hold her feet and suck on the cigarettes.

She laughs and jerks back and forth. 'You devils, you're tickling me. You sex fiends. When you die, you'll get what's coming to you.'

'Listen, listen. The bombers are coming back.' I hear the droning of aircraft.

We sit up stiffly in our bunks.

The roar comes toward us.

It's twilight in the Gorge, the time when day can't be distinguished from night, or clear dusk from a cloudy day.

The captain and the crew are in the bow.

'Hey, the bombers are coming. Come and hide in the cabin. Don't endanger everybody's lives!' shouts the old man.

No response.

'Look at that,' says the captain, 'three planes in each formation. Nine altogether.'

'Motherfuckers, those traitors. Only traitors aren't scared of bombers.' Refugee Student gnashes his teeth.

A boat comes downstream. People on board are yelling. Gongs are crashing.

The bombers are overhead. We sprawl on the bunks. I cover my head with the quilt, the rest of my body exposed.

The yelling, the gong, the roar of the planes get louder.

'I can't hear you,' the captain is shouting to the people on the other boat, 'say it again.'

Shouting, gongs, bombers.

'The Japanese have surrendered!' the captain finally yells.

We rush to the bow. A flame shoots up in the sky, bursting into colourful fireworks. A huge lotus flower opens above the Gorge.

The airplane sprinkles coloured confetti and flies off down the river.

The boat, separated from us by the churning rapids, glides downstream to the sound of cheering and gongs.

'Victory, victory, vic . . . tory . . . tory . . .'

The echoes of their cheers, the confetti swirl around us and disappear into the river.

'There are thunderheads on those mountains,' shouts the captain. 'It's going to rain. We'll float away.'

Dark clouds appear overhead.

Refugee Student, still dressed as the flower drum girl, snatches up a drumstick and pounds on the drum. The drum is thundering.

PART II

ONE

Peach's Second Letter to the Man from the USA Immigration Service

2 February 1970

CHARACTERS

PEACH, she tells the Immigration Service agent the story of cannibalism among a group of pioneers trapped in a snow storm for six months by Donner Lake in the Sierra Nevada mountains. With her letter she encloses the notebook Mulberry kept in Peking in 1949 when the city was under siege by the Communists.

THE MAN FROM THE IMMIGRATION SERVICE.

Dear Sir:

I'm heading west on Interstate 80, just leaving Wyoming's Little America. I found a ride in a camper going to Donner Lake when I was in the gas station diner. The owner of the camper, Mr Smith, just got back from Vietnam. As soon as he got back, he got married. The newlyweds are going to Donner Lake for their honeymoon.

This is the newest model camper trailer. It's a moveable house: living room, bedroom, kitchen. It has every kind of electrical appliance imaginable: refrigerator, stove, air conditioner, heater, TV, radio, stereo, vacuum cleaner. The camper is full of second-hand store antiques: Victorian armchairs with torn satin covers, cracked Chinese vases (made in the reign of the Ch'ien-lung Emperor in the Ch'ing Dynasty), filthy sheepskin wine bags from Spain, fuzzily engraved silver platters from Iran, rusty Turkish swords, chipped Indian powder horns. A picture of a naked woman wearing a man's tophat is painted

59

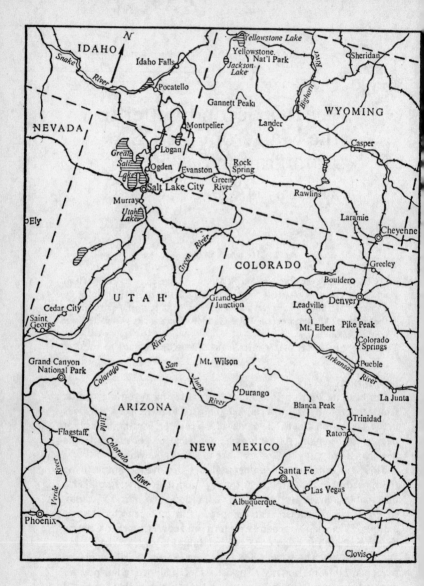

on the outside of the camper. She is kneeling with her back turned, head to one side looking over her shoulder, smiling. Her body is mapped in different coloured sections, labelled like a butcher's chart: ribs, loin, rump, soup, bone, chuck, shank.

Here I am, Peach, sitting in this honeymoon trailer writing you a letter. Mr Dark, you can see this trailer from far away. I'm sending you a map, too, to show you where I've been and where I'm going. If you want to chase me, then come on.

There are too many roads to explore. There are too many interesting things to tell you: changing scenery, changing climate, different animals (Wyoming's mountain goats, Utah's deer, wolves on the plains, foxes, jack rabbits . . .), so many different people. The further west you go, the friendlier the people get. In the East, not even little children will pay attention to you, but in the West, even policemen wave! (Mulberry, who is scared to death of the police, would faint at that!) In New York, you're only another worn-out foreigner, like thousands of others.

I've found out that I'm not the only hitchhiker. All along the highway, many lonely people are standing by the roadside, trying to thumb a ride. Some cars stop for you, some keep right on going. If you catch a driver's eye, he'll wave (they always wave at miniskirted girls on motorcycles, or bored children in backseats about to fall asleep), lightly lifting his hand from the steering wheel, waving, then lowering his hand; drivers always wave that way: solemn and self-assured.

Of course, it's dangerous. Someone in Colorado said to me, 'A woman hitchhiking alone! Didn't you see the newspaper yesterday? Several girls hitchhiking were killed; the murderer cut out their hearts and ate them, and then threw their bodies over a cliff. And then there was the male hitchhiker who disappeared; they found his clothes floating in the river, but they never found his body. There were some young people hitchhiking and . . .' I've heard a lot of those stories.

I just got a ride in Rock Springs, Wyoming during a blizzard with a very strange man. After I got in the car, he couldn't stop laughing. 'Aren't you afraid of me, uh, Little Woman? Ha, ha, ha!' (He was even shorter than I am!) When he wasn't laughing, he was making strange noises: 'Wu–wu–wu–', like a yelping coyote. Then he would slide next to me and say, 'Do you know how porcupines have sex? Uh, Little Woman? Do you know how porcupines have sex? Wu–wu–.' The only time he stopped laughing was when the road got icy. Then he concentrated on driving. Waves of swirling snow billowed in front of us. His expression became serious. 'I can't hear the tyres hitting the pavement. That means black ice has formed on the road. This road will be the death of someone yet.' We struggled over that road all the way to Little America. From the distance we could see the huge billboard–

FOOD AND GAS

Before the car came to a complete stop, I jumped out and waved good-bye to the little porcupine. There was a nice diner at the gas station. The owner used to be a truck driver and had been stranded there in a blizzard many years ago. So he opened a rest stop on the very place. People passing through stop to eat and get gas. Inside the diner was all red; red walls, red lights, red carpet. But the tables were black. Blonde waitresses wove back and forth among the black tables. I sat down at an empty table near the door. A young couple at the table next to mine smiled at me; perhaps they smiled because I was a foreigner. We began to chat. They told me they were going to Donner Lake for their honeymoon. As soon as he started talking about Donner Lake, Mr Smith got excited, as if it were the most beautiful place in the world. Before he was sent to Vietnam, he went ice-skating every winter at Donner Lake.

He told me that Donner Lake is an important point between California and Nevada. Transcontinental highways pass through there. You can also get there by train. The trains have special equipment which protect them from being buried by avalanches. Or, if you want, you can abandon modern machines and get there on horseback, taking trails through the mountains to the lake.

Donner Lake lies in the basin of a valley. It's surrounded by mountains several thousand metres high. In the summer the lake is a green mirror reflecting forests of willow and pine. Quail, grouse, and antelope live there. The pure lake water reflects mountains capped with glittering snow, brooks, wild-flowers, and granite slabs. In the winter, Donner Lake is the West's largest skating rink. The mountains echo with bells from the ski lift and with the skaters' laughter on the lake. Everyone there is relaxed and carefree, looking for a good time.

It was getting dark. The snow fell harder; gust after gust of whistling wind and swirling snow. Someone in the diner put a quarter in the juke box and several young people started singing along with the Beatles' 'Blackbird'.

> Blackbird singing in the dead of night
> Take these broken wings and learn to fly.

All your life you were only waiting
For this moment to be free.
Blackbird singing in the dead of night . . .

Mr Smith said that the wind and snow reminded him of the story about the Donner Party. I asked him what the Donner Party was. He explained that it was a group of California-bound pioneers who were stranded, snowbound by the lake for six months. After that, the lake was called Donner Lake.

This is the story: In 1846, 'California Ho!' was a catchy phrase. The Gold Rush hadn't started yet and there was no overland route west. About one hundred people from the Midwest formed a group to go to California and Mr Donner was elected leader of the party. They started out in the spring, crossing valleys and deserts where there were no roads, pushing on through settlements of hostile Indians. When they reached Donner Lake it was the end of October. They found themselves facing towering cliffs. Winter set in earlier than usual that year. The oxen slowed down as they pulled the wagons, looking for grass under the snow. They could see that the pine forests on the mountains in the distance had already turned white. A blizzard was coming. They abandoned the wagons. They left the cattle to fend for themselves. They went on foot with the children and horses, trying to get through the mountain pass. It was hard for them to throw away the things they had brought with them. A tin of tobacco, a bolt of cloth: it took a long time to decide what to get rid of. They needed to rest. Then they started to climb the mountain in the snow. By evening they weren't far from the top. But it was too cold and they were too tired and they couldn't go on. They finally got a fire started and nothing could make them leave the fireside. They lay in the snow and fell asleep. While sleeping one of the men felt a weight pressing so heavily on his chest that he couldn't breathe. He woke and discovered he was buried in the snow. The people and the animals had vanished; around him was a vast expanse of whiteness. He yelled. Heads poked up through the snow. The animals were scattered. Snow blocked the pass.

They climbed down to the valley and built several small huts beside the lake. Again and again they struggled to cross the mountain and when they failed, they would climb back down. When the food supply ran out, they ate wild animals. Later they couldn't even find wild animals to eat. Blizzard followed blizzard. They were starving and didn't have the energy to gather firewood. After one month, the snow was piled up eight feet high, as tall as their huts. The winter had just begun. Some of them collapsed from hunger and cold. Some died. They tried to think of ways to escape. They used the U-shaped ox yokes to make snow shoes. Whether they tried to escape or whether they remained there, death was certain. Those who tried to escape struggled with fate. Those who remained were resigned to the will of heaven. Their fate was the same, but they responded differently. Some gave in and some didn't.

Ten men, five women, and two boys set out wearing the ox-yoke snow shoes. They spent several days climbing the mountain. Wind and snow kept coming and they were snowbound again. Later the place where they were stranded was called the Death Camp. Bitter cold, exhaustion, hunger. They lay in the snow beside the fire. Those who fell asleep had their hands burnt to a crisp. Several people died. Those who survived starved for five days. Then someone chopped off the legs and arms of the corpses and roasted them over the fire. As they ate, they turned their heads aside and cried. After two days, even those who had refused to eat human flesh in the beginning were eating it. There was only one rule: they wouldn't eat the flesh of their own kin. One girl stared wide-eyed at her little brother's heart which was stuck on a twig, roasting over the fire. A wife agreed that the others could eat her husband's corpse in order to save them from starvation. They cut off as much flesh as they could eat; the rest was made into jerky. Two men discovered deer tracks in the snow and they knelt down and wept and prayed, although they really weren't religious. They killed the deer and lay on top of its body, lapping up its blood. They sucked the deer dry and their faces were smeared with blood. (Too bad that Mulberry, who is scared by the sight of blood, couldn't have heard this story!) After thirty-three days, they finally reached safety. Only two men and five women were left.

Back by the lake, more people were dying. Others tried to escape. One mother set out alone so that her child could have her share of the food. They lived in the snowpit, subsisting on animal skins, bones, and rats. The children slurped spoonfuls of snow from fine porcelain teacups and pretended it was pudding. Everyone lay in his own little hut. Going to others' huts became an important affair.

A man named Boone kept a diary. He referred to the people in the other huts as strangers. The rescue team finally reached them in February. One woman, crying, asked if they had fallen down from heaven. Snow blocked the mountain pass and was still falling. A group of women and children, the sick and the weak, went with a rescue team.

64

Two men, three women, and twelve children remained at the lake. They didn't have the strength to leave.

When the remaining survivors at Donner Lake had eaten the last animal skin, they dug up the corpses of those who had died of starvation and ate them. In March, a second rescue team arrived. As the rescue team approached, they saw a man carrying a human leg. When the man saw them coming, he threw the leg down into a pit in the snow. At the bottom of the pit lay several heads so frozen that their faces were not distorted, torsos with legs and arms missing, chests ripped open, hollow where the hearts were dug out. Outside Donner's tent several children were sitting on logs, blood smeared on their mouths and chests. They were holding their father's heart, tearing off pieces to eat. They did not respond when they saw the rescue party. Around the fire were strewn bones, hair, and pieces of the limbs. The children's mother was lying in the hut. To save the children she told them to eat anything they could. But as for herself, she wouldn't eat her husband's flesh even if it meant she would starve to death.

In April the last of the survivors were rescued. Only half the people in the Donner party had survived.

Mr Smith finished telling the story. He asked me where I wanted to go.

'Donner Lake!'

He laughed. 'I've got a new recruit.'

> He's a real nowhere man,
> Sitting in his Nowhere Land
> Making all his nowhere plans for nobody . . .

The Beatles sang on. More people got up to dance.

'Nowhere Man, can you see me at all?' Mr Smith was singing along with the Beatles. He stood up, bowed to his bride, and stretching out his hand, swept her close to him and they began to dance. His hand was stainless steel.

Peach
2 February 1970

P.S. I am enclosing Mulberry's Peking diary.

TWO

Mulberry's Notebook
Peking, The Besieged City

(December 1948–March 1949)

CHARACTERS

MULBERRY, she flies north to Peking, surrounded by the Communists. She is the only passenger on a one-way plane. She left her home at Nanking, because she was afraid of being arrested by the Nationalist government, which was still in power in the South of China, for her connection with some young people suspected of being Communist. In addition, she could not bear living at home: her brother had run away to the Communist-occupied area, her father had committed suicide, her mother is still having an affair with the family butler. In besieged Peking, she stays with the Shens, an old, traditional family in decay. The Communists have taken most of the country.

AUNT SHEN, (in her sixties), she has been bedridden several years, covered with a red satin quilt embroidered with gold love birds. Joy, the slave maid, massages her paralysed legs. For many years after her marriage, she had no child. It was one of the most important Confucian values for any family to have a son who would carry on the family name. She 'promoted' one of the young slave maids to be concubine for her husband, and thought that she would take over the boy if the concubine bore one. The concubine bore a son, Chia-ch'ing. But Mrs Shen found that she could not control her when she was more favoured by the husband and became more and more powerful in the family. When the concubine became pregnant again, Mrs Shen murdered her with poison (more sons meant more favour and power). Mrs Shen represents the traditional order in its dying throes.

CHIA-KANG, (in his twenties), Mrs Shen's son. He represents the bourgeois class in traditional China. He has leisure, fine tastes and delicate fingers with long nails. He sings Peking Opera, flirts with girls. He is fondled, indulged and possessed by his mother. He wants to marry Mulberry to assert himself as a *man*.

66

HSING-HSING, (in her twenties), a lively, seductive girl. She lives with her mother, and grandfather on her father's side. Her father is an official working for the Nationalist government in Nanking and lives with his concubine. Hsing-hsing was in love with Chia-ch'ing before he left home and became a Communist. She expects the Communists to come and the world to change.

JOY, (in her twenties), Mrs Shen's slave maid. She is always smiling. She has waited on Mrs Shen many years, sitting on the edge of her bed and massaging her legs. When the Communists approach Peking, Mrs Shen sends her to Hsing-hsing's grandfather as concubine.

MR WAN, Hsing-hsing's grandfather.

AMAH CHIEN, Aunt Shen's maid.

I'm the only passenger on the plane.

At the airport in Nanking as I was boarding, an airline official repeated to me, 'The Communists have already surrounded Peking. Everyone is fleeing south.'

And I repeated to him: I understand the situation completely, but I have decided to go on to Peking.

We are flying above the clouds.

Beneath the clouds Nanking slips by: strikes, hoarded rice, suspended classes, marches, demonstrations, bloody riots.

My past disappears under the clouds.

The only thing I've brought with me is the broken jade griffin.

Peking is a square inside a square, shaped like the Chinese character: 回

The Forbidden City.

The Inner City.

The Outer City

The Communists are outside the city.

In the alleys and lanes the hawkers are crying out:

> Sweet apples
> Fresh dates
> Popcorn
> Who will buy my altar flowers?
> God of Wealth for sale.

The Shens live in the western part of the city, in a house with two courtyards.

The Main Gate.

The Gate of the Dangling Flowers.

The Gate at the Entrance of the courtyard.

The central part of the house is divided into three rooms.

The centre room is the parlour. Aunt Shen and her son Chia-kang live in the two rooms off the parlour. It was just a year ago, when the situation in the North deteriorated that Chia-kang moved from the west wing to the central part of the house and dismissed the cook and the chauffeur.

The tenants in the east and west wings come and go in an endless stream. They arrive here, having fled from the area beyond the Great Wall: from Shantung, and Shansi, from Honan, Hopei and other parts of the country. They usually stay less than two months, then flee south. Since September, the Communists have occupied the whole of the North-east and war has erupted again in Hsü-chou and around Peking and Tientsin. The east and west wings are hard to rent out. If they are left empty, army units or refugees will probably take them over. The east wing is now rented by the Chengs, who, born and bred in Peking, swear they will never leave. They sold their own house. Their monthly rent is ten dollars. In November ten dollars could still buy twenty packs of cigarettes. In December it only bought ten packs. Amah Ch'ien and the maid, Joy (mentally retarded), live in the west wing. The two rooms in the south section of the house, beyond the Gate of the Dangling Flowers, are occupied by a group of more than twenty students who fled from T'ai-yuan in Shansi. T'ai-yuan has been surrounded by Communist forces for half a year now. I live in a small room off the corner courtyard. It was Chia-kang's father's study when he was alive. It is isolated from the rest of the house and has a cobblestone patio.

The sky is black and silent. In the central courtyard the old acacia tree, bent and blacker than the sky, its blossoms shed, stretches its branches upwards.

Two low explosions sound in the south horizon. The south sky reddens suddenly. Red sparks sprinkle down. Above the acacia branches the dark sky begins to glow.

Chia-kang and I race to the central part of the house to see his sick mother, Aunt Shen. She is lying on the brick *k'ang* facing the wall. A thin knot of ash-coloured hair sticks out from the thick red silk quilt. Amah Ch'ien has just finished styling Aunt Shen's hair. She goes to get the spittoon. Joy is sitting on the edge of the *k'ang* massaging Aunt Shen's legs.

'Chia-kang,' she says, still turned to the wall. 'Was that the Eighth Army?'

'Mother, the Eighth Army is still a long way away. They wouldn't just fire two shots. It's probably some local explosion.'

'Do you think the Eighth Army is responsible?'

'Mother, the Eighth Army is still a long way away.'

'The Eighth Army took over the airport the day after I arrived,' I say.

'Mulberry, that's only a rumour. It's not certain. There are rumours everywhere these days; that the Eighth Army has occupied the Summer Palace, that the Tower of Treasures has collapsed, that the glass arch in front of the Confucian temple was smashed. That the ancient cypress grove by the temple of Heaven was chopped down, that the Golden Buddha of Yung-ho Palace was stolen! That the temple of the Reclining Buddha . . .'

'All right, all right, Chia-kang. That's enough. Don't say any more. What you don't know won't hurt you.'

'Mother, don't worry. Peking has always been an imperial city. It has a way of turning disaster into good fortune. The Mongols, Manchus, the Allied Army, the Japanese, none of them could swallow her; it's Peking that swallowed them up.'

'Well, that cheers me up a little, Chia-kang.'

'Mother, if you stop worrying, you'll get better.'

'And when will that happen? I've been to see doctors, I've gone on, I've drawn lots, made vows, it's all useless.'

I look at Joy. 'Since I've been in Peking, Joy is the only person I've seen who is still smiling.'

Aunt Shen glances at her. 'I wish I were an idiot girl, with no responsibility except massaging someone's legs. If the sky fell, I'd still be massaging and grinning from ear to ear.'

'And I'd like to be a nightsoil collector,' says Chia-kang. 'I'd carry a large barrel on my back and take a long iron shovel in my hand and scoop it up from the ground and toss it into the barrel on my back, all the while humming lines from the opera.'

'Joy,' Aunt Shen cires out, still facing the wall.

'Hai,' she answers.

'Your day has arrived. You're going to have a better life from now on. But what about me? There will be no one to massage my legs. You better be good to old Mr Wan.'

'Hai.' Joy nods vigorously.

69

'Joy, do you really like that old guy?' asks Chia-kang with a smirk.

'L-l-luv bim.' She stutters.

'What about "bim" do you "luv"?'

'I l-l-uv bim.' Joy is still grinning.

'"Luv" to sleep with "bim"?'

'L-l-uv bim.'

'Chia-kang,' laughs Aunt Shen, 'I won't let you intimidate her.'

'What's wrong with a little joke? Nothing else to do in Peiping. There are soldiers and refugees all over, you can't go anywhere.'

'Go make fun of someone else then. It wasn't easy to find a master for her. If it doesn't work out this time I'll marry her off to you. Mulberry!' Aunt Shen suddenly turns to face me, 'Do you still have that little gold chain I gave you when you were little?'

I unbutton my collar and take out the necklace. 'I wear it all the time. After the war was over and I left Chungking and went back to Nanking, Mother gave it to me.'

'I gave it to you before the war. Was it '36? I took Chia-kang with me to Nanking and we stayed at your house. You were only six or seven then. Chia-kang was ten. You two played so happily together. I gave you that little gold chain for your birthday. Your mother laughed and pointed at you, "Twenty gold ingots. I'll sell her to you for that!" she said. In the wink of an eye twelve years have passed. Your father, Chia-kang's father, those two sworn brothers have both passed away . . .'

'Mother, all those years Mulberry's family has been in the South. We've been in the North. Just think, it was only after the end of the war with Japan that we got in touch again. Mulberry said that it was the strength of that little gold chain that brought her to Peking.'

'Now that you are here, there's no way to leave, Mulberry. The railroad from Peking to Tientsin has been cut. Thousands of people have made plane reservations, but you have to pay gold. We aren't able to do that.' Aunt Shen pauses, then suddenly cries out. 'Chia-kang! Chia-kang, I've got a cramp in my foot!'

Chia-kang runs over and shoves Joy aside. He pulls back the red silk quilt embroidered with mandarin ducks. He uncovers her small foot, no longer bound, pointed and wrinkled, the toes twisted.

'Ai-ya! Ai-ya! It hurts!'

'Mother, I'll massage it for you. Every time I do it, you get better,' says Chia-kang, cradling the small foot in his hands, massaging the muscles along the top of the foot with his thumbs.

'Good, that's good. Chia-kang, don't stop!'

Chia-kang cradles the calf of her leg as he massages. He presses his thumbs along the top of her foot. 'Mother, is it better? Is it better now, Mother?' he says over and over.

She doesn't answer. She stares at the foot in her son's hand. Then she says, 'Chia-kang, dig into it with your fingernails.'

Chia-kang presses his long nails into the top and arch of her foot.

'Chia-kang, harder. That's good, there . . .'

'Mother, I've pinched so hard that you're bleeding. Does it hurt?'

'If only I could feel pain. When I saw that foot in your hand, I was shocked. It wasn't my foot anymore.'

'If it's not yours, then whose is it?' Chia-kang laughs.

'I've been sick too long, Chia-kang. I'm in a daze all the time. Sometimes when your face suddenly flashes before my eyes, I even think it's your father.' She withdraws her foot from his hands and wiggles her toes at him, laughing. 'Look, it's alive again.'

Joy, still grinning, returns to her place on the *k'ang* and begins massaging Aunt Shen's legs.

The oil lamp on the table sputters and almost goes out. We haven't had electricity or water for two days. Now the fire in the stove is dying down.

Chia-kang opens the door to the stove and throws in a shovelful of coal. The fire flares up again, the flames licking higher and higher, about to leap out of the stove. He hurriedly slams the door shut. The shadow of the acacia tree, with its branches stretching up to the sky, appears etched in the paper window.

Suddenly the clamour of shouts and a dog's barking come toward us. The noise moves from the main gate to the Gate of the Dangling Flowers. The barking comes into the main courtyard. The howls lengthen into low muffled whimpers.

Aunt Shen turns to face the wall. 'Dogs cry at funerals. Chia-kang, get that dog out of here.'

I go with Chia-kang to the courtyard. Ice has formed on the ground. The sky is dark. Seven or eight of the students are beating a black shadow by the wall with clubs and poles. The shadow darts from corner to corner, whimpering. The rest of the students stand aside, cheering.

I ask them whey they are beating the dog. 'There's nothing to eat in this city. When you're hungry, you want to eat meat!' replies one of the students, grinding his teeth.

'Mulberry, last night I dreamed you were at the Altar of Heaven.'

'I've never, ever been there, Chia-kang.'

71

'Maybe that's just as well. The Temple of Heaven, the Imperial Park, the Imperial Temple, the Confucian Temple, Yung-ho Palace, now they're all overrun by refugees. The holy grounds of the sacred temples of the past are now contaminated, but when I dreamed about the Temple of Heaven, there was one tiny part untouched.

'You know, the Temple of Heaven is the place where the Ming and Ch'ing emperors sacrificed to Heaven and prayed for a good harvest. All around, as far as you can see, are old cypress trees. The Hall of Prayer, the Imperial Circular Hall, and the Altar of Heaven are all located at the Temple of Heaven. The Hall of Prayer is where the emperors prayed for a good harvest. It's a huge round triple-roofed hall with double eaves. The ceiling of the dome is decorated with golden dragons and phoenixes, glazed blue tiles; there are no beams. The three roofs and the double eaves are supported solely by twenty-eight giant pillars. The Imperial Circular Hall houses the memorial tablets of the emperors. It's a small circular shrine with a golden roof, glazed blue tiles, red walls, and glazed doors. The Altar of Heaven is where the emperors sacrificed to heaven. It's a three-tiered circular terrace built of white marble. The centre of the altar is a round stone encircled by nine rings of marble. Each ring consists of marble slabs arranged in multiples of nine. The rings radiate from the centre like ripples on a pond. When you stand there, you feel like you've touched heaven. If you whisper in the centre of the altar, you can hear a loud echo.

'The Temple of Heaven I dreamed about wasn't like that at all. The Hall of Prayer, the Imperial Circular Hall, the Altar of Heaven were crowded with refugees' straw mats, quilts, and sheets. Ragged pants were hanging out to dry in the sun on the white marble balustrades. The memorial tablets of the emperors had been thrown down to the ground, and the Hall of Prayer was full of excrement.

'The old cypress trees had been cut down.

'Only the shrine of the Altar of Heaven was still clean: white marble stones. The sky above the shrine was still clear blue. Mulberry, I dreamed you were lying in the centre of the altar, naked, looking up at the sky. You were so clean and pure. I had to make love to you. We rolled over and over on top of the altar, shouting. The space between heaven and earth was filled with our shouting. Between heaven and earth there was only you and me, two naked bodies entwined together.'

He gently pushes me down on the sofa in my room and begins stripping off my clothes.

I suddenly sit up. 'No, Chia-kang, you must respect me.'

'I know you're a pure, clean girl. I want to marry you right away. Even if we sleep together now, it's all right because we're going to get married.'

'Even if I sleep with my own husband, it's still dirty.'

The parlour door opens. Large flakes of snow whirl around the doorsill. Tiny icicles dangle from the acacia branches. A crow, immobile, sits on a branch, a black statue in ice.

Hsing-hsing hurries in, removes the red scarf from around her head and brushes the snow from her clothes. Her long pigtails swish back and forth. She goes into Aunt Shen's room, saying, 'A bomb went off at the airport, killing and wounding more than forty people!'

'Who did it?' asks Chia-kang.

'Someone said that the Nationalists did it as they were retreating from the airport. Someone else said the Eighth Army did it as they were seizing the airport . . .'

'Then the Eighth Army is really going to fight its way into Peking.'

'Second Master Shen, the Eighth Army is already at the base of the city wall. Grain and vegetables can't get into the city. The city's food supply is almost gone. My mother hoarded up twenty sacks of flour and forty heads of cabbage. The Nationalist government just released a lot of prisoners in order to save food, but the prisoners didn't want to leave the prison. No one would feed them if they left. The guards forced them out with bayonets. The government has declared a general amnesty. They have even released traitors from the Japanese occupation and a lot of students who had been jailed for demonstrating. Five or six students from our university were released. Some people say that Nationalist Commander Fu Tso-i is talking peace with the Eighth Army, and that he wants to form a coalition government with them. Other people say that Fu Tso-i is withdrawing to the Northwest to join forces with Ma Hung-k'uei. Anyway, Peking will never be the same. Someone else said . . .'

'Hsing-hsing, stop it, don't go on!' says Aunt Shen lying on the *k'ang* with her face to the wall.

'Hsing-hsing,' laughs Chia-kang. 'Tell us some good news, not bad news. We're just doing fine here, and then you come bursting in like a firecracker with all this bad news. May I ask where you got all these rumours?'

'Rumours? Things are changing out there. You are still shut up at home playing Second Master Shen. There are all sorts of reports on the bulletin board at school. We don't even go to class anymore. Everyone is wriggling and dancing to the Rice-sprout Song.'

'Hsing-hsing, are you happy that the Eighth Army is coming?'

'Why should I be happy? I'm just not afraid, that's all.'

'Do you think that once the Eighth Army arrives, your family will have an easy time? Your grandfather was a wealthy landlord and your father is an official in Nanking!'

'That has nothing to do with me. My mother and I are victims of the old society. My father hasn't paid any attention to my mother for more than ten years. He took his concubine and her children to the South to live in luxury. We never had any part of it. My mother stayed home and took care of his parents. When the old lady died, she was the one who had to find someone for the old man. Joy!'

'Hai!' Joy is still sitting on the *k'ang*, massaging Aunt Shen's legs. She is still grinning.

'Joy, my grandfather has your new room all ready for you. He has even bought the flowers you'll wear!'

'White lilies.'

Hsing-hsing laughs. 'Silly girl, even if it were summer now, you couldn't find white lilies in Peking. No fresh flowers or vegetables can come into the city. You have to pay gold for cabbages. Aunt, I came today about Joy . . .'

'Has the old gentleman changed his mind?' says Aunt Shen, suddenly turning over.

'He won't change his mind! He wants her to come earlier. He says that things are getting worse and worse. When the Eighth Army enters the city, he won't be able to marry Joy.

'He had wanted to invite enough guests to fill two tables at the wedding banquet. Now the guests can't come. Some suddenly left for the South. Others are moving to smaller houses. Some have set up stalls in Tung-tan selling things. Others are trying to get plane reservations to escape. The old gentleman asked me to come over and ask Auntie if Joy could come over tomorrow.'

'How can I bear to see Joy leave? For the past few years, I have had to have my legs massaged day and night. These days you have to give up whoever wants to leave and whatever you have to throw away. Come and get her tomorrow.'

'Joy!'

'Hai!'

'Pack up your things. I'll come get you early tomorrow.'

'Hai!' Joy's grin widens.

'Lately the old gentleman has been very cheerful, even praising my mother for being a good daughter-in-law. Things are getting worse and worse. All the scrolls in the house have been taken down and packed away. He took out a painting of the sun rising in the East above the ocean and hung it in the parlour. He said it had a double meaning: it's supposed to bring good luck and decorate the room, but it also could welcome the Red Army. Mulberry,' Hsing-hsing suddenly turns to me, 'I really envy you. You came up here to the North all by yourself. The South really is more open-minded. I've never been to the South, but I really want to go. When I think of the South, I think of willow trees.'

'I've wanted to go to the South for a long time, but I couldn't get away,' says Chia-kang looking at his mother's tiny, flower-like chignon of grey hair. 'To me the South is an endless rampart of stone, an old monk, bent over, tugging on the rope to ring the bell at the Temple of the Crowing Cock, his whole life spent like that, just ringing the bell.'

'To me Peking is grey cranes flying over the Gate of Heavenly Peace, it's mansions of the Manchu Monarchs, lots of gates, secluded courtyards. It's houses haunted by fox spirits,' I say.

Chia-kang laughs. 'So you escaped to Peking. Hsing-hsing and I want to escape to the South.'

'But now both North and South are in chaos.'

'Did you hear that? Did you hear that, Chia-kang?' says Aunt Shen, still facing the wall. She raises her arm and shakes her finger in the air, 'The North and South are both in chaos. You better listen to me and stay at home.'

"Inside Peking there's a big circle. In the big circle is a smaller circle. In the smaller circle is the imperial yellow circle where I live." Chia-kang begins to sing the role of the disguised emperor in the opera *The Town of Mei-lung.*

Hsing-hsing immediately takes up the role of the flirtatious innkeeper who does not recognise him.

"I recognise you now."

"Whom do you recognise me to be?"

"You're my brother's . . ."

"Eh?"

"Brother-in-law."

"Ai, nonsense!"

"You military clerks aren't polite. You shouldn't flirt with women of good breeding."

"Good woman, good woman, you shouldn't wear begonias in your hair. You wiggle delightfully. But most bewitching are your begonia flowers."

"Begonias, begonias. You are making fun of me. I make haste to throw these flowers on the ground. Throw them down, crush them underfoot. Never again will I wear begonia flowers."

"You, my lady, aren't being polite. You should not crush these begonia flowers. I, in all my dignity, shall retrieve them. I shall place, place, place these begonia flowers in your hair."' Chia-kang throws the red scarf over Hsing-hsing's head.

"'You're nothing special!'" Hsing-hsing brushes off the scarf and eyes Chia-kang flirtatiously, her taunting expression about to crinkle into a smile. 'Second Master Shen, return to your imperial yellow circle. Come on, Mulberry, sing a part.'

'How could a girl from the South know how to sing Peking Opera?' answers Aunt Shen.

'Do you know how to make dumplings, Mulberry?' asks Hsing-hsing.

'Sure I know. I roll out the dough really thin and then use the mouth of a glass to cut out the dumpling skins.'

Aunt Shen, Chia-kang, and Hsing-hsing laugh at my method. Joy, seeing them laugh, also chortles.

'Paper cutouts for windows!'

I don't know what they're selling outside.

'It's almost New Year's. We ought to put up fresh window paper. Well, we'll forget about it this year,' says Aunt Shen. 'Hsing-hsing, since you've been here, I feel a little better. Don't go. Stay and sleep on my bed. There aren't many good times left. That way you won't have to come again tomorrow. You can take Joy away early in the morning.'

I'm still an outsider at the Shen's.

Joy giggles as she goes out the door with her bags.

Mr Cheng, who has been staying in the east wing pays a visit to the Shens. He announces that his family is leaving tomorrow to fly to Nanking. He has a friend in Nanking named K'ung who wants to bring his whole family by plane to Peking. The Chengs will live in the K'ungs' house in Nanking. The K'ungs will come to stay in the Chengs' place in Peking. He asks Aunt Shen if it's all right for the K'ungs to live in the east wing.

Aunt Shen says, 'As long as they are decent people, anybody can come live here free. It's better than having it occupied by troops or refugees. What's the use of fleeing south, though? Mulberry just came from there. The South is as chaotic as Peking.'

I look at Mr Cheng and nod. 'Hsü-chou has been taken. The Communists will cross the Yangtze River any moment now. I just fled from Nanking to come here.'

Chia-kang says, 'Well, I'm not going to run away. In the last war we fought the Japanese. If you saw a short "devil" you could tell it was Japanese. But now it's Chinese fighting Chinese. You can't tell the people from the "devils". They are all devils. There are devils everywhere.'

Mr Cheng chuckes ironically. 'Escape today, add one more day to your life. We've sold everything. And already bought plane tickets. We'll first go to Nanking, then on to Shanghai and Canton, and if we have to, we'll go to Taiwan as a last resort.' He continues to chat about 'meeting again sometime in the future' and other polite topics of conversation. Finally he asks Aunt Shen if we could keep a trunk of antiques and a trunk of scrolls for him, all priceless heirlooms.

Aunt Shen, lying on the *k'ang*, waves her hand. 'Do us a favour, Mr Cheng. Get those things out of here as quickly as possible. When the Eighth Army comes, they'll think they are ours. We have a roomful of our own furniture, furs and antiques that we haven't thrown out yet.'

A loud cracking noise comes from the courtyard.

Mr Cheng laughs. 'Don't worry. The students in the south section of the house are helping out. They're chopping up your furniture for firewood.'

Explosions.

The city gates are closed.

All connections with the outside world have been cut off: railroads, telephone lines, air routes.

'. . . Those of you living in the areas controlled by Chiang Kai-shek, please listen carefully: The Chinese People's Liberation Army is about to liberate the whole country. Please don't try to flee. Please remain where you are and take all steps necessary to protect people's lives, property, buildings and provisions. Please don't try to flee. Wherever you go, the People's Liberation Army will follow. The Liao-Shen campaign has already ended victoriously. The Huai-Hai campaign is in the last, decisive stages of victory. The People's Liberation Army is ready to cross the Yangtze River. The Peking-Tientsin campaign is in the last decisive stages of victory: The People's Liberation Army has already completely cut off and surrounded enemy forces in Peking, Tientsin, Chang-chia-k'ou, Hsin Pao-an, and T'ang-ku, five isolated areas, and cut off the enemy's escape south and west . . .'

'. . . As she listened, the ghost became afraid. Most honoured King of Hell, please listen to my plea. It was my parents' cruel hearts, they should not have sold me to the land of mist and flowers. At twelve or thirteen I learned to sing and play the zither. At fourteen or fifteen I began receiving men. Chang San comes when he wants me; Li Ssu comes when he wants me. The money I earned went to make the old Procuress happy. Yee-hsia! If I didn't earn money, she would beat me and whip me. Yee-hsia-hsia! . . .'

'. . . the Communist rebels, unconcerned about the lives and property of the people in Peking, have been savagely bombing Peking since December thirteenth. Commander-in-Chief of the Extermination Campaign Against the Communist Rebels in North China, Fu Tso-i, has announced that he has utmost confidence in wiping out the rebels. He will fight to the finish. The six hundred thousand troops under Fu Tso-i's command have already undertaken rapid measures to protect Peking and Tientsin. Several thousand workers are working around the clock to construct temporary landing strips at Tung-tan and the Temple of Heaven. The cypress groves at the Temple of Heaven have been completely uprooted. . . .'

'I, the commander, am mounted on my horse, and I am busy looking for signs of movement. Chu-ko Liang sits drinking in the watchtower playing his lute. Two servants are at his side. The old, worn-out soldiers are cleaning the street. I should send down the order to take the city. Kill, kill, but no. . . .' Chia-kang keeps moving the radio dial back and forth.

The radio blares all day long in the parlour. Chia-kang and I sit by the radio for hours, and listen to the news of the war. The radio is our only connection with the outside world.

Shells whiz above the courtyard.

'Hey, why don't we take over those rooms,' the students are shouting in the courtyard. 'The east wing is empty. There's no one living there now.'

'You students, you have no respect for the law,' shouts Chia-kang from the doorway. 'You took over the south section and now you want the east wing. The government has declared that anyone taking over residences by force will be severely punished!'

'Listen, there are more than two hundred thousand troops in Peking. Three or four hundred prisoners have just been released. The days that one family can occupy a whole house are over!'

'You rebels! The east wing has already been rented to a family from the South. They should arrive any day now.'

'I'm sorry, but from now on no one can get in or get out of this city.'

'Hey, what are you doing with those trunks? They belong to the Chengs. Hey, there are valuable things in those trunks . . .'

'Sorry, mister, it's cold and we need a fire.'

The students begin carrying their belongings into the east wing.

Broken antiques and torn scrolls litter the courtyard; a shredded picture of the Yangtze River, a cracked bamboo brush holder, a green gourd shaped vase split in half. Bits and shreds of mud-splattered scrolls, calligraphy copybooks, and classical texts are strewn everywhere. The only thing intact is a statue of the folk hero, The Foolish Old Man Who Moved the Mountain, lying in the corner of the courtyard. The Foolish Old Man is wearing a yellow robe and straw sandals. There's a pack lashed to his waist. He is holding a black axe in his right hand and with his left hand he strokes his long white beard. A boy, dressed in a white robe, blue pants and red smock, stands at his side, shouldering a yellow basket. The old man and the boy are standing on a cliff looking up.

The artillery booms. There's an explosion and the main gate blows open. Wind and sand whirl in around us.

Scraps of the Yangtze River flutter in the courtyard.

The Shens are dismissing Amah Ch'ien. They give her three months' wages. Amah Ch'ien mentions her mistress's jewelry. Aunt Shen gives her a gold bracelet. Amah Ch'ien continues: She is old, the mistress has suddenly dismissed her. Where is she supposed to go? She has waited on the same mistress for twenty years, and although she may not have been an exceptional servant, she did work hard. She deserves something more. In addition she is given a sheepskin jacket.

Amah Ch'ien leaves, the students take over the west wing. To celebrate, they kill another dog in the courtyard.

'Chia-kang, it's dark all of a sudden. Light the lamp.'

'There's no oil, Mother.'

'Well, then let's sit together and wait until it gets light outside.'

'Mother, are you better today?'

'I get worse every day.'

'Auntie, let me massage your legs.'

'All right, Mulberry, massage my legs. Chia-kang, come sit on the *k'ang* with me. It'll be warmer if the three of us crowd together.'

'OK.'

'Chia-kang, the jewelry box is beside my pillow. I want to go through it and put my jewelry in order, then you can bury the box under the floor boards.'

'Mother, can you find everything in the dark?'

'Eh. Right now I'm feeling the brocade pouch.'

'You mean the black, blue and pink brocade one? Don't forget the belt braided with blue and pink silk floss.'

'That's right, Chia-kang, you remember it exactly. All my prize possessions are in this pouch. Now I can feel the gold locket.'

'Mulberry, you've got to see how Mother looks in the photograph inside the locket.'

'Too bad we don't have any electricity.'

'You don't need light to see it, Mulberry. I can describe it for you. Mother had her hair in a chignon, with a magnolia flower tucked in it, bangs on her forehead. She is wearing a black satin dress with bell sleeves, a high mandarin collar, and high slits on the sides, a white silk scarf and gold-rimmed glasses. She is holding a deluxe edition of a foreign book and she is posing by a small bridge over a stream, standing with one foot on tip-toe as if she is about to take a step, but can't.'

'Chia-kang, you remember so clearly how I looked. The next thing will be more difficult to guess. Guess what I'm holding in my hand now?'

'The jade bracelet?'

'You're wrong. It's the jade Buddha that you played with when you were one year old. I bought it at the market outside Hartman city gate. I sewed it to your hat and you wore it for a picture. In the picture you were naked, sitting on a prayer mat, and giggling like a little laughing Buddha.'

'Mulberry, why are you so silent?'

'I'm looking and listening, Chia-kang.'

'It's so dark you can't even see your own hand. What can you see?'

80

'I can see everything you and Auntie are describing.'

'Chia-kang, now I'm holding the white jade bracelet. In the spring of 1933, there was a festival at the Shrine of the Fire God. There were many pearl and jade stalls set up there. I saw this white jade bracelet at the jade stall there. A lot of things happened that year. Your grandmother died, your grandfather died. Phoenix, your father's concubine, had a miscarriage and died. At that time we still had two maids, Ch'un-hsiang and Ch'un-hsia.'

'Mother, does Chia-ch'ing know he is Phoenix's son?'

'How could he not know? He just pretends not to know because Phoenix was a maid. Chia-ch'ing ran away from home in the summer of '39. Some people said he went to Yen-an to join the Communists. If he comes back with the Eighth Army, we'll have a little protection.'

'Mother, Father is dead. You aren't his real mother. I'm afraid he might cause trouble for us.'

'It's not my fault his mother died.'

'That's not what I mean. I mean, he might come and carry on about class struggle and throw people out of their home and things like that.'

'Live each day as it comes, Chia-kang, don't talk about troubling things. Mulberry, can you see this wedding crown in my hand?'

'I can't see anything but a black shadow.'

'It's a red phoenix with two little black pearl eyes, wings outstretched with a string of red tassels in its tiny pointed beak. When I was carried into the Shen's house on a flower-decked brocade sedan-chair, I was wearing this crown and a pink silk cloak.'

'Mother, what about the jade frog ring?'

'It's in here somewhere. Here, I've found it. This was part of my dowry.'

'Auntie, your whole youth is in that pouch.'

'You're absolutely right, Mulberry. What I'm touching are the most splendid days of my life. Now I'm just an old, broken kite, unable to fly.'

'Mother, we ought to bury this jewelry immediately. I've been thinking, that jade frog ring . . .'

'Chia-kang, the fire is going out. Go and try to find a little coal.'

'All right.'

'Mulberry, don't massage me anymore. Just sit and talk to me. The whole country is fighting and here you are in Peking. You don't know how happy that makes me. When I saw you in Nanking, such a tiny little thing, I loved you so much. I said to your mother, "Let's hope our two families will be united in marriage." That's why I gave you that little gold chain. After all these years of war and fighting, you and Chia-kang are together again. Everything is decided by fate. I'm old now. I'm anxious to get a daughter-in-law and hold a grandson in my arms. There's only Chia-kang left in this branch of the family. Chia-ch'ing has become a Communist. He doesn't count any longer as a Shen family heir. Chia-kang told me he wants to marry you immediately. No one knows a son like his mother. I have something I have to make clear to you. My Chia-kang is happy with his life, a loyal and generous person, but he has been spoiled. He has never had to struggle. If you marry him, you've got to give in to him in certain ways. He has only one fault, the same as his father. He likes to play around with girls. The best maids I had were ruined by his father. Later I bought this idiot maid, Joy. I had to be careful about the father and then I had to watch the son. It was like a mute taking medicine, can't even say it's bitter. Do you know why Hsing-hsing comes to visit so often?'

'I know. I realised that a long time ago.'

'That young girl is all right, but she is just fickle. When Chia-ch'ing was at home, she led him on. Now she and Chia-kang are having an affair. Did you know that?'

'Why doesn't he marry her?'

'Because I don't approve. There are only two sons in our family, if there were three, four, five, six or seven, she could have all the others. I'm telling you this so you'll be prepared. If you marry Chia-kang and he behaves himself, you're lucky. If he doesn't, you'll be prepared for it and it won't be so bad. I know what that kind of bitterness is like. It happened to me. I . . .'

'Mother, we don't have much coal left.' Chia-kang comes into the room.

'Don't waste it then. We don't know how long this siege is going to last. Chia-kang, I was just talking to Mulberry about the two of you getting married.'

'Mulberry, let's get married on New Year's. Today is the twentieth of the twelfth lunar month. Oh, no, wait a minute, we can't get married on New Year's. Ever since the city has been surrounded, there have been more and more wedding announcements in the paper. Everyone gets married on New Year's. There probably won't be an empty banquet hall we could rent. Let's get married on New Year's Eve. The sooner the better. Mother, do you think that's all right?'

'Of course it is. I've got the ring all ready for you. Here, Chia-kang, take it.'

'Oh, the glittering green frog. I can even see it in the dark. Mulberry, let me put the ring on your finger. Give me your hand.'

'Chia-kang, I want to go back to the South.'

'It's getting late, Chia-kang, will you bury my jewelry box under the floor now?'

Chia-kang has found a second-hand dealer. The redwood furniture, furs, silks and satins, painting and scrolls . . . Aunt Shen and the dealer settle on a price. The money she gets is exactly enough to buy four sacks of flour and twenty cabbages.

It's getting late. The second-hand dealer carts the things away.

'. . . The People's Liberation Army recaptured Chang-chia-k'ou on December 24. Fifty-four thousand enemy troops were wiped out . . . *Wild geese fly over the sand flats, frost on the road, landscape of the barbarian North* . . . Fu Tso-i, Commander-in-Chief of the Extermination Campaign Against the Communist Rebels in North China, announced that Peking's defense is secure. The Communist rebels do not dare make any reckless moves . . . *Hand in hand, we climb into the gauze-curtained bed. I unbutton your gown, I will put on my sleeping slippers. Tonight, I will stay by your side and do my best to serve you. If they kill me, my head will fall to the ground* . . . An authoritative spokesman for the Chinese Communist Party has announced the names of the forty-three most wanted Kuomintang war criminals. On January 1, Chiang Kai-shek announced that he is seeking peace negotiations. He outlined three conditions under which he would consider negotiations with the Communists: maintaining the invalid constitution, the invalid system of justice, and the Nationalist armed forces . . .'

'The Wall of Nine Dragons is falling down. The Wall of Nine Dragons is falling down! The Wall of Nine Dragons! Falling down! Falling down!' Aunt Shen murmurs unconsciously, lying on the *k'ang* with her face to the wall.

She has not eaten for two days.

The artillery fire becomes more frequent. The windows to the courtyard rattle with each explosion. The main gate keeps banging open. The sandy wind blows stronger.

I walk into Chia-kang's room and discover him and Hsing-hsing squeezed together on a chair. Hsing-hsing is sitting on his lap. His hand is inside her blouse. They stand up suddenly.

I run outside and hail a pedicab and hurry to the Peking Hotel to inquire about the airplanes. The airline has managed successful landings at the temporary landing strip at the Temple of Heaven. Because of the fuel shortage, there are only two flights a week. I make a reservation. I'm number eight thousand and twenty-one, scheduled to depart in three months. The solar New Year has just begun.

I walk through blowing sand to the lake, Pei Hai, which has just recently been opened to the public.

Golden Turtle and Jade Frog.

Double-Rainbow Pavilion.

Hall of the Serene Way.

Hall of Rippling Waters.

Five-Dragon Pavilion.

I approach the Wall of Nine Dragons. Nine colourful dragons are prancing between the blue heavens and the green waters, playing with their golden dragon pearls and their tongues of fire. The dragons, the sky, the water, the pearls, the tongues of fire are a mosaic of glittering glazed tile. The Wall of Nine Dragons stands more than twenty feet high. It has been standing here for seven or eight hundred years, since the Yuan dynasty.

I go home, back to my room off the corner courtyard. Chia-kang is waiting for me there. He tells me that I'm the only one he loves and that Hsing-hsing is really in love with his brother Chia-ch'ing. When they are together, he always hopes I will walk in and discover them because she is really thinking about Chia-ch'ing.

I tell him I've already made a reservation to go south and that his mother had already told me how things were.

'My mother! My mother! She is going to make me kill myself,' says Chia-kang stamping his foot. 'Mulberry, if you want to go away, then let's go away together.'

When he comes back from his mother's room, there are red marks on his face.

'. . . New China News Agency cable, 14 January: Mao Tse-tung, Chairman of the Central Committee of the Chinese Communist Party, has already rejected Chiang Kai-shek's January 1 request for peace negotiations. Comrade Mao Tse-tung announced the eight conditions under which peace negotiations can be held. (1) Punish all war criminals; (2) Abolish the invalid system of justice; (3) Abolish the invalid constitution; (4) Reorganize all counter-revolutionary armed forces according to democratic principles; (5) Confiscate property of the bureaucrats; (6) Reform the land system; (7) Abolish traitorous foreign treaties; (8) Convene a political negotiating conference of all non-counter-revolutionary parties, and establish a democratic coalition government.

'The People's Liberation Army Broadcasting Station announced from Tientsin: The People's Liberation Army liberated Tientsin today, and took the puppet mayor of Tientsin, Tu Chien-shih and the Nationalist Party Garrison Commander Ch'en Ch'ang-chieh and others, captive. More than ten villages in the suburbs of Tientsin are still burning . . .' The students cut out the wire from the doorbell to repair their radio.

The Shen doorbell is now mute.

The Communists are bombing the centre of the city.

The landing strip at the Temple of Heaven is closed.

The gates to the city have been opened and the refugees who fled into the city are now pouring out. Daily there are four or five thousand people waiting by the gates to get out.

Amah Ch'ien and her son come to the Shens and demand that half the house be given to them. The Shens only offer her one ounce of gold.

She sews the gold into her belt and wraps it around her waist. She stands in the long line waiting for the guard to check her before leaving the city. The sun is setting. The gates will be closed before dark. When it is Amah Ch'ien's turn to be inspected, a donkey pulling a cart of nightsoil passes by. The donkey, excited by the crowd, starts galloping. The guards chase the donkey and manure splatters all over the ground. When the donkey is finally subdued the gates have been closed and no one can leave the city. Suddenly an artillery shell falls on Amah Ch'ien's head. The donkey, excited again, gallops off.

Amah Ch'ien's son comes to tell us about her death and demands that the Shens pay for the coffin.

A loud thump comes from Aunt Shen's room.

Chia-kang and I run from the parlour into her room. She is sprawled on the floor. She stares at us, her eyes unnaturally bright. But she really doesn't see us.

She is no longer here in the house with us.

Chia-kang goes to lift her to the bed. She waves him away with her hand.

'Don't touch me. I have something to say. Your father and Phoenix have returned. I have been talking with them for a long time. I've told lies my whole life and I've heard lies all my life. Now I can tell the truth. Chia-kang, I haven't treated you fairly. I have suffocated you. I didn't want you to be a success. I only wanted you to spend your whole life quietly here with me. I held you back on purpose, telling you that you were too soft that you couldn't take it. I encouraged you to play around with the maids, even sleep with Hsing-hsing. I know you don't really care about them. I let your father have Phoenix so I could keep him under my control. But now you are serious about Mulberry. When the two of you are together laughing and talking, I lie here crying alone. I said bad things about you in front of Mulberry. You want me to let you go. You told me that you can't spend your whole life with me. And I said to you that I have remained a widow my whole life for your sake. After your father died, there were men that were interested in me. You said you wanted me to remarry. I slapped you. You went to Mulberry's room. I held the jacket you had left in my room and cried the whole night. I pinched my feet, the way you used to pinch them, the way your father used to pinch them . . .'

'Mother . . .'

'Don't interrupt me.'

'Mother, I only have one question. Father always had other women. How could you stand it?'

She rolls on the floor laughing, pulls down her pants and reveals part of her buttock and slaps it, saying, 'I have one precious possession: a good figure. Although I'm getting old and my body is drying up, this part is still good. This part of me has committed so many sins! Your father and I are even on that account. But not you. Chia-kang, I was a widow all these years for your sake. You . . .'

'Mother . . .'

'Don't interrupt me. I must say this: Chia-kang, you're not a true son of the Shen family. Chia-ch'ing, the runaway, is the only legitimate son!'

'Then whose son am I?'

'You were given to me by the gods at the White Cloud Temple . . .'

'Mother . . .'

'Listen to me. Phoenix was the maid who came with me when I married. I couldn't have children. I thought I could raise the sons she bore. But once she had a son, she became too haughty. Whoever bore sons had power in the Shen household. I was frantic. I went to see doctors – useless. I just couldn't get pregnant. The eighteenth of the first lunar month in 1925, I made a trip to the White Cloud Temple with some of the women that I used to play mahjong with. That evening the festival of the Immortals was celebrated at the White Cloud Temple. Late in the evening, two or three hundred male and female devotees chanted Taoist sutras in the great hall. There was chanting and chanting, the painted lanterns glowed, and cymbals and drums clashed as the Immortals descended to earth: there was the Primordial Heavenly Master, the Secluded Holy One, the Master of Penetrating Heaven, the Emperor of Dark Heaven, the Immortal of the Golden Cap, the Black Cloud Immortal, the Golden Light Immortal, the Youths of the White Crane, the Youths of Fire and Water . . . all the important and unimportant immortals appeared. The Immortal of the Golden Cap told me that if I wanted a son I would have to borrow an embryo. He took me to the Hall of Four Emperors to steal a porcelain baby-image, and then he led me to the store house behind the great hall and taught me how to use it to borrow an embryo. Nine months later I gave birth to you, Chia-kang. I could have shared the glory with Ch'un-feng. But who could have known she was pregnant again? . . . I took some arrowroot dug up in the dead of winter, made it into powder and put it in her tea. She drank it and had a miscarriage and died from hemorrhaging. Now, Chia-kang, everything I have kept secret has been said. Go ahead and curse me. The burden has been lifted from me.'

She turns suddenly and points at me: 'Mulberry, I have something to say to you, too. When you first came to Peking, I didn't like you the minute I saw you. Your eyes are too watery. You're a girl who dreams wild and ridiculous dreams. You try to seem clean and pure, but in your heart, you're like a snake or a scorpion. You're the kind of girl who could even fantasize about your own father. You're an evil star – a jinx on your father, mother, husband and sons! Chia-kang, do you still want to marry Mulberry?'

'If she is willing.'

'You are aware of all her faults?'

'Yes.'

'Chia-kang, why do you want to marry her?'

'Because she is different from girls from the North. I've been in Peking too long.'

'Mulberry, do you want to marry Chia-kang?'

'Yes.'

'Chia-kang, are you really sure you want to marry her?'

'I decided that a long time ago.'

'My son. You're being a real man. You played around with the maids and Hsing-hsing because you wanted to be a man. But you couldn't escape your mother's clutches. Now you're a real man . . . You . . .'

'Mother, it's too cold on the floor. Mulberry and I will lift you back up to the k'ang.'

'Only on one condition: I can still go on talking when I'm back on the k'ang and you won't interrupt me. If I stop, the Wall of the Dragons will fall on me.'

'Go on and talk, Mother, you don't have to stop.'

The ideogram for double happiness, written in gold, hangs in the middle of the wall, between two scrolls with auspicious sayings. A red felt tablecloth has been spread out on the long table on which sit two burning red tapers. The Shens' parlour is the ceremonial hall.

There are thirteen guests: Hsing-hsing, her mother, her grandfather old Mr Wan, and his bride Joy – the whole family has come. Joy is pregnant.

My wedding dress, flowered velvet, is borrowed from Hsing-hsing. Hsing-hsing is styling my hair: long curls hanging down to my shoulders. She says that this hairstyle is worn by European aristocrats and that it brings out my classic features. The small notch in my right earlobe is covered by the curls. The mole below my right eye looks darker after I put on my makeup. Hsing-hsing leads me from the room near the garden into the ceremonial hall.

The groom is waiting. He stands between the tall red tapers, and facing old Mr Wan, the legal witness. The others lead his mother into the hall. She sits in the seat of honour at the long table. (She didn't stop talking for two days and nights, but she has calmed down.)

Artillery fire sputters over the roof.

President Chiang, due to reasons not yet disclosed, has announced that he will resign . . . The students' radio blares from the courtyard

They come and go in front of the parlour and peer in at the ceremony.

I am standing beside the groom.

The master of ceremonies announces: 'Let the ceremony begin.'

The legal witness, Old Mr Wan, delivers a speech: '. . . This modest gentleman and this fine and charming lady are a true match made in heaven. We Chinese value virtue above everything else in this world. If one must choose between a man of talent or a man of virtue, how much better it is to choose the gentleman of virtue . . .'

'. . . *The Headquarters of the Extermination Campaign Against the Communist Rebels in North China has announced that forces of more than fifty thousand soldiers have already safely withdrawn to T'ang-ku . . .*'

'. . . From ancient times, many treacherous ministers of state and dissipate sons have had great talent, but have lacked virtue. Those who have wrecked the state and ruined their families are too numerous to count. Thus, Chia-kang's virtue is especially precious in these troubled times. And his virtue is due to the efforts of his wise and saintly mother.'

'. . . *After eight years of the War of Resistance Against Japan, there followed three years of civil war. Not only has this destroyed the only thread of hope that survived the victorious war of resistance, but slaughtered by the tens of thousands . . .*'

'The first commandment in *The Way to Manage a Household* is: Do not listen to the words of women and do not treat your parents ungenerously. Then the household will be at peace and although there may be chaos in the world outside, one will find refuge in the joy of family love . . .'

'*Our armed forces have safely retreated from Feng-p'u and Ho-fei and have destroyed the main bridge over the Huai River . . .*'

'. . . For generations the Sangs have been a family of distinguished scholars. Mulberry Sang herself is a virtuous and capable woman. I will quote from *The Classic for Girls* the following words of advice: "A woman must submit to her husband. A wife should serve her husband's parents with the same attention with which she would hold an overflowing cup and cultivate herself as carefully as if she were treading on ice." Finally, I wish that the new bride and groom be as harmonious together as the lute and zither. May your sons and grandsons be without end.'

'. . . *Fu Tso-i and the Communists are holding peace talks in the Western Hills. Two bombs exploded in the house of one of the negotiators, the former mayor . . .*' Several students stand talking in the doorway.

Next the appointed matchmaker makes a speech. He first solemnly announces that he was forced up on the platform at the last minute and made to play the role of the matchmaker. When he gets to the word 'platform' he looks all around and adds in a low voice: 'There is no platform. In these troubled times, everything must be simplified.'

There are two loud blasts of artillery. The door to the ceremonial hall swings open and shut.

The matchmaker clears his throat and says that his virtue is his brevity. He doesn't want to delay the bride and groom's enjoyment of this happy occasion. 'The scenery was of mountains collapsing, the earth cracking open, bright and dazzling, revealing the golden light. Branches, leaves, flowers, and fruit too: a peach with a hard, solid seed wrapped in tender flesh.' He tells two more jokes and finally finishes by warning the new bride and groom, 'On the wedding night you must watch out for spies and be careful not to divulge your secrets. The city must be protected or else everything will be disrupted.'

My room off the corner of the courtyard becomes the wedding chamber. In the room there is a bed, a desk, and a wardrobe. The rest of the furniture was sold to the junk dealer. Chia-kang's father used to work at the long desk. His things are still arranged on it: a large marble brush stand, two rows of bamboo brush holders holding twelve unused brushes of different sizes. In the white flower-embossed ink box are two pieces of white silk wadding. There's a stack of writing paper with a red inscription 'The Room of Retreat'.

Two large red candles are burning on the desk. In the stove the fire is burning briskly. Chia-kang ran around the whole afternoon looking for a basket of coal to buy especially for the wedding.

The artillery suddenly stops.

Chia-kang takes the flashlight and examines every corner of the room, even under the bed, and then goes out to inspect the courtyard.

He comes in, closes the door, and locks it.

I am sitting on the edge of the bed.

He motions to me, pointing first at me and then at the bed.

I don't move.

He tugs at my dress.

I still don't move.

He paces up and down. He must not say anything. If the groom speaks first he will be the first to die. His shadow leaps from the wall to the ceiling. Then it suddenly looms larger and jumps down at me from the ceiling.

He walks over to me and sits down and begins to unbutton my dress. As soon as he undoes a button, I quickly fasten it up again.

He pushes me down on the bed and strips off all my clothes. Then he takes off all his clothes. Our clothes lie in a heap on the floor.

I slip under the embroidered quilt. He lifts the quilt and falls on top of me. His whole body caresses my body. Suddenly I start itching. I wriggle underneath him and try to scratch. He cocks his head and pouts at me. I pick up his hand and bring it near the candlelight. I can't see anything in the dark. My scalp and the soles of my feet begin to itch. I shove him aside and begin scratching wildly.

He begins scratching himself.

The two of us scratch on the bed: scratch lying down, sitting up, rolling over.

He gets out of bed and picks up one of the candles, still scratching himself.

Some sort of furry substance has been spread all over the bed.

We don't understand who would play a joke like this on our wedding night.

We brush ourselves off and then brush off the bed.

As soon as we get back into bed, a dog starts barking. Then we hear voices and a gong.

'Kill that beast,' the students are yelling.

The sound of the dog, the voices and the gong rush from the main gate through the Gate of Dangling Flowers into the courtyard.

An oil lamp is hung on the courtyard gate. Shadows of men with clubs in their hands appear on the paper window.

The dog is still barking.

The shadows vanish.

A gong sounds.

Six shadow puppets appear on the paper window. Six heads on six sticks nod and bow towards the barking dog.

Voices come from under the window. 'Congratulations to the bride and groom. Today is a happy occasion for the Shen family. If you don't make merry, you won't prosper. We are shadow puppets gathered together from all corners of the world: Pigsy, Monkey, Cripple Li, Chung Li, the God of Thunder, the Fox Spirit, and White Snake Spirit. We have heads but no bodies. You people have bodies but no heads.'

Two voices mimic the voices of clowns, an old man and a woman:

Chao Ch'ien Sun Li (*Old Man*)
Next door threshing rice (*Female Clown*)

Chou Wu Cheng Wang (*Old Man*)
Steal rice and take sugar (*Female Clown*)

Feng Chen Chu Wei (*Old Man*)
Dog climbs up God's altar (*Female Clown*)

Chiang Shen Han Yang (*Old Man*)
Eat the child and be silent (*Female Clown*)

The gong sounds again. The two voices begin to improvise nonsense variations on the Confucian text, *The Great Learning*:

The way to great learning (*Old Man*)
is to knock down Teacher (*Female Clown*)

To understand enlightened virtue (*Old Man*)
is to pick up Teacher (*Female Clown*)

To be close to the people (*Old Man*)
is to carry Teacher out the door (*Female Clown*)

To achieve great goodness (*Old Man*)
is to bury Teacher in a muddy hole (*Female Clown*)

The flickering shadow-clowns on the window sing to us. Chia-kang and I roll on the bed, scratching ourselves wildly. The shadows lurch towards the dog and the dog howls. The shadows swing toward us and we freeze on the bed. Their voices begin counting, the male and female clowns alternating the count:

One two (*Male Clown*)
Two one (*Female Clown*)

One two three (*Male Clown*)
Three two one (*Female Clown*)

One two three four (*Male Clown*)
Four three two one (*Female Clown*)

One two three four five (*Male Clown*)
Five four three two one (*Female Clown*)

One two three four five six (*Male Clown*)
Six five four three two one (*Female Clown*)

One two three four five six seven (*Male Clown*)
Seven six five four three two one (*Female Clown*)

One two three four five six seven eight (*Male Clown*)
Eight seven six five four three two one (*Female Clown*)

One two three four five six seven eight nine (*Male Clown*)
Kill! (*Male and Female Clowns*)

Suddenly the heads plunge towards the dog. Then all we hear is the crashing of sticks against the wall.

The dog howls and the door to our room bursts open. The dog darts into the room.

It rushes from corner to corner and finally scrambles under the bed. It yelps hysterically and its back thumps against the mattress as it twists and turns. It rubs against the furry substance that litters the floor.

The students stand in the doorway. They hold the sticks with the puppet heads, and they laugh at us: the two of us on the bed and the dog under the bed.

Chia-kang and I throw off the quilt and get out of bed.

They clap and cheer.

I stand in the corner naked. Chia-kang, also naked, picks up the mattress and the dog chases madly in a circle under the bed frame, barking.

The students drive the dog out with their sticks.

Chia-kang shuts the door.

The dog howls in the courtyard.

There is a loud thumping of sticks and the dog stops barking. It is dead.

Chia-kang and I lie on the bed and listen to the sound of fur rubbing against the stone slabs. They are dragging the dog's carcass away. I curl up into a ball.

Chia-kang turns over and straddles my body.

'Mulberry, you're not a virgin!' He pushes into my body and blurts out the first words of the wedding night. Then he clenches his teeth. He is the first one to speak tonight.

'Peace has been restored to Peking. Fu Tso-i has announced a peace communique. From 22 January on, more than two hundred thousand troops under his command will be garrisoned outside Peking to await reorganisation by the People's Liberation Army. The Peking-Tientsin campaign has finally ended . . .'

Suddenly the shelling stops. The lights come back on.

The hawkers begin yelling in the lanes again.

'Sweet apples!'

'Fresh dates!'

'Popcorn!'

It is snowing. Powdery snow flutters in the air. It's one of the few times it has snowed since I arrived in Peking.

Chia-kang sprawls on top of me, his head dangling over my shoulder. Suddenly he collapses.

He makes me tell him about Refugee Student in Chü-t'ang Gorge. I tell him that I have forgotten what happened in the past. I tell him that the night I married him I made up my mind: even if he had to roll down the Mountain of Knives I would roll down with him and if he died, I would be a widow all of my life. He says I shouldn't have thought about being a widow on our wedding night. It's an unlucky omen. He rolls off my body and stretches out beside me.

The wet smell between my legs makes me want to vomit. I pick up his hand and place it on my breast. He slides his hand down my body.

When his hand reaches below my stomach it stops. He asks if Refugee Student touched me like that. I repeat: I forgot what happened in the past a long time ago. But he is obsessed. He caresses me but he thinks about him.

I say, then don't touch me. He says he can't help it, he has to touch me. Then go on, I say.

His hand slides down my stomach. The winter sun shines on the window paper.

He drives into my body several times, then turns over and sprawls beside me. He wipes his leg with a washcloth and laughs, saying that next year the Communists will discover that the population of Peking has dramatically increased. In a city under siege, there's nothing to do except make love. We can call our children the generation of the siege.

'It's New Year's. God of Wealth for Sale.' A hawker selling paper images of the God of Wealth yells from The Gate of Dangling Flowers.

'It's getting windy. Don't let the flame go out. Chia-kang, hold it carefully . . . At last, here we are, the five branches of the Shen family together again. Dozens of burning flames, like little flowers. Look,

94

the flames of great-grandfather and great-grandmother are arranged in the first row. The flames of the sons and daughters-in-law and grandchildren and the flames of the concubines all arranged in order in front of the altar. See how they stretch across three courtyards to the entrance of Li-shih Lane. Pass the lighted flames along, hold them carefully. Chia-kang, be careful. It's getting windy . . .'

'Mother,' Chia-kang is standing beside the *k'ang*. 'Mother, are you awake? The Eighth Army has entered the city. There is going to be a huge parade today. Mulberry, Hsing-hsing and I want to go watch it from the Gate of Heavenly Peace.'

'Oh, have all the flames gone out?' She turns over on the *k'ang*. 'Chia-kang, where is my flame?'

'This is no time to think about flames, Mother. The Eighth Army has entered the city.'

'Oh, I thought we were at our old house on Li-shih Lane.'

'That was twenty years ago, Mother. Today is 3 February 1949. Eighth Army has entered the city. We're going to the Gate of Heavenly Peace to see what they look like.'

'Don't go. Be careful. You might run into Chia-ch'ing.' She stares hard at us for a while. 'Chia-kang, Mulberry, Hsing-hsing, are you all here in this room with me?'

'Yes, Mother, we're all here. You have been lying in bed too long. When you get better we'll go out for a walk with you.'

'Good. Just like before, in the spring when we went to see the black peonies at the Temple of Reverence. They are the same flowers for which Empress Wu held a ceremony to make them bloom faster, but it didn't work. But *I* saw them in bloom.' She laughs and turns back to face the wall.

'That's right, Mother. You even saw the hortensia bloom in the imperial garden. In all of Peking, there is only one hortensia flower and it only blooms once a year. The peony is the flower of wealth and nobility and the hortensia flower is the flower of peace. And you have seen them both.'

'Yes, Chia-kang, I am one of the lucky ones. Chia-kang, with all this fighting, we didn't really celebrate the New Year. All we did to celebrate was to paste up the Gods of the Door. Next year we really have to do things right.'

'That's right, Mother. I'll go with you to do the New Year shopping. We'll buy New Year pictures at the flower market: "Fortune and Longevity", "Three-fold Happiness", "Good Fortune as One Wishes", "Wealth and High Rank Overflowing", "Plump Pig Bows at the Gate",

"Summon Wealth and Gather Treasures", we'll buy them all. We'll buy some pretty lanterns and hang them in the courtyard, in the house, everywhere. We'll buy some long strings of firecrackers and set them off and scraps of red paper will fly all over the courtyard. And I'll buy you some pretty velvet flowers, red and green, to wear in your hair.'

'You want to dress me up to look like a coquette,' laughs Aunt Shen. 'There are many different festivals for the New Year. On the eve of the twenty-third of the twelfth month, there is the offering to the Kitchen God. On the night of the thirtieth, you must welcome back the Kitchen God and the God of Happiness. The second day of the New Year, you make offerings to the God of Wealth. The eighth day of the New Year, you make offerings to the God of Wealth. The eighth day of the New Year, you pass around lighted flames to thank the ancestors for their protection and blessings in keeping our family healthy and safe. From the thirteenth to the seventeenth is the Lantern Festival. We'll buy a glazed glass lotus-flower lantern to hang at the Main Gate . . .'

'Those students tore off one side of the Main Gate for firewood,' Hsing-hsing says to me in a low voice. 'If she goes on talking like this, we'll miss the parade.'

'Chia-kang, Mulberry, Hsing-hsing, sit down and chat with me. A little conversation cheers me up. You know what? I've been walking all over the main streets and the alleys. I went back to all the places I had been before: The White Cloud Temple, the Peach Palace, Yung-ho Palace, the Temple of Exalted Wealth, the Temple of the Fire God . . . all the festivals at those temples. The Wen-ming Tea House where T'an Hsin-pei, Yang Hsiao-lou, and Yu Shu-yen sang opera. The Chi-hsiang Tea House where the great opera singers Mei Lan-fang and Yang Hsiao-lou sang. The tiger stalls at Tung-an Market and Hsi-tan Market. The Old Imperial Palace, the Pavilion of Sudden Rain, the Summer Palace. I visited the First Balcony overlooking the river in the northern part of the city and ate sesame biscuits and listened to the eunuchs of the Ch'ing dynasty telling stories. And I saw all the imperial parks. And the Wall of Nine Dragons still hasn't fallen down. And . . .'

'Mother, we really have to go now. If we don't go now, we'll miss the parade.'

'Chia-kang, what you don't see can't hurt you. Why do you want to go see the Communists?'

'Everyone's going, Auntie,' says Hsing-hsing.

'Chia-kang, what if you run into Chia-ch'ing?'

'If Chia-ch'ing is there, there'll be a big family reunion, won't there?' says Hsing-hsing.

No one answers. Chia-kang reaches over and turns on the radio.

'. . . *I serve in the camp of the Hegemon of Western Ch'u. I am Yü-chi. I was well versed in the classics and in swordsmanship at an early age. Ever since that time I have followed my lord to campaigns and battles east and west. There have been hardships and difficulties. When will peace come . . .*'

'OK, you may go,' the old lady says. 'I'll listen to Mei Lan-fang sing *The Hegemon Bids Farewell to His Concubine*!'

A strong wind full of sand and grit swirls along the ground. Eventually, everything, everyone crumbles into sand at the touch of a finger. Peking has turned to sand. The streets in front of the Gate of Heavenly Peace, Kung-an Street, Ch'i-p'an Street, Ministry of Justice Street and East and West Ch'ang-an Street are filled with shadowy figures, moving through the sand.

'Can you see the Gate of Heavenly Peace?' Chia-kang asks me.

We are walking on West Ch'ang-an Street toward the Gate of Heavenly Peace.

'I can't see anything. The sand is too thick.'

Chia-kang and Hsing-hsing compete with each other to tell me, the outsider, about the Gate of Heavenly Peace.

The Gate of Heavenly Peace is the main gate into the Imperial City. Inside the Imperial City, there's a moat. The Forbidden City lies across the moat. Inside the Forbidden City are the Imperial Palaces. Each palace is surrounded by a high wall. The Gate of Heavenly Peace is a many-tiered tower on the city gate which sits on a white marble pedestal. The roof is covered with glazed yellow tile. The walls and the pillars are red. Inside and outside of the Gate of Heavenly Peace statues of beasts and dragons are standing. Prancing along the edge of the roof are dragons, phoenixes, lions, horses, seahorses, fish, fire-eating unicorns, and one Immortal. On each end is a beast with a dragon head, with a sword stuck in his back to keep him from escaping. There are also strange beasts whose tails stir up waves to make rain. The River of Gold Water runs in front of the Gate of Heavenly Peace. Seven stone bridges straddle the river and on each bridge a pair of white marble pillars stand propping up the heavens. A plate has been placed on top of each pillar to gather dew. On each plate a dragon-headed wolf squats, facing south, watching for the emperor's return. A dragon curls around each pillar, his four five-clawed feet dance in the folds of the encircling clouds. Two stone lions squat in front of the Gate of Heavenly Peace. They have broad foreheads, curly manes. They lift their heads up and grin. Their plump glistening bodies are draped with fringed harnesses and bells. The lion on the left is playing with an embroidered ball with his right paw. The lioness on the right plays with a lion cub with her left paw. All these beasts and dragons protect the Imperial palaces. There is a lance wound on the lioness's stomach. At the end of the Ming Dynasty the rebel, Li Chih-chen, fought his way into Peking as far as the Gate of Heavenly Peace. The stone lioness came to life and leaped at him. He lunged at her with his lance and she became stone again. Even now, when it rains, blood flows from the wound on her stomach.

'We welcome the People's Liberation Army to Peking,' shouts from the distance the woman announcer with a precise, distinct voice.

The Gate of Heavenly Peace is in front of us. We are standing beside the wounded lioness. The five-star flag, a huge portrait of Mao Tse-tung and banners with slogans are hung on the Gate of Heavenly Peace. 'The Gate of Heavenly Peace is the sacred ground of the people's liberation!' 'Celebration of the Liberation of Peking!' 'At the Gate of Heavenly Peace burns the eternal flame of struggle!' A whirlwind of sand beats against the flags, the portrait, the banners.

The shadow of the parade moves through the vast expanse of the square and approaches the Gate of Heavenly Peace.

'. . . We welcome the strong, the victorious People's Liberation Army. The People's Liberation Army is the defender of peace in our fatherland! And the builder of socialism in our fatherland . . .'

The voice gets louder. The parade is still invisible in the sandstorm. There is only the voice.

'. . . The liberation of Peking is in accord with the eight conditions for peace which were laid down by the Chinese Communist Party and this is the first good example of ending the war by peaceful means. The liberation of Peking hastens the victorious conclusion of the War of the People's Liberation . . .' A procession of shadows is passing by in the sandstorm.

A giant portrait of Mao Tse-tung appears out of the sand and wind and is hoisted above the heads of a crowd of young men riding in the broadcast truck.

'Long live Mao Tse-tung!'

'Safeguard Chairman Mao's eight conditions of peace! Punish the war criminals! Abolish the invalid constitution! Abolish the invalid legal system . . .'

The cries swirl away in the sandstorm.
Workers.
Students.
Children.
Civil servants.

Groups of people shouting slogans and waving banners in the blowing sand file past the Gate of Heavenly Peace.

Suddenly comes the noise of drums, cymbals, trumpets, and whistles. Children on stilts dressed in loose robes with wide sleeves appear, waving coloured fans and dancing with their instruments to the Rice Sprout Song.

The People's Liberation Army emerges from the sandstorm.
Infantry.
Cavalry.
Armoured Corps.

Tanks equipped with machine guns and mortars are followed by ambulances and jeeps. Hundreds of vehicles, all US-made, rumble past the Gate of Heavenly Peace. Soldiers, dressed in full uniform, their faces wrinkled and expressionless, very young yet very old, stare straight ahead as they march – six abreast, past the soaring, circling dragons and beasts which protect the Gate of Heavenly Peace. They vanish into the blowing sand. Rows and rows of soldiers emerge from the sand and wind.

'Look, it goes on and on,' an onlooker in the silent crowd remarks as we watch from the Gate of Heavenly Peace.

'That's him!' Hsing-hsing grabs my arm.

'Who?' asks Chia-kang.

'. . .'

'Who, Hsing-hsing?'

'Your brother!'

'Where?'

'There! The one in uniform, back to us, leading the troops in shouting slogans.'

The three of us stand on tiptoe to see, but we can only make out half his face. A gust of sand and wind whirls around us. When we open our eyes again, he has vanished in the sandstorm.

The God of the Door that we pasted up for New Year is still there on the half of the main gate that remains. He is dressed in colourful armour. His chest is stuck out and his stomach protrudes. He has two swords. He leans on one sword and brandishes the other.

Some of the students come out of the house and tear the God of the Door off the gate. They rip him apart and throw the pieces on the icy ground.

They paste up a slogan in his place on the ruined gate:

PROTECTING THE PEOPLE'S PROPERTY IS THE NUMBER ONE DUTY!

Through the gap in the main gate another slogan can be seen on the Gate of the Dangling Flowers:

THE FRESH BLOOD OF REVOLUTION BRINGS FORTH BEAUTIFUL FRUIT.

'Phoenix your son has returned. You have come back too. Good, you have both come to settle accounts with me . . .' I enter the room and hear the old lady talking to herself as she lies on the *k'ang*. 'Phoenix, your son has become a Communist and you're acting too proud . . . you have come to take me to the Western Heaven. But I know I am not allowed to go there. "When the Goddess of Mercy was engaged in the deep course of wisdom, she beheld the Five Substances and saw that these substances in their self-nature were empty. O Sariputra, here form is emptiness and emptiness is form . . ." The Wall of Nine Dragons is falling down. It's falling on top of me. I can't get out from under it. Phoenix, help me. Phoenix, Phoenix . . .'

'It's not Phoenix. It's Mulberry.' I sit on the edge of the *k'ang* and massage her legs.

'Ah, Phoenix isn't here.' She is still facing the wall. 'Is Chia-ch'ing here?'

'No, he has never been here.'

'Didn't you see him at the Gate of Heavenly Peace?'

'We could only see half his face, and we couldn't really tell if it was him or not.'

'If only Phoenix were still alive. Chia-ch'ing wouldn't do anything to us in front of his own mother.'

'Maybe he hasn't come to Peiping yet. Don't try to think too much.'

'My brain won't listen to me. I don't want to think, but it keeps on thinking, what I owe to other people, how I deceived others. I remember it all. Mulberry, do you hate me?'

'No, not anymore.'

'Mulberry, I have something to tell you.'

'All right.'

'That year when I couldn't get pregnant, I went to the Divine Astrologer of the Imperial Polarity at the festival of the Fire God to have my fortune told. My horoscope said that if I were to conceive the child would be famous, but since there have always been few males born into the Shen family, I would have to be careful with the child. He meant that the Shen family line was about to end. Chia-ch'ing is a Communist. We can't depend on him to pass on the family name. Only Chia-kang can do that.'

'I'm pregnant.'

She suddenly turns over and takes my hand. 'Mulberry, you're pregnant? Then I won't worry about it anymore. I don't care about money or position, all I want is a big bunch of children around me. No, no, enough children to fill the whole main hall, each holding a flower flame – a long line of burning flames like a huge fire dragon.'

'That day will come for you. I want a lot of children.'

She presses my hand and laughs.

'. . . Fox fur . . . The People's . . . Communists . . .' The refugee students are discussing something in the courtyard.

'Mulberry, don't go out there, it's dangerous.'

There are footsteps in the main hall.

'Chia-kang?'

'He went to the barber shop on the alley to get his hair cut,' I lie. I don't want her to know that he is at the People's Court.

'Someone's coming. He has come back already.'

Hsing-hsing comes into the room. 'Auntie, I came especially to tell you something, to prepare you for it. I saw it with my own eyes, on Wang-fu-ching Boulevard. The Nationalist slogans that used to be there are now all changed to Communist slogans. They were making a well-dressed woman in a fox fur coat crawl on the ground. A group of students surrounded her singing the Rice Sprout Song and taunting her, saying, "People in New China don't wear fur coats, only animals wear fur coats." Auntie, I know you have a lot of furs. By all means, don't wear them. The students in the courtyard are saying that they won't let anyone wear a fur coat in this courtyard.'

'I sold some of my furs. The rest I gave away. The only thing I have left is my fox fur jacket. It's hanging over there by the bed. When I get up I always put it on. Hsing-hsing, what should I do with it?'

'If you try to give it away now, no one would want it.'

Chia-kang comes into the room. Hsing-hsing repeats the story again and imitates the woman in the fox fur coat crawling on the ground.

Chia-kang throws the fur jacket on the floor and stamps on it. 'What kind of world is this anyway? If I knew things would turn out like this, I would have gone South even if I had to be a beggar.'

Hsing-hsing laughs, 'Second Master Shen, the South is about to fall, too. The executive government has already moved from Nanking to Canton. The Nationalist representatives are at the peace talks: Shao Li-tzu, Chang Shih-chao and three others have already arrived in Peking.'

'Hsing-hsing,' Chia-kang stares at her. 'How do you know so much about what's going on outside? Are you . . .'

'Chia-kang, I'm not a Communist,' Hsing-hsing says, staring back, curling her lip in a smile. 'I couldn't be one even if I wanted to. I wasn't born in the right class. But the world is changing and we have to learn things all over again, learn how to be new, different people or else we can't go on living. The Peking Military Control Committee of the People's Liberation Army has already been established. All sorts of discussion groups have been set up, too. There are discussion groups, demonstrations, speeches every day. Yesterday two hundred thousand people held a meeting at the Gate of Heavenly Peace. Now everybody is busy: workers, students, peasants, merchants. And here you are, Second Master Shen, still at home clutching an old fur jacket and you are not able to decide what to do with it!'

'Throw it in the outhouse!' Chia-kang picks up the fur jacket, signals to me, and heads for the door.

I follow him into the main hall.

'From now on, you've got to be careful about Hsing-hsing,' he says in a low voice as he caresses the fox fur. 'Maybe she's a spy for the Communists.'

'What happened at the People's Court?'

'Amah Ch'ien's son sued us saying we exploited her and tormented her to death. He wants half of the house as well as the expenses for her burial.'

'What did the court decide?'

'The house belongs to the people. It's not the Shen's nor the Ch'ien's. We'll have to give him more money to settle it. One of these days, we're going to get kicked out of here. You stay inside and don't go out. Those students are getting pushy.'

Chia-kang wraps the jacket up. When it's dark, he takes the package and steals past the students dancing the Rice Sprout Dance in the courtyard.

When he returns, Hsing-hsing is laughing as she tells us about her grandfather and Joy. Joy's belly is swelling. The old man had his fortune told: Joy will certainly have an outstanding son. The old man was delighted and strutted around joyfully. 'Marriage at sixty, a grand birthday celebration at eighty. There are twenty good years left to enjoy.'

After Hsing-hsing leaves, the old lady calls Chia-kang to the *k'ang*. She faces the wall and says listlessly, 'Chia-kang, remember this: no matter what happens, the Shen family line must not be broken. Mulberry is pregnant. You two must get away to the South.'

It's spring. A narrow coffin is carried out of the courtyard. Chia-kang and I aren't dressed in mourning. We bury the old lady outside the City Gate in the paupers' graveyard, the Muddy Hole.

Chia-kang and I take a train for the South.

Peking. Tientsin. Ching-hai. Ch'ing County. Ts'ang County. Tung-kuang. Te County. P'ing-yüan. Yü-ch'eng. Chi-nan. Chang-ch'iu. Ch'ing-chou. Chu-liu-tien.

Everyone has to get off at each stop where we are inspected by Communist guards. It's always the same routine. The same questions. The same answers. Each person walks forward, gives the Eighth Army guard his travel pass, shows him his empty hands and turns around. What's your name? Where were you born? Where are you going? Why are you going there? What do you do? All those questions.

Chia-kang and I pretend not to know each other. He's a cloth seller from Shantung. I'm from Hsu-chou; I sell fritters of twisted dough. We sit in two separate sections of the freight train.

The Peking-Tientsin railroad already has their passenger trains running. Between Tientsin and P'u-chou, there are only freight trains. I left my wedding ring and the broken jade griffin in Peking.

We come to another station. Wei County is the last stop in the Communist-controlled area. Beyond Wei County is no man's land; the trains can't connect the two sides. Beyond the no-man's land lies Nationalist-held Ch'ing-tao.

Twelve men and women have been travelling in the same car since Tientsin. Now each of us picks up his own luggage and walks to the Inn. There's a sign in big black characters on the mud wall at the Inn:

> EVERYONE ALLOCATED LAND MUST JOIN THE ARMY
>
> ANYONE NOT JOINING THE ARMY IS REACTIONARY

The twelve of us, strangers, sleep on a large communal *k'ang*. I lie next to the wall, beside Chia-kang. We are silent, all twelve of us. I haven't said a word for six days. Now I have to say something. I take Chia-kang's hand out from under the covers and write on his palm with my finger. We talk on his palm.

CAN'T SLEEP
COME HERE I'LL ROCK YOU TO SLEEP
NO
?
AFRAID
SLEEP DON'T BE AFRAID
FIRST, SAFETY
SAFETY WHERE
CH'ING-TAO
COMMUNISTS ALMOST THERE
NANKING
COMMUNISTS ALMOST THERE TOO
RETURN PEKING
CAN'T RETURN
MUST KEEP GOING
UNTIL WHEN
UNTIL GOOD PLACE FOR CHILD
TAIWAN
BEAUTIFUL ISLAND
I WANT A SON
I WANT A DAUGHTER
SON CALLED YAO-TSU
DAUGHTER CALLED SANG-WA

No man's land.

The sun is setting. Only a few more miles to Ts'ai Village. No sign of the village in sight. The twelve people on the narrow path are silent. We are still strangers. We have to hurry. Wheelbarrows piled with luggage creak over the dry, cracked earth. Dust rises in veils, separating each of us from the others. Each figure is blurred, hidden in a tent of dust. The faster we walk, the quicker our hands swing: clenched fists poking through the swirling tents of dust. Wherever we go, the tent of dust whirls around us, no matter how fast or how far we walk.

It's growing dark. Still a couple of miles. the twelve of us are lined up on the narrow path. Chia-kang and I are at the end.

At the front a lantern is lit.

Ah, we all murmur. Someone coughs, spits loudly; another stumbles on a rock, and curses.

The lantern is held up, lighting the path for those at the back.

'Mulberry, I still want a son,' says Chia-kang in a low voice, leaning forward.

'And I still want a daughter.'

'Only sons, no daughters allowed,' he says and punches me playfully on the back.

Ahead of us a man from Shantung chuckles, 'I could tell all the time that you two were married.'

The lantern goes out.

Ah, we all murmur again.

'Excuse me, anyone have a match?' asks the one carrying the lantern.

'Here!' Chia-kang yells.

The man stops and lets the people behind him pass. 'Watch out, A pit. Be careful, folks, there's a pit. Be careful, ma'am.' He stands in the dark and helps people across.

Chia-kang walks up and hands him the matches.

The lantern is lit again.

'Thanks, sir.' He hands the matches back to Chia-kang.

'Keep them, man, you have to hold the lantern.' Chia-kang threw the matches back into the man's hand.

There are several cottages at Ts'ai Village. All empty. On the slope stands a temple with a broken signboard above its entrance. The name of the temple is in fading gold characters.

The twelve of us relax in the main hall. The Buddha with a thousand arms lies on its back on the mud floor. The child in the Goddess of Mercy's arms is headless. Only the Laughing Buddha is intact, laughing. We light the altar lamp, untie our luggage and sit on bedrolls and eat our dry food. The main hall comes to life.

'Well, now!' someone suddenly yells. 'Let me sing you a passage from *Beat the Drum and Condemn Ts'ao Ts'ao.*

> Although you serve as Prime Minister
> You can't tell the virtuous from the stupid
> Your thief's eyes are impure
> You can't take good advice
> Your thief's ears are impure
> You don't study the classics
> Your thief's mouth is impure
> You cherish thoughts of usurping the throne
> Your thief's heart is impure.'

Someone else chimes in:

> 'Beyond the mountains are beautiful lands
> Where people toil dawn to dusk
> To eat, you must work with your own hands
> No one serves as another man's slave.

'. . . Hearing that, Huang Chung gets on his horse. He points his sword and shouts, "Master Kuan," the Great Han Army has been defeated. From the four corners of the empire gallant men rise up in the chaos . . .

'. . . Suddenly something jumped out at me. And you know what it was? A tiger. Where did that tiger come from? He was living in a remote valley on South Peak.

> Look, there's a dragon on my head
> a dragon on my body
> on my left side is a dragon
> on my right side is a dragon
> there's a dragon in front of me
> and a dragon behind me
> nine dragons all around me
> golden dragons with five claws . . .

'Hey, all you opera singers, storytellers and folk singers. Stop all that noise and listen to my ghost story.'

The singing and chanting stop. Only the voice telling the story is heard:

'Yü and the girl in the green dress finish making love. Yü asks the girl to sing him a song. She laughs and says that she doesn't dare. Yü caresses her tenderly and repeats his request. The girl in green says that she doesn't mean to be inhospitable, but she is afraid someone might overhear. She lowers the gauze curtain and leans against the bedpost and softly begins to sing:

> The Han River ceases its flow
> Birds soar high
> Where will they land
> Here and there they fly
> Tall peaks not so low
> As city walls nearby.

She finishes her song and gets down from the bed. She looks out the window, looks in the corners, inspects the room. Yü laughs at her timidity and coaxes her back to bed. He begins to make love to her again, but the girl in green remains passive and melancholy, unwilling to make love. Yü entreats her and finally succeeds once more. At dawn, she gets dressed and climbs down from the bed, walks to the door, hesitates and returns to his side, quite frightened. Yü accompanies her to the door and watches as she vanishes down the corridor. Suddenly he hears her scream for help. He races over but sees no one, only hears a faint moan under the eaves. Looking closely, he sees a spider web under the eaves. The moan appears to come from the web. Looking again he sees a big spider with something in its grip. He tears down the web. A large green honey bee falls to the ground.'

'Hey, I'd like to meet a bee like that!'

'Does anybody know if the Communists have crossed the Yangtze yet?'

'Hey, you motherfuckers, still talking about the war. In all of China this is the only place where there's no fighting. Look, see how beautiful the moon is, feel how soft the spring breeze is. The trees on the hill outside the temple are sprouting green leaves.'

'Hey, old man, thanks for carrying the lantern for us. What's your name?'

'Don't ask me my name. And don't ask where I'm going. I'll stay here in this dilapidated temple and become the ancestor of later generations. I'll take the first name in the Book of the Hundred

Names; just call me Chao, as in Chao founder of the Sung Dynasty.'

'Master Chao, may I ask where Madame Chao is?'

'That's something I haven't thought about yet. I'm still a bachelor.'

Chia-kang glances left and right, looks at my stomach and laughs. 'I'm the one who is going to be the ancestor of later generations. My wife is pregnant. I'll take the next name in the *Book of the Hundred Names.* Call me Ch'ien.'

'If you're going to be the ancestor of later generations, you better take care of your wife. On the road, you really tried to fool us. You avoided your woman as if she were a locust. But I knew a long time ago that you two were together.'

'We'll take the third name in the book,' a young man who looks like a student takes the hand of the girl sitting next to him.

'You too? Now that I couldn't tell.'

'We have just gotten engaged.'

'Get married tonight,' Master Chao jumps up. 'The main hall will be the wedding chamber. The mud floor the wedding bed. You can roll around and turn somersaults on the floor. Make love in front of the Buddha. The god of heaven, the god of earth, the god of man, none will bother you. No need for a minister, the witnesses or a matchmaker. The hell with them all.'

'Good idea!'

'No ceremony whatsoever. All you do is get into bed, no, get down on the ground to sleep.'

'What could be a better ceremony?'

The student and the girl look at each other. He pinches her. She pinches him. They lean against each other and laugh.

Chia-kang runs over and beats the drum in the hall three times. The wedding ceremony begins.

We all retreat to the courtyard. The bride and groom are the only ones left in the hall.

In a woodshed in the corner of the courtyard, we find a huge butterfly kite and a small red lantern.

A half moon shines on the hill. A soft breeze. We light the lantern and tie it to the kite with some string. The kite flutters upwards. The wings spread wide. As it goes higher, the lantern becomes a tiny point of light. We run; the string whispers in the wind. We race on the hill toward the mountain top. The kite soars higher, flickering like a firefly off the darkness. Suddenly the kite catches fire, blazes red above the village.

We return to the temple. Through the door to the hall we can see the bride and groom sleeping soundly on the mud floor, the quilt has slipped off half-revealing their nakedness. The bride sleeps cuddled in his arm; her mouth against his cheek, right arm curled around his neck.

Her right breast touches his chest and shimmers in the moonlight.

Chia-kang leads me to a small shed where hay is stored. For the first time, he tells me that I have a beautiful body.

PART III

ONE

Peach's Third Letter to the Man from the USA Immigration Service

(22 February 1970)

CHARACTERS

PEACH, she lives with a tree cutter, a Polish Jew, in an abandoned water tower in Mid-west of America; they call it 'The Womb'. With her letter, Peach encloses Mulberry's diary kept during her life in the attic in Taiwan.
THE MAN FROM THE IMMIGRATION SERVICE.

Dear Sir:

I'm living with a lumberjack in a water tower in an open field south of Des Moines. The water tower is a round wooden tank supported by three legs, like the Eagle space capsule that landed on the moon. It stands in the middle of a vast expanse of corn and from the highway you can see it a long way away. If you want to chase me, then come on. I'll be sending you reports all along the way because I want to convince you that I'm not Mulberry.

I was hitchhiking in Des Moines when I saw a very muscular man pulling a thick rope. The rope was tied around a huge termite-eaten elm tree; there was a semi-circle cut deep into the trunk and a large saw lay beside the tree on the ground. It was cold and dry outside. The man's face was bathed in sweat. He gritted his teeth as he pulled. The elm cracked and the gash opened wider. He suddenly jumped aside and the huge tree crashed to the earth.

I was standing by the roadside, watching him fell the huge tree.

He straddled his motorcycle and was about to start it up, when he suddenly turned around and looked at me.

'I'm waiting for a ride.'

'Where are you going?'

'Anywhere is fine with me.'

'Let's go get a drink.'

'OK.'

I climbed onto the back of his motorcycle and clutched him around the waist. The motorcycle moved like wind, like lightning. We rode up and down the undulating backroads of the Midwest, rising and falling, rising and falling. Dry flecks of fine snow were suspended in the sun.

The motorcycle stopped at the water tower. All around the earth was black and frozen. The grass around the water tower was very tall and the weeds had been hacked down unevenly. A large scythe was sunk in the grass. I was half-buried by the weeds.

'I'll make a path for you. This is where I live.' He picked up the scythe, hacking at the weeds with one hand, pulling them aside with the other, each stroke harder than the one before. 'Where are you from?'

'I'm a foreigner.'

'I could tell. I am, too. This is the age of the foreigner. People drift around everywhere. I'm a Polish Jew.'

'I'm an Asian Jew,' I joked.

He bent over, gripping the scythe and cut a path open through the weeds, all the way from the road to the foot of the water tower.

I climbed up into the water tower from that newly cut path. He had made the furniture in the tower from logs all by himself. We drank gin. He said that when he was thirteen he had been in Auschwitz. The Nazis had used his father, mother and older sister for bacteriological experiments, and they had died in the camp. After he got out, he became a drifter. He makes a living by cutting down termite-infested trees. By chance he discovered this abandoned water tower. He felt very safe there. No one could harm him there. During the time of the Indians, the water tower had supplied water to the soldiers. But now it's the space age. Who would want such a broken-down wooden tank? Deer, antelope, squirrels, and rabbits live around here, but no people. When he was small, he dreamed of having a zoo when he grew up, a zoo without tigers. When he was four he was almost eaten by a tiger. His father had taken him to the circus. They sat by the gate where the animals enter the ring. The tiger was supposed to come out and jump through hoops of fire. When he saw the tiger coming out, shaking its head and swishing its tail back and forth, he jumped up excitedly. The

114

tiger suddenly turned and clamped his head in its teeth. He heard the crowd's startled screams. He wasn't frightened but his neck hurt a little. He couldn't see anything; the tiger's mouth was a black cave. Then the trainer came and pried the tiger's mouth open. The teeth left holes in his head and neck, and its claws had ripped the skin on his shoulders. As he felt the blood dripping from his head, he told his father that he wanted to grow up in a hurry. He wanted to be as big as Tarzan so he could kill tigers.

I like boys who want to kill tigers, so I have settled down in this water tower. I have decided to have my baby here. Right now I feel that little guy kicking in my stomach.

I'm sending you Mulberry's diary written in the attic in Taipei, the T'ang poems and the Diamond Sutra which she copied out by hand, and Shen Chia-kang's pile of newspaper clippings.

Peach
22 February 1970

TWO
Mulberry's Notebook
An Attic in Taiwan
(Summer 1957–Summer 1959)

CHARACTERS

MULBERRY, she is now 28. She and her husband and child have lived in Taiwan since 1949. They are now hiding out from the Nationalist police in an attic. Her shattered past, her guilt, and life in the attic begin to wear away at her sanity. She begins to show signs of schizophrenia.

CHIA-KANG, is now in his 30s. He is wanted by the police for embezzling. Never very strong or independent he has become more and more self-pitying and bitter.

SANG-WA, their daughter, born in Taiwan.

MR TS'AI, an old friend of Mulberry's father who allows them to hide in an attic in his storage shed.

AUNT TS'AI, his wife, dying of cancer.

(A) Summer, 1957

The noise on the attic roof has started up again. It's like rotting ceiling beams splitting apart, or like rats gnawing on bones, gnawing their way slowly from the corner all along the eaves, stopping just above the place where I am lying. Gnawing overhead from my toes to my forehead, then back down again. Gnawing up and down, finally stopping at my breasts. Gnawing my nipples. Two rows of tiny, sharp rat teeth.

I am sleeping on my *tatami* mat.

Chia-kang is sleeping on his *tatami* mat.

Sang-wa is sleeping on her *tatami* mat.

Clothes are piled on half of the remaining *tatami* mat. The moon shines down on a small patch of the *tatami* mat where the clock sits. It's twelve thirteen.

Overhead the rat stops and gnaws at my nipples. Chia-kang writes something on my palm with his index finger. We talk on my palm.

SOMEONE ON ROOF
RAT
MAN
WHO
SOMEONE IS FOLLOWING US
WHAT SHOULD WE DO
WAIT
FOR WHAT
WAIT TILL HE LEAVES
SHOULDN'T HAVE RUN AWAY
BUT YOU'D BE IN JAIL
NO WAY OUT EITHER WAY
IT'S GNAWING MY HEART

Chia-kang reaches over to feel my heart, then continues writing on my palm.

I LET YOU DOWN
I CHOSE THIS
YOU'RE NOT A CRIMINAL
I AM
WHAT CRIME?
HARD TO SAY
MAYBE SPEND WHOLE LIFE HERE
THAT'S OK
WHY
CLEAN CONSCIENCE
HOW ABOUT SANG-WA
SHE HAS NO CHOICE
HE'S GONE
HOW DO YOU KNOW
HE'S GNAWING MY HEAD
MY HEAD
NO, *MINE*
CAN'T HEAR IT

117

```
GNAWING MY NOSE
CAN'T HEAR IT
GNAWING MY STOMACH
CAN'T HEAR IT
HE'S LEAVING
HOW DO YOU KNOW
NOT GNAWING ANYMORE
HAS HE GONE
YES
ALIVE AGAIN
SLEEP WELL
```

Taiwan is a green eye floating alone on the sea.

To the east is the eyelid.

To the south is a corner of the eye.

To the west another eyelid.

To the north, the other corner of the eye.

The sea surrounds the eyelids and the corners of the eye.

It's now typhoon season.

The little attic window looks out over the street. Peering out from the left side of the window, we can see the roof and the fence of the house at Number Three. Peering out from the right side we can see the roof and fence of the house at Number Five. Crows fly above the rooftops. Directly across from the window is the blackened chimney of a crematorium. We don't dare stand in front of the window for fear someone might see us.

The attic and the Ts'ai's house are enclosed by the same wall. Underneath the attic is a shed where the Ts'ais store junk.

The attic is the size of four *tatami* mats. The ceiling slants low over our heads. We can't stand up straight; we have to crawl on all fours on the *tatami* mats. Eight-year-old Sang-wa can stand up. But she doesn't want to. She wants to imitate the grown-ups crawling on the floor.

I sit on my *tatami* mat and read old newspapers. Old Wang, the Ts'ai family servant, piles the old newspapers for us at the foot of the attic stairs. Every day I go down to pick them up. Chia-kang crawls over to read them with me. He wants to read the international news. I want to read the police news, and we both want to see who is on the wanted list. I imagine how the story would appear:

At-large: Shen Chia-kang. While acting as Director of Accounting

118

of the Public Transportation Service, Shen Chia-kang embezzled 140,000 Taiwan dollars and fled with his wife and daughter. A warrant is now out for his arrest.

I also look to see if there is any news about Chao T'ien-k'ai. I imagine that the story would be written like this:

Chao T'ien-k'ai has been found guilty of collaborating with the Communist rebels. While attempting to flee the country, he was captured. Before his attempted escape, he was seen in the Little Moonlight Cafe with a mysterious woman. The police are now trying to find out the identity of this mysterious woman.

I arrange kitchen matches in the shapes of ideograms on the *tatami* mat, three characters:

LITTLE MOONLIGHT CAFE

Chia-kang also takes some matches and writes:

HAVE YOU GONE THERE?
TWICE
WHY
THIRSTY
BAD PLACE
I WAS THIRSTY
BE CAREFUL
CAN'T GO NOW
I'LL GIVE MYSELF UP
NO
WHY NOT
SINCE WE'RE HERE, ACCEPT IT
IF I GIVE MYSELF UP, WHAT WILL YOU DO
WAIT
HOW LONG
UNTIL YOU GET OUT
GOOD WOMAN
BAD
BAD GOOD WOMAN

I raise my head to look at Chia-kang. He opens his mouth in a silent

119

laugh. There's a big grin on his face.

He turns over and tries to repair the broken clock.

I take a pair of rusty scissors. I pick up handfuls of my long hair and begin snipping it off.

We have a big box of kitchen matches. They help pass the time. We use matches to talk and to play with our child. It's like playing with blocks. Sang-wa loves to play the word-making game. I write the easiest words for her.

THE WORLD IS AT PEACE

She scrambles the matches with her hand. She says that easy words aren't any fun. She wants harder ones. She copies complicated characters from the newspapers. She arranges them one by one, then scrambles up our matches, content, giggling.

COUNTRY
KILL
WARFARE
THIEF
ESCAPE
CRIME
POLICE
DRAGNET
UNDERGROUND
HIDE
CHEAT
DRUGS
DEFORMED
RIFLE
WOUND
CONFUSION
DESTROY
DIFFICULT
DREAM
INSANE
BURN
DEATH
PSEUDO

ANIMAL
PAIN
PRISON
INVASION
LOVE
MONEY
SEARCH
FOOD
HAPPY
GRIEF
CHANCE

On the roof the gnawing is beginning again. This time it's daylight outside. The noise starts in the corner and gnaws along the eaves. It gnaws as far as my head and stops. I am sitting on my *tatami* mat. The rat's sharp, tiny teeth gnaw into my head.

Chia-kang sits on his *tatami* mat, repairing the clock.

The time on the clock is still twelve thirteen.

He is working with a small drill. I take a pencil and write in the margin of an old newspaper:

DON'T FIX IT
I HAVE TO
NO USE FOR TIME HERE
CLOCK STOPS, THE WORLD STOPS
WORLD WON'T STOP. CLOCK WILL
JUST GO IN CIRCLES. DOESN'T
 MATTER IF IT STOPS

Chia-kang continues working with the drill.

The rat teeth on the roof gnaw into my body. They gnaw into my heart and liver. They gnaw into my vagina.

I recite the Heart Sutra silently.

Newspaper clippings are piled beside Chia-kang's pillow, all cut out from the old newspapers he has read in the attic.

MASTER SAN-FENG'S TECHNIQUE
TO PRESERVE POTENCY

This technique is based on secret manual handed down from the

Taoist master, Chang San-feng. It enhances conjugal bliss in the bedroom. It cures impotency and premature ejaculation. Immediate results. May heaven and earth destroy us if any deceit or fraud is intended. Write for information. Include self-addressed stamped envelope. Mail to P.O. Box 14859, Taipei.

DREAM OF GOLD IN DESERTED MOUNTAIN

More than a thousand tons of gold are thought to be buried in the remote mountains of Hsin-yi Village in Nantou County. The gold was allegedly buried there when the Japanese army withdrew after World War II. Kao Wan-liang went bankrupt after spending three years digging for the treasure. It is said that the gold buried there is worth three hundred billion Taiwan dollars. At present, the government has only twenty-six billion dollars of currency in circulation. The government has already signed an agreement with Mr Kao. Ninety per cent of the treasure will go into the government treasury. Ten per cent will be awarded to the finder of the treasure.

DIGGING FOR TREASURE OR DIGGING A GRAVE?

Kao Wan-liang is digging for the treasure with a group of workmen. Fifty metres under, traces of dynamite used when burying the treasure were discovered. The workmen diggers were elated and speeded up the digging until the earth was piled high in the tunnel, narrowing the entrance to the tunnel to only six feet wide. There was no way to remove the earth. At this time, the diggers have been trapped in the poorly ventilated tunnel for three days. It is not known if they are still alive.

REALITY OR DREAM?

Kao Wan-liang and the other treasure hunters are still trapped in the tunnel. Informed sources are now expressing doubts concerning the possibility of buried treasure in these remote mountains. The road from Hsin-yi to the excavation site is steep and hazardous. It takes two hours to get there by car. During the Japanese occupation of Taiwan, there was no road and travelling by automobile was impossible. Transporting the gold, which weighed more than 1,000 tons, into the deep mountains on foot would have been virtually impossible.

Chia-kang also has a pile of clippings about a British cabinet official's affair with a model. Included is a photograph of the model lying in an empty bathtub with a wash cloth covering her vulva.

There is also a pile of clippings about a dismembered corpse. Included are photos of the body, head, and each of the arms and legs.

There is a pile of clippings of scenes of old Peking. Wedding and funeral ceremonies. The flower market. The morning market. The night market. The ghost market. Opera theatres. Streetcars with bells. Mutton shops. Wine vats. Barber tents. Rickshaw pullers. The ruins of the Manchu palaces.

Chia-kang never tires of reading these clippings.

I've already copied out two books of the Diamond Sutra by hand, and two books of classical poetry. I keep copying and copying. I don't even know what I'm writing . . .

> The woman of Shang-yang Palace. Lady of Shang-yang Palace.
> Her fresh face slowly fading, hair suddenly white.
> Prison guards in green watch at the palace gate.
> How many springs has the palace been closed?
> Chosen at the end of Emperor Hsüan-tsung's reign,
> She was only 16 then, but sixty now.
> More than one hundred were chosen then.
> Alone, the years pass, wilted by time.
> She recalls how she accepted her sorrow and bid farewell to her family.
> She was helped into the chariot daring not to weep.
> Everyone said that she would be the emperor's favourite.
> Her face like hibiscus, her breasts like jade.
> But before the emperor met her
> Jealous Consort Yang ordered her sent away.
> All her life sleeping in an empty room, sleeping in an empty room sleeping in an empty room sleeping in an empty room empty room

Tonight there is no gnawing on the roof. Everything is black, inside and outside. The only light comes from the house at Number Three across the way. Chia-kang is asleep on his *tatami* mat. The clock, which is still being repaired, sits beside his pillow. In the dark I can't see what time the clock says.

Sang-wa is asleep on her *tatami* mat.

I lie wide awake on my *tatami* mat, waiting for the gnawing noise to begin on the roof.

Suddenly someone bangs at the gate, shouting, 'House check.' The police often use the pretext of a census check in order to search for fugitives.

I sit up with a start.

The main gate is opening. Someone comes into the courtyard. He shouts at Old Wang. He is ordering him to wake up everyone in the house. Tell them to get out their census papers and identification cards.

Chia-kang suddenly turns over and sits up. He lies down again and then sits up.

They've come? They've come? Have they finally come? He can't stop mumbling.

I nod and motion for him to be quiet.

We sit side by side. Each sitting on our separate *tatami* mats. Backs against the wall. Holding hands.

I hear them go into the Ts'ais' house.

Chia-kang writes on my palm:

> TS'AI WILL TURN US IN
> NO, MY FATHER SAVED HIS LIFE
> OLD WANG?
> NO
> I DON'T TRUST HIM
> HE HAS BEEN WITH THE TS'AIS
>   MORE THAN 20 YEARS
> THE TS'AIS HAVE SAVED OUR LIVES
> YES
> THEY'RE QUESTIONING HIM
> MAYBE
> THEY'LL SHOW HIM THE WARRANT
> MAYBE
> THEY ARE COMING UP TO THE ATTIC
> I'M READY
> I'LL GIVE MYSELF UP
> NO

124

WHY NOT
PERHAPS WE CAN ESCAPE
THEY'LL COME SOONER OR LATER
I'LL GO WITH YOU
YOU SHOULD BE FREE
FREEDOM WHERE
THEY'RE COMING
I'M LISTENING
IN THE COURTYARD
SOMEONE IS LAUGHING
LAUGHING AT WHAT
WHO KNOWS
ARE THEY COMING
WHO KNOWS

Hey, Old Wang, the inspection is over. Go on back to bed. They talk loudly as they walk out the gate. The gate is closing. Sound of boots on the stones in the alley. They knock on the gate to Number Three. In Number Three the lights go on one by one.

Chia-kang lies back down. I am still sitting by the window. He reaches out and tries to pull me over to his *tatami* mat. I can't move.

He wants to sleep. He wants to forget. It will be all right when the night is over. He mumbles and writhes under the blanket. I pull aside the blanket and lie down beside him. I let him crawl on top of me. With one jerk he wets my thighs like a child squirting urine.

Finally he falls asleep.

The noise on the roof starts up again. It gnaws from the corner along the eaves. I suddenly remember that there's a woodpecker that lives on the roof. Old Wang told me about it before we moved into the attic.

(B) Summer, 1958

The time on the clock in the attic is still twelve thirteen. It makes no difference if it's midnight or noon. The humidity and the heat are the same. The dampness seeps into the marrow of my bones and mildews there.

Chia-kang doesn't try to repair the clock anymore. We have our own time.

Sang-wa's *tatami* mat is near the window. The sun is shining down on her. Nine o'clock in the morning.

The sun is licking her body. Licking. Licking. Suddenly I look

125

up. The sun has disappeared. Twelve o'clock noon.

The man who sharpens knives comes by, banging his iron rattle. Two in the afternoon.

In the distance the train whistles. Three in the afternoon.

The government commuter bus stops at the intersection. Civil servants in twos and threes walk down the lane. Five in the afternoon.

The woman who sings in the local street opera suddenly bursts into tears over a lover's quarrel on some nearby street. Seven in the evening.

The blind masseuse is blowing her whistle in the dark alley. Midnight.

For a long time there have been no house checks after midnight.

Chia-kang sits on his *tatami* mat telling his fortune over and over with a deck of cards, three cards are fanned out in his hand. He hunches over and studies them, mouthing words.

Three sworn brothers.

He motions to himself in a gesture of victory. He peers into the small mirror in the corner of the room and nods his head and laughs silently.

My hair has grown long again. I don't bother to cut or brush it. I let it flow over my shoulders.

I spend most of my time on the *tatami* mat writing the story of 'Her Life'. I no longer copy the Diamond Sutra out by hand.

She is an imaginary woman. I describe the important and unimportant events of her life. A collection of odd, disjointed fragments. She marries a man who once raped her. She is frigid.

When I'm not writing, I look at old newspapers. First I read stories about people running away. There are all sorts of escape stories in the newspaper.

There's a story about someone who goes to prison in place of her husband. Lai Su-chu's husband was a merchant who went bankrupt before he died. He used her name to write bad cheques. Lai Su-chu didn't have the money to cover them. She was sentenced to six months in prison. She took her two-year-old son with her and served out sentence in the prison.

I cut out the picture of this woman embracing her child in prison and stick it up on the attic wall.

Sang-wa is sitting on her *tatami* mat drawing. She draws the *Adventures of Little Dot* on the margins of old newspapers.

1. Little Dot

2. Little Dot, Papa and Mama live on their *tatami* mats

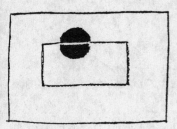

3. Little Dot wants to go away

4. Mama gets angry

5. Little Dot goes away

6. Little Dot wants the horse to take her away

7. The horse takes Little Dot to play on the sea

8. The horse carries Little Dot to play on the mountains

9. Little Dot pats the horse and says she is happy

10. Little Dot goes back to her *tatami* mat. Papa and Mama are very angry

11. The horse tells Little Dot to fly out the window and marry him

12. Papa kills the horse with an arrow

13. The horse's hide is hung up to dry in the sun

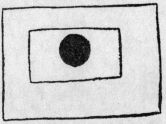

14. Little Dot looks out the window

15. The horse's hide rushes to hug Little Dot

16. Little Dot changes into a silkworm with a horse's head

I look out the window at the world outside. The world is covered with dust and cobwebs.

A white cat is dragging its black tail across the opposite rooftop.

Uncle Ts'ai and several friends come into the courtyard. They gesture and move their mouths. I quickly dodge to one side. Sang-wa crawls over to the window. I tell her not to look. However, I return to the window. The little window isn't big enough for two people to look out. I push her head down below the window sill.

Why can those people in the courtyard come and go as they please, Sang-wa asks me. Sometimes she presses her face to the window.

I explain. They can't go wherever they want to, either. There's a wall around the yard. Beyond the wall is the sea. Beyond the sea is the edge of the earth. The earth is a huge attic. The huge attic is divided into millions of little attics, just like ours. I want Sang-wa to understand that the other people in this world live just like us.

Chia-kang lies on his *tatami* mat mumbling to himself. His heart is pounding, it's about to burst. He has heart disease. He wants to die in the attic. He embezzled from public funds only for his family. If he were single, he would be innocent. Even if he has committed a crime, he could get out of the country. He could go to America or South America. Become a foreigner, just like that. His voice grows fainter and fainter. Finally he is just babbling and moving his mouth up and down. Whether his voice is loud or soft doesn't make any difference. Sang-wa and I ignore him completely. Besides, we aren't afraid of speaking in the attic anymore. We haven't used palm writing or writing with kitchen matches to converse for a long time.

Sang-wa sits on her *tatami* mat singing 'The Girl on the Great Wall' over and over in a small voice.

She sings and draws on the newspaper. One whole page is devoted to the important events in the history of modern China beginning with the founding of the Republic 47 years ago on January 1 when Sun Yat-sen took office as provisional president in Nanking, all the way to the present, to the Communist bombing of the Straits of Taiwan. In between there were the wars against the warlords, the war of resistance against Japan, and the Civil War. Sang-wa scrawls thick, crooked lines of ink all over those important events with her writing brush. Under the lines she draws little circles. Every circle has two eyes and a nose. She makes an ink blot on the thick line. She writes a caption:

Little Dot Plays on the Great Wall

She sings 'The Girl on the Great Wall' over and over.

I tell her not to sing anymore. That song is too old.

She says that it's the first song I taught her to sing. If Papa can talk to himself, then she can sing to herself. She keeps on singing the song.

> With the New Year comes the spring
> Every house lights red lanterns
> Other husbands go home to their families
> My husband builds the Great Wall.

Suddenly she stops singing. Suddenly Chia-kang stops talking. They turn. They glare at me.

I have put my hand on the window.

I tell them I want to open the window. But I don't open it.

The people in the yard have left. A fan made of palm fronds has been left on the grass.

It's twilight again.

The sun sets behind the attic. We can see only a few rays of red and purple light spreading through the sky. The further the rays of light extend, the fainter they become. Finally they blend with the darkening sky outside the attic window.

There are people in the courtyard.

This time I open the window. Just a crack. Now, not only can I see them, I can also hear their voices.

Uncle Ts'ai throws his head back in laughter. That's a good sign: as soon as I open the window, there is the sound of laughter.

They are speaking in Shanghai dialect. Peking dialect. Nanking dialect. Hu-nan dialect. Different voices. Different dialects. All tell the same story.

They are talking about a ghoul that eats people alive.

It happened on Lin Huo-t'u's thirtieth birthday in a village in the south of Taiwan. He invited three friends to his home to drink *t'ai-pai*. The four of them drank themselves into a stupor.

The next morning a monk walked into the yard of Pao-tz'u Temple. He saw a man lying under the palm tree. The monk carried him on his back into the temple and poured ginger water down his throat. When he came to, he said his name was Lin Huo-t'u.

Lin went home. At home he found his three friends dead. They were

130

lying in pools of water and they stank. The families of the dead men objected to the idea of having the coroner do autopsies. Instead, they held a ceremony to invoke the Ma-tsu Goddess to come. Speaking for the Goddess, the exorcist announced that an evil spirit was lurking in the tomb beside Pao-tz'u Temple. The coffin would have to be moved. Only then could the people of the village avoid calamity.

A girl, Pan Chin-chiao, was buried in the tomb. Six years before she had left the village to go to Taipei. Someone from the village had run into her when she was working as a prostitute in the red light district. She was beautiful and clever. She had acquired quite a reputation for herself in the district. Then, four years ago, Pan suddenly killed herself. There were only two sentences in her suicide note:

> This time I die just for fun
> To see what death is like

The people of the village moved Pan's coffin, but it was still buried in the same grave.

The third day, just as Lin was waking up, his own dog that he had had for three years, suddenly leaped at him. He fell to the ground and expired. In rapid succession, three young men between twenty and thirty died in the village.

After Lin's death, a story began circulating in the village. On Lin's birthday, the four drunk men had fallen asleep in their chairs. Dazed, Lin heard silk rustling. He opened his eyes and saw a girl in a red dress and hat. She had a lovely face and long hair; waves of cold came from her body. He pretended to be asleep. The girl in red breathed into the faces of the three other men. Lin jumped out of his chair and ran away. The girl in red chased him. He saw the lights of Pao-tz'u Temple. He thought to himself: Inside the temple, the gods will protect me. He ran up and pounded on the gate. There was no answer. The girl in red caught up with him. Lin grabbed hold of a cypress tree outside the temple to protect himself. The girl in red reached her arms around the tree and tried to grab him. He ducked left and right to get away from her. Her fingernails were like hooks and sank deep into the cypress bark. She couldn't pull them out. Lin jumped over the temple wall and rolled under the palm tree. Then he passed out. The next day the monk from Pao-tz'u Temple revived him. On the cypress tree there were four fingernail cuts each a foot deep. A trail of blood went from the gate to the temple all the way to Pan's grave.

. . . The ghoul devours people. Another young man died. The people

131

of the village went to find the monk from Pao-tz'u Temple to have him verify the traces of blood left by the corpse. The monk had disappeared. It was rumoured that he did not keep his vows of chastity. It was said that he kept a woman from a good family at the temple. The district magistrate wanted to punish him according to the law, but the monk had run away. Someone found part of a corpse in a clump of straw in the mountains behind the village. All that remained were the thigh bones, pelvis, fingers, and head. His spine was missing. The coroner could not establish the cause of death. He guessed that the dead person had died while sitting in the clump of straw. It was sitting, facing south, looking at the village at the foot of the mountain. The people of the village claimed that it was the monk of Pao-tz'u Temple. He was sitting in the lotus position in the clump of straw when the ghoul found him. The girl in red ate human spines.

Two more people died in the village, both under strange circumstances. The people of the village went to Pao-tz'u Temple to ask for help from the gods. The exorcist said that Pan's body had not yet decomposed, so she had become a ghoul who ate human flesh. Though at first, she was only eating men, later she would eat women. In two months she would eat all the people in the village. In six months she would eat all the people in the city. In a year, she would finish off all the people on the island and not even the fishermen would be spared. Taiwan would become a deserted island. The people of the village must burn her body.

On the next day the exorcist died.

On the third day the statues of the gods in the temple disappeared.

The people of the village decided not to disturb the corpse.

Then the people in the village began to attribute calamities to a different spirit – the spirit of the 11th century Judge Pao, who returned to avenge secret crimes and reward good deeds. Sometimes he inhabited the body of the victims; other times he appeared in the flesh. It was said that he had two black horns on his head.

A seventy-two-year-old carpenter quarrelled with his wife over an egg. Suddenly he lost consciousness. When he came to, his wife was lying in a puddle of blood. He was holding a bloody cleaver in his own hand.

A woman dreamed that a man with two black horns on his head wanted to take her to heaven. From then on she saw that man with black horns during the day. She burned incense and lit candles to seek his forgiveness. But the man with black horns did not spare her. She hanged herself.

132

A woman visited her mother's house. When she saw her younger brother, she grabbed his hand and shouted for the Goddess of Mercy to save them from disaster. The two shouted as they raced toward the pond. When the family got there, the brother and sister had already drowned in the pond. Before their death, neither had shown any signs of depression. The sister had been married for ten years and had four children. The younger brother had just gotten married. The two were both happy, optimistic people, and not the least bit insane.

The people of the village decided that those people were all guilty of some secret crime and that was why Judge Pao had settled with each of them. Within one month, fourteen people died in the village. It had become a village of death. Every house kept the main gate shut. Pao-tz'u Temple was a temple without statues of the gods. No one chanted sutras. No one went there to ask the gods for help. The grave where the corpse lay became a taboo area. No one dared to go near it. When people from the outside walked past the grave they could hear the villagers' loud curses from far away. The more they cursed, the more impassioned their voices became, as if their cursing could appease the ghoul and they would escape death. No one dared to mention the ghoul. They would just say that 'the Granddaddy' was back which meant that the ghoul was out eating people again. Everyone was terrified. They all felt they were guilty of secret crimes. They lived waiting for death. Every time someone died, they didn't need to tell each other. They immediately smelled the odour of death. Then every household would hurriedly burn incense and chant sutras. They weren't paying homage to the gods. They were begging 'the Granddaddy' to spare their lives.

Ch'ing, who returned to the village from Taipei, didn't believe in evil spirits. He wanted to help the people of the village. He advocated cremating the corpse. But no one dared to remove a handful of dirt from the grave where the corpse lay buried. No one dared carry the corpse to the crematorium. Ch'ing took a shovel and knocked down the gravestone. He broke into the grave. He opened up the coffin. She was a sleeping beauty, looking very much alive. Dressed in a pink gown flecked with gold. Long, black hair. Sleek, supple arms. Eyes wide open, staring at the sky. Ch'ing sprinkled gasoline over the corpse and coffin. The fire burned from early morning until midnight. In the evening Ch'ing dug out her intestines with a stick. They were dripping with blood. The blood spattered on the grass of the grave. The odour of the smoke mingled with the smell of blood and fresh grass. A slight breeze carried the odour throughout the village.

The people of the village recognised the smell, that's what it smelled like when the ghoul was out eating people.

Four days after the corpse was cremated, Ch'ing died suddenly.

Twilight again. I open the window. No one is in the yard. A heavy rain mixed with hot air presses in the window.

A truck with a loudspeaker drives down the lane, warning that a typhoon has hit the northeast coast.

The people are asked to inspect their roofs, doors, and windows to make sure they are secured. They should collect flashlights, candles, and matches in case the electricity goes off. They should store drinking water in case the water supply is cut off. They must be careful with burners and stoves to prevent fires.

I speak to Chia-kang about leaving the attic. We have already gone through half of the ten thousand dollars that he embezzled from the government treasury when we fled. We can't depend on the Ts'ais for left-overs for the rest of our lives. He should give himself up. He can still get a reduced sentence. He can still get his freedom back someday.

He turns over suddenly and sits up. He says life in the attic is imprisonment. If he leaves, he'll just go to another prison. He simply won't flee anymore. He asks if I plan to escape alone. He wants to know that.

I say even if it came to rolling down the Mountain of Knives, I would roll down with him. But Sang-wa is an innocent child who should not suffer.

'I'm sorry. She was born at the wrong time.' When Chia-kang says this, he looks at Sang-wa and grits his teeth.

Over the past year I have unconsciously collected a lot of newspaper clippings about escapes. There's a large pile of newspaper clippings on my *tatami* mat.

NO WAY OUT FOR OUTLAW
ESCAPE ATTEMPT UNSUCCESSFUL
KITE FLIES FAR, BUT STRING IS
  LONG
END OF THE ROAD FOR RUNAWAY
HOODLUM SURRENDERS
BIG DRUG SMUGGLER AT LARGE
SEARCH THROUGHOUT PROVINCE
CRIMINAL CAUGHT

134

Chia-kang says that all those fugitives were extraordinarily clever. But they were all caught and sent back to prison. What's the use of trying to escape? With one finger he lifts the pile of clippings and weighs them.

It's late at night. The typhoon snarls above the green eye. The green eye is still open wide.

Downstairs I hear the sound of chiselling at the shed door.

They have really come for us.

The door is creaking open. The attic shudders with the wind and rain.

It is absolutely silent. I can see Chia-kang's eyes open wide, staring at the ceiling.

I am sitting on my *tatami* mat. He is lying on his *tatami* mat. They could come up for us at any time.

We wait out the night.

By morning the gale winds have died down. Downstairs Old Wang coughs when he comes to get some coal. I open the door to the stairway. He says that a burglar broke into a house on the lane during the storm. He was discovered when the owner returned. The burglar killed the owner with an iron, then fled. Old Wang discovered footprints leading from the wall to the door in the shed that goes up to the attic.

Did he get away? Did he get away? Chia-kang and I shout in unison from where we lie at the top of the stairs.

The three of us escape from the attic.

We are climbing a mountain a thousand metres high. Sang-wa climbs to the top without stopping to catch her breath. So she can really walk, after all.

We can't stop anywhere for long. If we stop we must report our place of residence to the police station. If we report our residence, we must show our identification cards. Our identification cards will give us away as fugitives. At night we stop in caves in the mountains to sleep. During the day we climb. We steal sweet potatoes and fruit. We drink water from ponds.

Sang-wa sees our reflections in the pond. She says there's an attic made of water in the pond. In the water attic there are three people made of water. Their faces are covered with dirt, their eyes open wide in fright. The water people change shape when the wind blows. Their bodies gleam and sparkle. She throws in a pebble. The three water people shatter. The

135

shards toss about on the ripples, then are reassembled into people again.

Look, there's somebody. Sang-wa points halfway down the mountain. Two people have climbed midway up the path. They look up and see us.

From then on we are on the run, we hide in the mountains. We find a wanted poster lying in the road. The police have notified the mountain people to be on the lookout for fugitives. In a single day, we see people five times. Twice, they are passers-by. Three times they are policemen, combing the area in a search. We evade them all.

Finally we find our way into a virgin forest. Red cypress. Hemlock spruce. Japanese cypress. Trees a thousand years old. The forest is dark and endless. No sign of human beings. We climb to the top of a tree and hide among the leaves. They can't see us here. Bullets can't reach us here.

More and more people are searching for us. Waves of people encircle the whole forest.

On the mountain, a bullhorn screams.

ATTENTION, Shen Chia-kang and Mulberry. You cannot hold out anymore. We all know you are hiding in the forest. This mountain is shaped like a sack. Several hundred policemen are surrounding the mouth of the sack. We have cut you off. There's no way you can escape. You can't last in the mountain. There's no food in the forest. You will all starve to death. When winter comes you'll freeze to death. You are not murderers. You are ordinary criminals. Many people have committed your crime. If you give yourselves up now, you can still get lighter sentences. Your attempt to escape is endangering the safety of all the people on this mountain. If you try to get away, we have orders to shoot. We will set the dogs after you. It is pointless to try to escape. Shen Chia-kang and Mulberry, come out now and give yourselves up.

There is no one on the beach. Not a boat on the sea. Beyond the beach rows and rows of pine trees have been planted to break the wind. The tongue of the beach stretches out into the sea. There are two large trees near the shore. A straw hut is built between the trees.

The three of us are hiding in the hut. Ah Pu-la is here with us. He has arranged for us to slip out of the island. We are all looking out to sea.

A grey dot appears on the horizon. It gets larger. It turns into a fishing boat. The boat fires a white signal flare. Ah Pu-la drags the bamboo raft from the hut down to the water. The three of us file out of the hut. The four of us climb onto the raft from a sandbar in the shallow water. We paddle

toward the fishing boat. The fishing boat stops. The raft approaches it.
We crawl aboard.

Ah Pu-la climbs aboard with us.

The captain of the boat informs the two sailors that they're smuggling
us to Hong Kong. When the boat reaches Hong Kong, each of them will
receive five thousand Taiwan dollars as a reward. We set out as though we
were setting out to fish.

The captain hoists the nationalist flag.

As the flag reaches the top of the mast, one of the sailors hands Ah
Pu-la a note. He asks him to take the note to his wife. He has decided not
to come back. He asks her to take good care of their four children, his
crippled mother, and his widowed sister-in-law. He wants Ah Pu-la to tell
her the news. There's nothing he can do about it.

The other sailor scribbles several sentences on the back of the note. He
asks Ah Pu-la to tell his wife that he's not going to come back either. He
asks her to take care of their five children and his blind elder brother.
He is sorry that he has let her down, but he has to leave.

Ah Pu-la says that his family is a heavy burden. His wife is dead. They
have three children and a seventy-year-old father. The family of five is
supported solely by his fishing. He wants to go somewhere else. He
doesn't intend to return either.

The captain orders the sailors to set sail at full speed. The name of the
ship is Heaven Number One. It's an old fishing vessel weighing more
than ten tons. More than twenty feet long, more than five feet wide. The
helm is in the centre of the boat. Behind it is a small cabin. We spend the
day hiding in the cabin. We're afraid of running into patrol boats who
might search the boat and find us. The cabin is the size of two tatami mats
and has a low ceiling. We still can't stand up.

A salty sun shines inside the cabin. We lie in that sun for two days. In
three days we'll be in Hong Kong. When we get to Hong Kong, we'll be
safe.

From the bow the captain announces that the wind is changing
direction. A high cloud, shaped like a fishtail, appears on the horizon. A
typhoon is approaching. They turn on the radio for the weather forecast.

The water gets rougher. On the radio an opera singer begins to weep.
She finishes weeping. Then there is an announcement:

Attention: Fishing vessel Heaven Number One is attempting to
smuggle Shen Chia-kang out of Taiwan. The authorities have already
cabled the International Police Organisation to arrest Shen and the
others at the moment they debark. They will soon be taken into custody
and return to our country where they will be punished for their crimes. He

137

is wanted for embezzling government funds. Attention: Shen Chia-kang.
It is useless to try to escape. The navy patrol boats are in close pursuit.
Every port of entry in the surrounding waters has been alerted. Turn the
boat around and give yourselves up.

The blind masseuse is blowing her whistle again as she walks past the attic.

I write page after page of escape stories. Getting away to the mountains, getting away to the coast. How else could we escape?

(C) Summer, 1959

Aunt Ts'ai is ill. The Ts'ai family has saved our lives. I must leave the attic to go and see her.

The most important consideration is his safety, says Chia-kang. It isn't time to repay them for what they have done for us. Anyway, Mr Ts'ai is a notorious sex fiend. As soon as I set foot outside the attic, I'll fall into his clutches. That old sex fiend has hidden us in his attic because he's got his eye on me. If he, Chia-kang, is caught and sent to prison, how will Sang-wa and I survive? He is lying on his *tatami* mat. He talks on and on. Beside his pillow is a spittoon. The spittoon is full of his urine.

It's dark out. I want to take the spittoon outside.

He grabs hold of my hair. It has now grown down to my waist. He tells me not to try to find excuses to go outside. He likes that pungent smell. It reminds him of sex.

I go downstairs to the door. The courtyard is completely dark. A white cat with a black tail is squatting on the wall.

I go back to the attic.

I go downstairs, out the door. Someone knocks on the main gate. I go up to the attic again.

I go out into the yard. In the lane a policeman speeds by on a bicycle.

I go back to the attic again.

I approach one of the windows at the Ts'ais' house. There's a light on. Uncle Ts'ai is sitting by his wife's bed. She is propped up on the bed. They are talking.

138

He says he can't get out of the island now. Earlier, before the Communists crossed the Yangtze River, they had proposed peace negotiations. He had written editorials in which he advocated continuing the war. The Communists branded him as a war criminal. Now in Taiwan, he is advocating free elections. The Nationalists also consider him ideologically suspect. A pedicab is always parked at the intersection. The driver is always napping in his cab. That driver must be watching him.

Aunt Ts'ai says the driver is really watching the people who are hiding out in the attic. She doesn't understand why he is taking the risk of concealing a family of criminals. He should convince us to turn ourselves in to the police. He should tell us to leave the attic. He should remain silent. He should cut off his ties with the outside world. He should do this, he should do that. A lot of 'shoulds'.

I go back to the attic.

Aunt Ts'ai has cancer of the liver. I will risk everything to go see her.

Evening. Chia-kang and Sang-wa are asleep. At last I go out.

Uncle Ts'ai is alone in his study. I halt in the doorway when I see the mirror on the wall. It's a cheap mirror that warps its image. The farther away you stand, the more distorted your face becomes. He also sees the distorted face of the woman in the mirror. He turns in terror and stares at me. He tells me to come in. I don't know how to walk anymore. Hands. Feet. Body. All out of place. He tells me to sit down. My mouth moves up and down several times. I can't make a sound. I sit on the sofa, just like people outside the attic sit. I am three crooked sections. My torso rests on the back of the couch. My buttocks sit on the cushion of the couch. My feet rest on the floor. Each has its own part. The parts that should curve, do curve. The parts that should be straight, are straight.

He says he is pleased that I have come out of the attic. He has been thinking about advising us to leave the attic for a long time. But you can't tell other people what to do. They must decide things for themselves. Chia-kang should turn himself in to the police. Even if he has to serve a prison sentence, it would be for a limited term. Living in the attic is a sentence for life. Completely meaningless.

I explain. I am used to life in the attic. In the attic, all greed, anger, craving and love disappear. It would be traumatic if I changed my life. I'm afraid of changing. I have only come out to repay him for saving our lives. I want to help them in their time of difficulty. I will risk coming here every day to help them. I am speaking very slowly and

139

softly. Sometimes I have to pause awhile before going on. As soon as I finish speaking I stand up.

He wants me to sit a little longer. He has just sent Aunt Ts'ai to the hospital and he needs to talk to someone.

The blind masseuse's whistle is shrieking again.

I go back to the attic before midnight. It's safer there.

It's dark.

I am walking down the road. One, two. One, two. One, two. My feet touch ground, one step after another. I pick up a pebble. The pebble rubs against my palm. I go on walking like that. Walking. Walking. Walking.

I pass the pedicab at the intersection. The police station. The funeral parlour.

I pass an obstetrician's clinic. A white sign with black characters hangs over the door. CONTRACEPTIVE INOCULATION. SCIENTIFIC CONTRACEPTION. FREE CONTRACEPTION ADVICE. MISCARRIAGE TREATMENT. RECONSTRUCTED BIRTH CANAL.

I pass a drug store. There's an ad in the window showing two Westerners talking on the telephone. The Westerner with black hair calls out wryly, 'Hey, old Chang, ha-ha, you know this Male 10 stuff has male hormones in it.' The white-haired Westerner, his eyes wide open, replies, 'Really? Then I'll buy a bottle and replenish my strength.'

I pass a newspaper stand. The headline is 'VICTORY SOON IN OUR STRUGGLE WITH THE COMMUNISTS FOR THE MAINLAND.'

I pass a school. The sign says: ADVANCE TO HIGH SCHOOL. ADVANCE TO THE UNIVERSITY. HUMANITIES, SCIENCE, MEDICAL SCHOOL, AGRICULTURAL SCHOOL. EXPERIMENTAL CLASSES, ADVANCED CLASSES, SPECIALISED CLASSES. TEST OF ENGLISH AS A FOREIGN LANGUAGE FOR STUDY ABROAD.

I pass an airline office. A yellow airplane hangs in the window. The nose of the plane slants toward the corner of the window. Black letters are painted on the body of the plane. The airplane's passenger service extends to major cities all over the world. Fast and Safe. Courteous Service.

I pass the intersection. OPEN YOUR HEART TO THE HOLY SPIRIT, black characters on a white dress flash past me. A woman's head sticks out from a white collar. A missionary. She smiles and hands a leaflet to me. SIN AND REDEMPTION. Please come hear the holy word. Please believe in the Lord.

A hand grabs my arm. On the wrist is a huge round watch with a luminous dial. The time on the watch is 8:20. A policeman is holding me by the arm. A train thunders past in front of me. Characters painted on the box cars, 'Beware of Communist Spies' flash by. The railroad crossing bar has been lowered in front of me. I duck under the bar and try to scurry across the tracks. The policeman says that the crossing bar is lowered to warn pedestrians and cars that a train is coming. Next time, remember that. Don't play around with your life.

A bizarre world.

I am walking down the long hospital corridor. The lights are glaring. At the end of the corridor is the morgue. I walk halfway down the corridor and then turn right. Past the patients' rooms. In a window of the building opposite a woman is crying.

I am standing in the doorway of Room Number Four. Aunt Ts'ai is propped up in bed. I am calling to her. She doesn't answer. She stares at me as though she is looking at a ghost.

I pick up a brush from the table next to the bed and brush her hair. I smooth down her hair with my hand. I braid her sparse hair into a pigtail.

She reaches out to feel my face. Arm. Hand.

She says she can feel me, so I must be real. As she says this, she squeezes my finger hard.

I tell her it really hurts.

My life splits in half. Daytime in the attic. Night-time at the hospital.

Chia-kang is lying on his *tatami* mat. His heart is racing. Head aching. He has a pain in his side. Back hurts. All his muscles are sore. Constipated. He says he's not going to make it.

He wants me to give him an enema. He squats over the spittoon. He wants me to look between his legs at his bottom. Has it come out? Has it come out yet? He is asking over and over. I want to turn around and vomit. He wants me to stick it in again. Stick it in. Stick it in. He shouts at me.

He blames me for destroying his whole life. I wasn't a virgin, he married 'a broken jar'. His illusions about me have been shattered. His illusions about everyone in the world have been shattered. That lousy bastard Ts'ai has hidden us in his attic, just so he can make believe he is God. Then Chia-kang brings up the subject of Refugee Student in Chü-t'ang Gorge.

141

Sang-wa wants to know who he's talking about.

That son of a bitch who raped your mother, says Chia-kang.

SANG-WA'S DIARY

Papa and Mama both have identity cards. Mama says that an identity card proves that you are a legal person. I'm already ten, but I still don't have one yet. Mama says that people in attics don't need identity cards. Only people on the outside need them. If they don't have identity cards, they will go to jail. I hate it when Mama goes outside every night. Papa says she goes to look for men. She wants to get rid of us. I want to tear up her identity card.

I hate my stepmother . . . She buys new dresses for her own daughter but I have to wear dresses made from grey flour sacks. I run away, Papa will beat her to death. Papa is an ugly old sick man. He lies on the tatami mat and always wants to hit us. I hate him, too. People on the outside hang their identity cards around their necks and let them swing back and forth on the chains. That's really neat. One chain for each person's identity card. Even cats and dogs have identity card chains. I don't have one and I'm afraid. I don't want to go to jail. I run back home. Papa and Stepmother are dead. I'm an orphan. I'm sorry, I shouldn't have run away.

Little Dot has an identity card. She is legal so she can go outside. She comes back and tells me lots of funny stories. People on the outside who have identity cards can even eat people. They grab pretty girls and plug up their butts and stick water hoses into their mouths. Their stomachs blow up like watermelons. Then they eat them. A watermelon that breaks open by itself tastes better than one cut with a knife. I lick my lips and say 'How sweet.'

Mama goes outside every night. Papa says, 'Oh that woman. She goes out to eat men.' I ask him if she eats someone so she can get his identity card chain. Papa doesn't understand what I mean. Mama brings back a whole trunk full of identity card chains. I make lots of dolls out of the grey flour sacks. Each doll has an identity card chain. When Mama finishes eating all the people on the outside, she'll eat Papa and me. But I'm not a boy so maybe she won't eat me. I want to run away and elope with someone. I don't want to eat anyone. Little Dot says people's meat is like watermelon, red and sweet, but I think people's meat tastes bad. I bite my own finger and it's salty.

Mama says Aunt Ts'ai is dying. I don't know where people go when they die. She says they go to paradise when they die. People are very happy there. They aren't afraid. Whatever they want they can have. When offerings of paper servants and paper coins are burned, they go to heaven and become real. I ask if paradise has attics. She says no. I ask if people in paradise wear identity cards. She says no. I ask if people in paradise eat people. She says no. I don't believe her. Papa says Mama tells lies.

Aunt Ts'ai is dead. When it gets dark Uncle Ts'ai and I take her burial clothes to the Ecstasy Funeral Parlour.

A white curtain hangs in the morgue. Outside the curtain is an altar with two burning white candles. There's a strong pungent smell of antiseptic.

He pulls open the curtain. His wife is lying on the stone table. A gauze bedspread is hanging on the wall. We stand on either side of the stone table.

Her eyes are wide open. He closes the eyelids. The eyes are still wide open.

He suddenly chuckles. He says they slept together for more than thirty years, but only now does he realise that she doesn't have any eyebrows. She painted her eyebrows on when she was alive.

The mortician comes into the morgue. He drops a bundle of burial clothes on the legs of the corpse. He picks up one shroud after another and places them inside each other. Red. Yellow. Green. Blue. Purple. He removes the white sheet which covers the corpse.

The nylon rustles as it glides over the naked corpse. Her hair has fallen out, except for a little tuft of pubic hair between her thighs. I look at Uncle Ts'ai. He is looking at the gauze bedspread on the wall. The mortician wipes the corpse with a large towel. The breasts quiver.

Uncle Ts'ai walks out of the morgue. He chats with some people from the funeral parlour in the yard.

The mortician throws the towel in a corner. Some yellow pyjamas with black lace are piled in the corner. A dragonfly buzzes over and lands on them. The mortician lifts the upper half of the body to dress her in the burial clothes. The body is stiff. The clothes make a ripping sound. The seams of the sleeves are splitting.

Uncle Ts'ai walks in and says the burial cap should have a few pearls on it. He wants to go home to get them. He asks the mortician to wait awhile.

The mortician lets go of the body. It falls back on the stone table with a thud.

Forget it, he says. Anyway, the body is going to be cremated.

No, no, no, says Uncle Ts'ai. Not cremation. Burial. The coffin will be taken back to our old home on the mainland someday.

All right. The mortician's mouth twitches in a smile. I'll wait.

Someone lifts up the curtain and asks when the corpse will be taken out. A child has died. There aren't any empty tables. They're waiting to bring the child inside.

The mortician looks up at Uncle Ts'ai. Uncle Ts'ai motions to him to continue. The pearls aren't necessary.

The mortician slaps creme haphazardly over the face. Then powders it. Finally, he draws two thin lines for eyebrows and puts on the cap without pearls.

Fine. It's finished. Do you want that pile of clothes? He points to the lemon yellow pyjamas with black lace in the corner.

No, says Uncle Ts'ai.

The mortician picks them up and goes out.

We leave. We are silent all the way home. We go immediately into Uncle Ts'ai's bedroom.

I tell Uncle Ts'ai that I would like to live a normal life: going out during the day, coming home at night. Coming home to the attic.

He says it's not feasible. If I go out during the day, I am a threat to everyone I meet. I'm the wife of a criminal.

But it's only fair, I tell him. I live all my days threatened like that. They should feel threatened, too.

He asks me, am I innocent or guilty.

Both, I say. And neither. You could call me an innocent criminal.

He says he doesn't understand that. An innocent person should live outside the attic entirely. A criminal should hide during the day and go out at night. Then he told me a story about a criminal.

A murderer named Chu escaped from the prison. During the day he hid in a cemetery. At night he went out begging. No one noticed him. He hid in the cemetery for twenty days. But he couldn't go on hiding there. One night he went to a gambling joint. He won lots of money. He went to Taipei and rented a room.

He was a master of disguise. He passed as a policeman, a scholar, a business manager, a reporter, air force pilot, university professor, American Ph.D. graduate. He swaggered into dance halls and bars.

144

Finally, pretending to be a writer he began living with a bar girl. He wouldn't allow her to go back to the bar. She wanted to marry him, but he didn't want to. She got pregnant. He wanted her to get an abortion. She didn't want to. They had a fight. Then he wanted to go to bed with her. She didn't want to do that either. He beat her up and went out gambling. She took an overdose of sleeping pills and killed herself. In her room the police found a photo of him wearing a doctoral mortarboard. It was the man on the wanted list: Chu.

Chu won some more money at the gambling den. He felt the others were cheating him. He pulled out a gun. No one was frightened. He fired at the sky. Still no one was frightened. He fired at the window. Someone happened to be walking by the window. The bullet hit him in the chest. When the police arrived, Chu had already gotten away.

These two incidents were added to his record. The police put several detectives on the case.

Chu fled to T'ai-p'ing Mountain. He hid in the mountain for two weeks. He saw fireworks in the sky. He wanted to celebrate New Year too. He wanted to play some mahjong. He went back to Taipei. During the Spring Festival, every family was playing several games of mahjong. He pretended to have gone by mistake to the wrong house for a New Year's celebration. He was admitted into a house on Nan-ch'ang Street. He pretended to be an overseas Chinese just returned and played dominoes with the housewives. He went there for three days. An undercover policeman in the area became suspicious. On the fourth day the policeman recognised him from a photo. They frisked him and found a knife.

Uncle Ts'ai says that Chu's mistake after escaping from prison was that he forgot he was a fugitive. He had tried to live like an innocent man, but he just set a deeper trap for himself.

I say that my situation isn't the same. I'm not a criminal, and I don't carry around weapons to murder people with. I don't go on explaining. I just want him to know the facts and I want to prove to him I can live a normal life outside the attic. But at night I will stay in the attic to hide from house checks.

Uncle Ts'ai is having a few guests over for a party. I disguise myself as a servant, the kind that is resigned but still proud. I invent a good story. My husband was a government official. I escaped from the mainland to Taiwan with my four children. He is still trapped on the mainland. I am working as a maid to support my four children.

I hesitate for a long time in the kitchen before I make my entrance to the sitting room. Right now they are discussing the case of a certain Communist spy.

Three years ago a passenger jet crashed en route to the south of Taiwan from Taipei. All thirty-four passengers died. One of them was an overseas Chinese leader who had gone to Taiwan to talk with government officials about financing an attempt to reconquer the mainland.

A week earlier, Ying-ying, a singer at the Central Hotel, had disappeared after singing her last song on the programme. It was rumoured that she was caught and shot by the Security Police. She was the leader of a Communist spy ring. The crash was her doing. While accompanying the Chinese leader to the airport, she put a bomb in his luggage. A Mr Yin, who had lived with her for three years, reported her to the Security Agency. After she was shot he died in a car accident.

The guests are discussing the rumours. What was Ying-ying really? No one could say. They supposed she was a Communist. Then who was Mr Yin? There were several possibilities.

The first: Mr Yin was a Nationalist spy. The Security Agency sent him to live with Ying-ying. After he reported on Ying-ying's work as a Communist spy, the Security Agency ran over him with an army jeep to keep him from talking.

The second: Mr Yin was a Communist spy. Ying-ying had fallen in love with a Nationalist. Mr Yin reported to the Security Agency that Ying-ying had revealed his identity, so he committed suicide by running out in front of a car.

The third: Mr Yin did not belong either to the Nationalist or the Communist party. He was simply a jealous lover. Ying-ying had another lover, so he reported to the Security Agency that she was a Communist spy. Afterwards, he felt such remorse that he lost his mind. He died in a car wreck.

There are still other possibilities. No one knows for sure who he really was.

At that moment I step into the sitting room. Uncle Ts'ai is surprised. It is the first time I have shown myself to so many people at once. I ask him, Sir, when do you wish to eat. He immediately informs the guests that I am Mrs Chiang, just arrived. One of the guests asks me where I'm from. I say Szechuan. We begin to chat.

I say that my husband, before his death, was deeply in debt. I took my daughter to prison with me and served in his stead. My poor daughter died in prison. When I got out I came to work for the Ts'ais. I

146

say whatever comes to my head with great confidence. It's completely different from the story I had prepared beforehand.

He introduces himself to me as Chiang. My name is also Chiang. He says I look familiar. My eyes and eyebrows remind him of his father's concubine. He says his father died in the war. The concubine became a Buddhist nun.

I burst out laughing. Mr Chiang, you are really confusing me. Which war are you talking about? The campaign against the warlords, the war of resistance against Japan, or the war between the Nationalists and Communists?

He doesn't answer, just stares at me as if in a daze.

Oh, Mr Chiang, I gesture toward him, don't stare at me so. If you keep staring at me like that, I'll turn into a Buddhist nun. If you go on staring at me, I'll turn into that concubine. Monkey could transform himself eighteen times. I really believe such magic exists.

All the guests laugh.

Chiang asks me when I left the mainland.

April 1949.

Where on the mainland.

Peking.

Chiang claps his hands. He also escaped from Peking in April 1949. Maybe we met on the way.

I murmur, uh. Was it possible? So many people were trying to escape then. Like ants in a hot frying pan, scurrying in all directions, not knowing which way to turn. I came from Peking, Tientsin, Chi-nan, Wei County, through no man's land.

Chiang claps his hands again. That's right. That's right. He escaped from Peking, Tientsin, Chi-nan, Wei County through no man's land.

Please have a cigarette, I interrupt and offer him a Long Life cigarette.

I light it for him.

Uncle Ts'ai says I should win an Oscar for the best performance by an actress. The name of the motion picture is *The Woman in the Attic*; the role is Mother Chiang.

I begin a new life. I go out during the day. Back to the attic at night. Uncle Ts'ai gets used to it.

I am now Uncle Ts'ai's maid, housekeeper and mistress.

Chia-kang sleeps twenty hours a day.

He bitches four hours a day.

When he isn't bitching, he masturbates under the covers.

SANG-WA'S DIARY

*Mama goes out every day to eat people. When they get someone they first
smoke him with nice-smelling grasses, then smear pig's blood over his
body and barbecue him. The fire is burning hot. A big fire is burning all
around the attic. They want to roast me and eat me, too. I have a way to
get out. I draw lots of bird feathers on my flour sack dress. I look pretty in
bird clothes. They are down below and laugh when they see the fire in the
attic. They say I can't get out. The attic is on fire. The fire is so hot. I
stand in the window and flap my wings at the sky. I turn into a bird. I fly
away from the window.*

*The sun is so hot and burning. They want to use the sun to roast me and
then eat me. I turn into lots of little bugs and fly in the sky. The little gold
spirits in the sky come to help me. They all turn into little bugs flying in
the sky and cover up the big sun. The sky becomes dark. The sun goes out.
It can't roast the attic anymore.*

*The typhoon is coming. It is raining so hard. They want to hurt the attic
with the wind and rain. They'll turn me into a wet chicken. They want to
drink soup with people's meat in it. I draw a dragon on my flour sack. I
wear dragon clothes then turn into a dragon girl. The typhoon breaks the
attic window. Rain comes in. When the rain hits me I become a dragon
and swim out the window. The more it rains, the happier I am. I give out
silver rays as I swim in the sky. They lose again.*

*The sun roasts our attic every day. It's so unfair. I'll bet it's the people
who eat people who do it. They tie the sun on the roof of the sky. The sun
can't move. The little gold spirits help me. They make a branch come
down from the sky. It dances in the window like a snake. I grab the branch
and climb up on it and go up into the sky, then cut the rope off. The sun
falls down with a boom. It turns into a big ball of fire. The earth catches
on fire. The people who eat people all burn up and die. Ha, ha, ha. I laugh
up at the sky. I pick up the rope with the sun tied on it and drop it into the
sea. The sun goes out. I kick the sun like a rubber ball.*

*The people who eat people are all dead. Papa and Mama are also dead.
I am left alone. I cry and walk to the sea shore. There is a big footprint on
the beach. I don't know whose foot it is. I step on it with my foot to see*

148

how big it is. It is bigger than my foot. I faint and fall down. When I
wake up I have a big belly. I'm so scared I cry. I don't want to have a baby.
A big round ball of meat comes out from inside of me. I cut the ball of
meat into little balls and wrap them all up in pieces of paper. The wind
blows and breaks the paper. The little balls of meat fly through the sky.
When they fall to the ground they turn into stones. I look and the stones
move, float and turn into clouds. The clouds float away and turn into
white birds. The white birds circle in the sky and turn into snakes with
heads like people. The snakes with people heads are playing in the sky. A
black cloud sucks the snakes with people heads in and they turn into rain.
It's raining outside the attic.

I must go back to the attic in the evening. I don't want to go back. I
want Uncle Ts'ai to take me out; I want to have fun for a while.

We go to the circus. The trapeze act has just ended. The ringmaster
on stage is announcing the next act.

Beauty and the Bear.

The Bear's name is Ah Ke. He is from South Africa. Four feet tall.
Two inches of black fur cover his body. Weight 220 pounds. A rare
animal in the world. He can roll a ball. Leap through a fiery hoop.
Walk on rolling barrels. Play the harmonica. Walk on his forepaws.
Dance the mambo.

Ah Ke is in his cage getting ready to make his appearance.

The gong sounds.

The ringmaster cracks his whip three times. Then shouts:

Hey. Ah Ke, come out.

Silence.

The whip cracks three more times. The ringmaster motions to the
audience. Hurray. Thundering applause.

Silence.

Ah Ke is temperamental. In Singapore, Bangkok, or Manila, he
refused to come out. In Saigon he came out only once. In Calcutta, he
came out twice. Ah Ke is happy in Taiwan. He will come out for sure.
He will come out for every performance here. The audience must be
patient. The ringmaster chats with the audience as he paces up and
down the stage. He's wearing a fancy flowered shirt that animal
trainers wear. He is holding his whip.

Hey. Ah Ke.

Another shout and more thundering applause.

The bear definitely won't come out, I whisper to Uncle Ts'ai. He
asks why. I say because the bear has seen a ghost in the audience. Uncle

Ts'ai laughs, that's just a circus superstition; we shouldn't believe it.

The whip cracks.

More shouts and applause.

More silence.

The audience begins whistling.

Don't get upset, I whisper to Uncle Ts'ai, wait till the bear forgets there's a ghost in the audience, then it will come lumbering out. Uncle Ts'ai says he doesn't believe in ghosts. I say there really are ghosts in the world, for example, ghouls who eat people alive.

The audience is screaming for a refund. Some people are standing up to leave.

Hey. Ah Ke, come out, shouts the ringmaster as he snaps his whip.

The ringmaster should put down his whip, I say to Uncle Ts'ai. The bear will come out on his own. No wild animal likes to be shut up in a cage. Uncle Ts'ai laughs. He says I have become an expert on training animals. The ringmaster's whip isn't just for taming the animals. It's also to give himself courage.

The ringmaster is strutting up and down the stage. He snaps the whip faster and faster. The audience is screaming for a refund. Some people have already left their seats.

Hey. Ah Ke is coming out. The ringmaster suddenly leaps on stage and yells.

The bear lumbers out from back stage.

Applause.

A large barrel comes rolling out.

The ringmaster stops the barrel. The bear climbs up on it. The ringmaster lets go and the barrel rolls away.

The bear spins on the barrel. The barrel spins under the bear. Spins and rolls. Rolls and spins. Faster, faster. It's as though the bear and the barrel were under a spell. Rolling, rolling. The audience is clapping. Flash bulbs are blinking. Reporters are snapping pictures.

A slender young woman steps out on stage in a skin-tight, flesh-coloured leotard. It's Beauty. The bear jumps down from the barrel. Beauty pats the bear. The bear rubs his face against her body. Beauty tells Ah Ke to kiss her. The bear stands up on his hind legs. He clasps her neck with his front paws. He licks her face. She tells him to kiss her neck. The bear licks her neck. Beauty turns her profile to the audience. She moves her face toward the bear. The bear embraces her and licks her on the lips.

Beauty murmurs with pleasure.

The audience claps. Flash bulbs blink. Reporters snap pictures.

Beauty smiles. The bear stands aside. She asks for someone in the audience to come up and meet Ah Ke.

Silence.

Two or three hands hesitate and wave.

Suddenly Uncle Ts'ai stands up. He climbs up to the stage. Beauty leads the bear over to meet him. He steps back a few paces. Laughter from the audience. Beauty tells him to come over and shake hands with Ah Ke. He doesn't move. Beauty laughs and calls him a coward. She signals to the bear. The bear gets up on his hind legs and walks over to Uncle Ts'ai. He leans back and then retreats. People are yelling for him. He can't move.

The audience is laughing.

Beauty points her finger at him. This is only the beginning. The best is yet to come, she says as she and the bear walk over to him. Ah Ke stretches out a front paw. Beauty takes Uncle Ts'ai's hand and gives it to the bear to shake. Uncle Ts'ai nods at the audience and laughs. Beauty says the bear wants to kiss his face. No, no, no, he quickly says. Bears never kiss men on the face. Beauty says it is a Western custom. She leads Ah Ke over to another part of the stage. The man and the bear are standing on opposite ends of the stage. Beauty signals to Ah Ke. The bear thrusts out his stomach and lumbers over to Uncle Ts'ai. Uncle Ts'ai stands there, leaning forward slightly, rubbing his hands together. His eyes are glued on the bear, waiting for it to attack at any time.

The people are cheering.

The bear walks to centre stage. Uncle Ts'ai comes to life. His feet start moving. At first he is hunched over and takes tiny steps. Then he straightens up and takes bigger steps.

The man and the bear stand staring at each other, face to face.

People are getting up.

The bear stretches out a forepaw and puts it on Uncle Ts'ai's shoulder.

I get up.

Uncle Ts'ai looks up. The bear draws close and licks his face.

Everyone is standing up. People in the back yell for the people in front to sit down. People are whistling at the man and the bear.

The bear is licking the man's face.

People leap and cheer. Flash bulbs blink. Reporters snap pictures.

The bear draws back.

The man and bear stand staring at each other, face to face.

Beauty takes Ah Ke's paw and bows to the audience.

Uncle Ts'ai stands there very stiffly. Staring in front of him, smiling.

A little girl comes out onto the stage and pins a yellow carnation on his lapel.

The audience is still screaming and clapping.

Frightened. Frightened, but with a strange sexual excitement, Uncle Ts'ai tells me after he leaves the stage. He laughs with satisfaction.

Chia-kang is sleeping. Sang-wa and I talk on paper:

> I'LL TAKE YOU OUTSIDE
> NO
> WHY NOT
> I DON'T HAVE AN IDENTITY CARD
> IF YOU GO OUT, YOU CAN GET ONE
> I'M AFRAID OF THE SUN
> WE'LL GO OUT AT NIGHT
> I'M AFRAID OF PEOPLE
> THERE'S NO ONE IN THE YARD AT MIDNIGHT
> IT'S TOO DARK
> IT'S PRETTY WHEN IT'S DARK, EVERYTHING GLITTERS
> WHAT MAKES IT GLITTER?
> THE SKY LIGHT
> I'M AFRAID OF DOGS AND CATS
> ANIMALS ARE AFRAID OF PEOPLE
> I'M A PERSON
> RIGHT
> DOGS AND CATS ARE AFRAID OF ME TOO
> RIGHT
> REALLY?
> REALLY
> I WANT TO GO OUT AND SCARE THEM
> LET'S GO OUT TOGETHER

Sang-wa is so happy that she hugs her pillow and rolls over and over on the *tatami* mat. I look over at Chia-kang sleeping. She calms down suddenly. She knows Chia-kang won't let me take her outside.

Evening. I go back to the attic. Chia-kang and Sang-wa are asleep. I tap Sang-wa on the shoulder. She opens her eyes. I point out the window. A full moon. She scrambles up, rubs her eyes. I point out the window again. She nods.

I pull her up on her feet. She hesitates. She ducks her head when she stands up because she is taller than the ceiling. I walk down the stairs ahead of her. She stops at the head of the stairs. I pull her hand. She walks halfway down the stairs, then turns around to go back to the attic. I jerk her hand again.

Finally she is standing on the ground in the yard. She is still hunched over. I tap her on the shoulder and she straightens up.

She stands there looking surprised. Her eyes linger a long time on each thing before they move to something else. She softly says the names of the things she sees:

GRASS
LEAVES
STONES
VINE
JASMINE FLOWERS
MOON
STARS
CLOUDS
BUGS
FIREFLIES
LIGHT ON THE CORNER OF THE
    WALL
CAT: WHITE BODY, BLACK TAIL

Sang-wa grabs my hand. The cat hisses and jumps to the top of the wall. It squats there, its pupils two gleaming discs. I pat her hands. She doesn't move. The cat jumps down the other side of the wall. She looks up at me and smiles.

She says being outside the attic makes her tired. She has never stood straight up like this on the ground before.

I take her back to the attic.

It's very late at night.

Someone is knocking on the door, yelling, House Check. A light flashes across the window.

Sang-wa isn't in the attic.

I crawl over to the window. Sang-wa is standing in the yard holding the white cat with the black tail in her arms. Two flashlight beams are riveted on the girl and the cat. Several other lights sweep in the air over her head.

Two policemen bend over to talk with Sang-wa. She is pointing at the attic. All the lights sweep over and shine on the attic.

I'm sitting by the window.

A flash of light nails me from behind. I turn. The white cat with the black tail is squatting on the *tatami* mat. Sang-wa is sitting behind the cat.

She says angrily:

'PEOPLE!'

She raises her hand and points at the attic stairs. A policeman's torso and another policeman's head emerge from the stairs.

House Check. Take out your identity cards, says the policeman whose torso is showing.

We took them to the Buddhist Lotus Society to get welfare rice, Chia-kang answers from his *tatami* mat.

Then take out your household registration papers, says the half-bodied policeman and he rummages through a file in his hand. The file has a copy of everyone's household registration paper.

I take my identity card out from under my pillow. Taipei, number 8271.

There's no stamp on the identity card. This woman has not reported to the police station yet, says the half-bodied policeman as he turns my card over and over. It's illegal not to report to the police station. According to the card, your spouse's name is Shen Chia-kang. He says the name; then suddenly pauses.

Right, his name is Shen Chia-kang, I repeat.

Chia-kang glares at me.

The clock in the attic still reads twelve thirteen.

154

PART IV

ONE

Peach's Fourth Letter to the Man from the USA Immigration Service

(21 March 1970)

CHARACTERS

PEACH, she informs the Immigration Agent that the area residents felt threatened by Peach and the woodcutter because the ruined water tower where they live was declared unfit for habitation. This threatened woman, who even seems a threat to others, starts out again on her endless flight, in search of a place to have her baby. With the letter she encloses Mulberry's USA diary.

THE MAN FROM THE IMMIGRATION SERVICE.

Dear Sir:

I'm on the road again. I'm roaming around these places on the map.

I couldn't find any peace of mind in the water tower either. First the lumberjack's big saw disappeared. Next, my mud-splattered snow boots disappeared. Many people came to look at the strange couple living in the ruined wooden tank. The people living nearby reported us to the police saying that we were of questionable background and identity. Since we lived in such a broken-down wooden tank – that obviously meant something strange was going on; perhaps we had escaped from prison; or perhaps we were lunatics who had escaped from an insane asylum; they felt that their lives were threatened. Two policemen came to the water tower. The lumberjack and I were sitting nude in the water tower, discussing the baby's birth. After asking us a lot of questions, they discovered that we were only two wandering

157

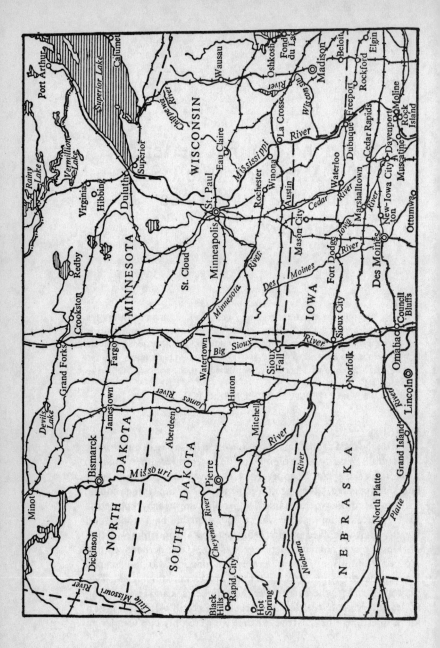

foreigners. We hadn't committed any crimes, and seemed very peaceable. We just wanted to live off the land naturally; we weren't threatening anybody. But they discovered that the dilapidated water tower was unfit for habitation. There were no sanitary facilities. The wood was rotten, and there was the danger that it would collapse at any time. Reporters came to interview us and take photos. We became newspaper headlines. They called us 'the people in the water tower'.

Finally, the police found the owner of the water tower, Mrs James. She had moved to California a long time ago. Her lawyer announced:

'Mrs James strove to preserve the water tower because it was a historic monument. But she doesn't want the water tower to endanger anyone's life. She has now decided to tear the water tower down.'

The lumberjack and I left the water tower. We hadn't planned on living there for the rest of our lives. He wanted to go east. I wanted to go west. We split up. He planned to cut down trees for people as he went, to save money to buy a camper to go to California. I told him the story about Donner Lake. He said he'd certainly pass through Donner Lake on the way to California. I want to find a place to give birth to my child. I'm going to give birth to a little life that's my own flesh and blood. Now I'm alone again.

When I left the water tower I hung a wooden plaque on the iron legs with the following words, imitating what was written on the plaque that the astronauts left on the moon:

A WOMAN WHO CAME FROM AN UNKNOWN PLANET
ONCE LIVED IN THE WATER TOWER
22 FEBRUARY 1970–21 MARCH 1970
I CAME IN PEACE FOR ALL MANKIND.

Peach
21 March 1970

P.S. I enclose Mulberry's diary in America, several letters from Chiang I-po, several letters Mulberry wrote in New York but didn't mail, and several letters from Sang-wa in Taiwan: she has fallen in love with a middle-aged married man. His wife is expecting their fifth child.

TWO
Mulberry's Notebook
Lone Tree, America

(July 1969–January 1970)

CHARACTERS

MULBERRY, she is now 41. She has applied for permanent residency in the USA. Everything in her life has been destroyed: her past, her traditional values, and her ethics have been shattered. She is schizophrenic.

PEACH, Mulberry's other personality, who plunges Mulberry into a life of promiscuity and adventure.

CHIANG I-PO, a Chinese professor. He cannot commit himself to anything and cannot choose between Mulberry and his wife. He lives in China's past and is neither Chinese nor American.

TENG, (in his 30s), a Chinese college student. He represents some young Chinese intellectuals in the USA.

BETTY CHIANG, (in her 50s), Chiang's bored, crazy wife.

TAN-HUNG, (in her 40s), Teng's older sister. Married with no children.

JERRY, (in his 40s), Tan-hung's husband, an American born Chinese, a stock broker in New York. He is in love with machines, especially cameras, and is remote and indifferent to Chinese problems.

I'm in Room 81 of the Immigration Service. I sit facing the window. The window is shut. The row of windows opposite me, in the tall grey office building, is also shut. The investigator from the Immigration Service is sitting across from me; we are separated by a grey steel desk. He is bald with a sharp chin, and a pencil moustache. He is wearing dark glasses. A red-lipped secretary is sitting behind another grey steel desk. On the desk is an electric typewriter. The man in dark glasses pulls a thick folder out the file cabinet. In the corner of the folder is my alien registration number: (Alien) 89–785–462. He opens the folder, and pulls out a stack of forms and asks me to look them over.

Name: Helen Mulberry Shen
Sex: Female
Place of birth: Nanking
Date of birth: 16 October, 1929
Nationality: Chinese
Present address: Apartment 5, 33 Second Street, Lone Tree
Permanent address: None
Occupation: Chinese teacher
Employer: Holy Conception High School, Lone Tree
Marital status: Widow
Name of spouse: Chia-kang Shen (deceased)
Name of children: Sang-wa Shen (presently in Taiwan)
Have you ever joined any political party? No
Passport Number: Taiwan 53–28895
Date issued: 2 September 1966
Place issued: Foreign Ministry, Republic of China
Type of visa issued: Exchange visit
Purpose of application: Permanent residency
Date of application: 8 December 1968
Previous residences (from 16 years of age): . . .

So many dates, so many addresses. I don't read it all the way through. I pass the form back to the man in dark glasses. He opens the folder and replaces the form. Inside the folder are many more forms. He presses the folder shut with his two hands and shrugs. 'Helen, are there any mistakes in the form?'

'My name is Mulberry. I haven't used the name Helen for a long time.'

'Mulberry – foreign names sure sound funny. Now, let's get back to business.'

He opens the folder, studies the contents, then shuts it again. 'This is the information we obtained from our investigation of you. If you want to apply for permanent residency, you must go through an investigation. We still don't know the result of the investigation. We want to continue investigating. Now we want a deposition from you.' He motions to the secretary. She immediately poises her hands on the typewriter keyboard.

'Helen, please raise your right hand and repeat the oath after me.'

I raise my right hand.

'I, Helen Mulberry Shen, on July 17, 1969, do solemnly swear . . .'

'I, Helen Mulberry Shen, on July 17, 1969, do solemnly swear . . .'

'That what I am about to say is the truth, the whole truth and nothing but the truth . . .'

'That what I am about to say is the truth, the whole truth and nothing but the truth . . .'

'So help me God.'

'So help me God.'

'Or else I will fully submit to punishment by American Law.'

'Or else I will fully submit to punishment by American law.'

Da-da-da. The typewriter types each word.

'Now, I want to ask you some questions. What is your name?'

'Mulberry Shen.'

'I'm sorry. Please use the name Helen Mulberry Shen. What is your nationality?'

'Chinese.'

'When were you born?'

'October 16, 1929.'

'What is your father's name?'

'Sang Wan-fu.'

'When did he commit suicide?'

'October 7, 1948.'

'Why did he commit suicide?'

'I don't know.'

'Was he a Communist?'

'I don't think so.'

'What is your mother's name?'

'Sang Chin-chih.'

'Where is she now?'

'Mainland China.'

'Is she a Communist?'

'She wasn't a Communist when I left the mainland. After that, I don't know.'

'What did she do before she married your father?'

'She was a prostitute.'

'Are you in contact with her?'

'In the beginning, we wrote several times. Later, we stopped.'

'What is your younger brother's name?'

'Sang Pao-tz'u.'

162

'When did he leave Nanking to go to the Communist areas?'

'October 6, 1948, the day before my father committed suicide.'

'Is he a Communist?'

'When he was in Nanking, I don't think he was a Communist.'

'Why did he go to the Communist areas?'

'He couldn't survive at home.'

'Are you in contact with him?'

'No. He died in the Korean War.'

'When did you leave Nanking to go to Peking?'

'December 1948. It was after my father died. I don't remember the exact date.'

'At that time did you know Peking was encircled by the Communists?'

'Yes.'

'Were you a Communist at that time?'

'No.'

'Did you go to Peking to work for the Communists?'

'No.'

'Why did you flee to an encircled city?'

'I couldn't survive in Nanking. My only way out was Peking.'

'What's your husband's name?'

'Shen Chia-kang.'

'Was he a Communist?'

'I don't think so.'

'What did the Taiwan police want him for?'

'He embezzled government funds.'

'Why did you hide in the attic as well?'

'To be with him.'

'Were you guilty?'

'I wasn't guilty of any crime I know of.'

'Do you know a person by the name of Chao T'ien-k'ai?'

'Yes.'

'Is he a Communist?'

'When he was on the mainland, some people said he was a Nationalist. When he got to Taiwan, the Nationalists said he was a Communist. I really don't know which he was.'

'Why was he sent to prison?'

'I don't know.'

'Did you help him?'

'No.'

'Someone said you saw him the day before he was arrested.'

'Yes.'

'Where did you meet?'

'In the Little Moonlight Cafe in Taipei.'

'Why did you see him?'

'We were classmates from Nanking, and went together for a while. I ran into him on the street in Taipei, and we went to the Little Moonlight Cafe for a cup of coffee.'

'Did you commit adultery with him?'

'No.'

'Whom did you commit adultery with?'

'. . .'

'In Taiwan, did you commit adultery with Ts'ai Ch'eng-te?'

'. . .'

'Did you commit adultery with Ts'ai Ch'eng-te?'

'. . .'

'Did you commit adultery with Ts'ai Ch'eng-te?'

The two black lenses move toward me threateningly.

'Please answer my question.'

'I was intimate with Mr. Ts'ai for a time.'

'I'm sorry. Please answer the question again. You cannot use generalizations like "was intimate." I am investigating your behavior. "Committing adultery" is behavior. You must use a definite "yes" or "no" in reply to my questions. Did you commit adultery with Ts'ai Ch'eng-te?'

'Yes.'

'Define the words: "commit adultery."'

'When a woman and a married man or a man and a married woman sleep together, that's adultery.'

'You should change "sleep together" to "have sexual intercourse." Please say it again.'

'When a woman and a married man, or a man and a married woman have sexual intercourse, that's adultery.'

'Was Ts'ai Ch'eng-te married?'

'His wife was dead.'

'Were you married?'

'Yes.'

'When did you and Ts'ai Ch'eng-te first have sexual intercourse?'

'I don't remember the exact date. I only recall it was after we left the funeral parlor.'

'What you're saying is, after you saw his wife put in the coffin?'

'Yes.'

164

'So that's how it was. How many times did you have sexual intercourse with Ts'ai Ch'eng-te?

'I don't remember. That was ten years ago.'

'How often did you have sexual intercourse?'

'There wasn't a definite schedule.'

'How long did intercourse last each time?'

'I don't know. I'd fall asleep after intercourse. I wouldn't look at my watch.'

'Have you ever participated in any anti-American activity?'

'No.'

'Are you now a Communist?'

'No.'

'Are you a leftist?'

'No.'

'Are you loyal to the American government?'

'I'm Chinese.'

'But you're applying for permanent residency in America. Are you loyal to the American government?'

'Yes.'

'Is there anything else you would like to explain?'

'No.'

The man in the dark glasses signals with his hands. The electric typewriter stops.

'OK. The Immigration Service must continue its investigation. You'll have to await the final decision.'

'When will that be?'

'I don't know. The investigative process must go through related Chinese and American channels. We still have to interview many different kinds of people, and gather information on you from various sources. Only then can we reach a decision: permanent residency or deportation.'

'Whom are you interviewing?'

'Some are your friends. Some are people you don't know.'

'Even if they are friends, they don't necessarily know me.'

'That doesn't make any difference. What we want to investigate isn't your state of mind, your emotions, or your motivations. I'll say it again: what we want to investigate is your behaviour. And that can be observed by anybody. Now please make a fingerprint on the deposition.'

I make a fingerprint with my thumb on the deposition.

'Excuse me. I'll have to have you sign this as well.'

165

I sign 'Helen Mulberry Shen' on the deposition.

'Good luck, Helen.' The man in dark glasses stands up and thrusts his hand across the grey steel desk to shake hands.

I am running on top of the stone wall in Nanking. The sun is about to set over the lake. Rocks are strewn at the base of the city wall. On each rock perches a white cat with black tail. The city wall is crumbling about to fall, about to fall – about to fall down on top of all those white cats with black tails. I turn and run toward the Temple of the Crowing Cock. Where is the Temple? And where is the old monk who rings the bell? A man in dark glasses chases me on the stone city wall. First one, then two, then three, then four, then five . . . close behind me, a file of men in dark glasses – all bald, with pointed chins and wearing dark suits. I turn around again and run toward the lake. The stone wall is about to fall down on the cats' backs. The cats glare at me. The men in dark glasses point at me shouting, '(Alien) 89–785–462, if you want to run, you'd better step on the cats' backs!' The stone wall collapses, the cats with the white bodies and black tails disappear. Corpses lie in heaps under the stone. My father, my brother, Chia-kang, my mother. Did mother die, too? Uncle Ts'ai? Did he die, too? He just married a young girl in Taiwan. He can't die! I step on the naked corpses as I run, leaving an imprint of my foot on each soft and pliant body and I babble, 'I treated you badly when you were alive and now you're dead and I still step on you. But I can't help it – I have to get away!' As I step on Chia-kang's body, he suddenly sits up. He doesn't speak but just looks at me laughing silently. Sang-wa stands far off to the side and points at my naked body yelling, 'Prostitute. The prostitute is going to give birth to a bastard!' 'I'm your mother. Come over here! We'll start a new life together.' I am screaming but no sound comes out. I look up to see Chiang I-po in a little boat on the lake. I call out, 'I-po! I-po! Come over here and take me back!' I still can't make any sound. I must already be dead. Only the dead can't make any sound. I'm already dead – dead – dead . . .

Last night I took too many sleeping pills, and had a nightmare. Now, I'm still dazed; I grope my way into the bathtub. As I sink down into the water, I become a new woman – my headache, all my pains vanish. All feelings of suspicion, fear, and guilt disappear. The water warms my whole body. I am translucent as the water.

It is wonderful to be alive. The elm, the rays of the sun and the squirrels outside the window are also alive. The water laps against my breasts. I suddenly discover they have grown a little: ripe and full, firm and supple, breasts men have fondled. I lightly rub my nipple with my finger. My nipple quivers, then stiffens.

After getting out of the tub I open all the windows, doors, turn on the lights, the stereo and the TV. The whole world comes to me.

'The commander of the space capsule for the moon landing requests that everyone, no matter who you are or where in the world you are, remain silent for one moment, to meditate on the events of the last few hours and in your own way express the gratitude in your heart . . . those words were just spoken by astronaut Aldrin on the surface of the moon. Now the astronauts are preparing for the moonwalk . . .'

> '. . . the birds singing wildly
> the flowers dizzily bloom
> You, what a happy, happy feeling . . .'

The astronauts are ready to descend. The singer on the record croons along merrily. Carrying a small overnight bag, Chiang I-po tiptoes through the open door of my apartment. There's a movie screen tucked under his arm. He closes the door gently. Braced in the doorway he stares at me without speaking. After a moment he says: 'What's happened to you? You're not acting like yourself!'

'Professor, what's happened to you?' I am standing naked in the middle of the room, right under the light, facing a painting on the wall: a large lion embracing a naked woman in its paws – the woman, her legs slightly bent, lies on her back looking up at the sky; the lion rubs her breast with his ear.

'I'm fine. This morning, I went to church. In the afternoon I played tennis for a while and beat a young guy!'

'I think there's something really wrong with you, Professor.'

'What's that? I have a physical every July 7th on my birthday. My blood pressure and heart are both normal. Not only that, but this year when more mentally ill Chinese than ever are jumping off buildings committing suicide, here I am totally sane!'

'What? There's a woman in front of you and you're sitting there talking about mental health? Isn't that a little bit weird?'

I-po laughs. 'What's the hurry. Anyway, you won't escape from Monkey's grasp tonight!' He switches to English, '*I've got a surprise for you.*' He points to the screen on the floor.

'. . . Sea of Tranquility basecamp, Sea of Tranquility basecamp, this is Houston Control Center. Aldrin, please tell us, at this moment what is your exact position on the surface? . . .'

> '. . . I don't want this mad, mad world,

167

this mad, mad, mad, mad world . . .'

A police siren begins to shriek.

I-po switches off the TV and turns up the volume of the stereo. 'We're Chinese. What do Americans on the moon have to do with us? Let's listen to Golden Voice sing. When I left the mainland she was really popular . . .'

>Here the morning is free
>Here the morning is good
>Rice vendors far away
>Fruit hawkers far away . . .

He sings along in falsetto with Golden Voice as he sets up the screen. He takes the projector out of the bag and fishes around for the movie reel. He lowers his voice. 'The only people who live in this apartment house are either widows or old maids. Every time I come to see you, I feel as if they are all watching me. As I was carrying this stuff up the back stairs I ran into your landlady. She looked at the stairs and then at what I was carrying. I felt foolish going on, but I couldn't turn around, so I just kept on walking toward your apartment with my back to her. When I turned around finally, I saw her standing in her doorway, glaring at me. Her TV was on and behind her on the screen I saw a close up of a black woman's face, her mouth wide open as if she were pleading for help, but there was no sound, the volume had been turned off. The landlady stood at her end of the corridor and I stood at the other end. She stared at me and I stared at the black woman who couldn't make a sound. Boy, that was weird. I suddenly started laughing and she waved and said, "Have a good time, Professor," I took off my hat and replied, "Thank you, madam!" and strutted in here with these porn flicks.'

I pour him some gin and fix myself a Bloody Mary. Still naked, I sit next to him on the sofa. His eyes are riveted on the porn flick, and he doesn't notice that I am drinking. I have never drunk before. It is as if he doesn't know there is a naked woman by his side. The movie shows various positions for intercourse: two girls making love; two men making love; a man and a woman; and a group of men and women. I-po's body begins to stir and twitch. The Golden Voice is singing about a pair of phoenixes flying up to heaven.

The red light atop the police car flickers onto the window like blood splattering.

I-po's hands and mouth race over my body. I spill my Bloody Mary on myself. He licks my body with his tongue. "Hey, bloody woman, why are you drinking today?"

I struggle out of his embrace and throw the empty glass to the floor. I run into the bathroom and turn on the faucet in the tub. The night breeze blows in the window. I stretch out in the tub. I-po walks in naked. I wash him, touch him, kiss him, lick him. He bends over me; he is breathing hard. The cool water covers our bodies. He suddenly crawls out and runs into the next room. When he returns, he is wearing a rubber. I repeat my performance: touching him, kissing him, licking him . . .

He slips inside me.

'I'm pregnant.'

He suddenly stops. 'You're kidding.'

'The doctor's already verified it.'

'That's impossible. I always wear a rubber.'

'Don't you remember? When we were in the tub, the rubber slipped. I pulled it out of my vagina but it was empty.'

'You'll have to get an abortion immediately!'

'That's illegal.'

'You'll have to get an abortion immediately!'

'The Immigration Service is investigating you.'

'What for? I've been an American citizen for a long time!' He goes soft inside me.

'They're investigating you because we committed adultery.' I tell him about the Immigration Service's questioning me.

'It's better that we don't see each other.' He pulls himself out of my body.

'You're lying on top of me right now, Professor!'

He laughs. 'You are my weakness: I can't do without you!'

'Then move in with me!'

'I can't do that. Betty and I are Catholics. We can't get a divorce; I have to protect my teaching position. Anyway, I'm too used to my freedom. I must retain some *dignity* in front of my friends. You know I wouldn't do anything rash.'

'I've decided to keep the child.'

'No, that won't do,' he frowns. 'You've got to get an abortion.' I grab his penis, and lightly rub it between my hands. 'New York. You can go to New York for the abortion. New York's changed the law: abortion is legal there. I'll pay for everything: travel expenses, medical expenses, all your expenses in New York.'

169

His penis stiffens in my hands.

He lowers himself back into the water with a grunt.

I suddenly leap out of the tub. I-po, lying in the water, yells at me. 'Hey, Mulberry, you can't leave. I'm about to come, I'm about to come! Mulberry!'

I turn on the T.V. The astronauts are speaking.

'. . . I'm climbing down the ladder. The feet of the Eagle only sink one or two inches into the moon's surface. Getting closer, you can see that the moon's surface is made up of very fine dust, like powder, very, very fine. Now I'm going to leave the Eagle . . . That's one small step for man, one giant leap forward for mankind . . .' Armstrong, moving slowly one step at a time, explores the surface of the moon. He is hunched over like an exhausted ape man.

I mix another Bloody Mary and go back into the bathroom.

I-po is lying in the tub, his eyes closed, holding his penis, a soft, wrinkled lump.

Again footsteps echo in the corridor. The sound of decisive boots, boots with cleats like policemen wear, approaching my door. I lock the door. The siren on the police car whines they're going to break down the door and get in I'm going to jump out the window. No, no it's not the police siren. It's the kettle on the stove whistling.

The footsteps stop knock on my door. The landlady watched I-po walk into my room and secretly listened to I-po and me on the telephone. She's definitely the one who reported me to the Immigration Service. One evening I called I-po more than ten times I told him that I felt ashamed about the incident in the tub that evening, he's a good person I shouldn't torment him like that – I've decided to do as he said and go to New York to get an abortion, I shouldn't make problems for him I shouldn't leave proof of guilt for the Immigration Service, for the time being we won't see each other, then the Immigration Service can't accuse me of any more bad behaviour, not seeing him is a matter of life and death, I need him if I don't see him I will have nothing at all.

The knocking on the door gets more insistent as soon as I open the door I will see two large black lenses I've never seen his eyes.

As soon as I open the door two eyes fix on me they're the listless eyes of an old man. He asks me if I want to buy an evangelical pamphlet 'Guide to the Truth of Eternal Life'. He says this world doesn't have any god we should bring god back, very cheap only twenty-five cents will bring god back. I buy the 'Guide to the Truth of Eternal Life' for twenty-five cents. I close the door lock the door lock the old man's eyes outside the door. I leaf through the truth pamphlet in it is written 'The Dead May Hope for Resurrection' perhaps I should keep the child because of that hope I shouldn't harm a single life. I've hurt so many people. Keeping the child is my only chance for redemption. Sang-wa hasn't written for a long time. She hates me she despises me she won't live with me.

I see that red bird again with the blue breast and yellow eyes it's perched on my father's fresh grave. I pick up a stone and throw it at the bird the bird is pecking at the dirt on the fresh grave. I burn paper money before the grave the bird flies into the room I go into my father's study the bird flies in the door. It jumps around bobbing and bowing on my father's red yoga cushion. I ask the bird are you my father's incarnation it nods. I light three sticks of incense in front of the bird confessing that I stole the jade griffin ran away from home I seduced many men I threw away many men I stole Mama's gold locket gave it to my younger brother so he could run away from home I must change and become a new person I want to start a new life. The bird flies out the window.

The hospital in Nanking. The civil war. I am lying in a sick bed Chao T'ien-k'ai stamps into the room wearing tall US army boots his eyes are blood-shot a stubble of beard crawling all over his face. He tells me he hasn't slept for three days. There was a riot at the student anti-hunger demonstration and the Nationalist police arrested a truckload of students his two roommates were taken away people say that the Nationalists put the rioters in hemp bags and threw them into the Yangtze River, someone found Lao-shih, my best friend, lying on a path on campus her body covered with blood they don't know who beat her up like that, some people say it was the leftists who beat her up because she was a reactionary other people say it was the rightists who beat her up because she was a leftist. Other people say she is just sex-starved and helps the leftist student cause so the leftists will sleep with her and then helps the rightists so they will sleep with her and when her lovers found out they beat her up, Chao T'ien-k'ai isn't sure what she really is he doesn't even know what he himself is, some people says he's a reactionary, some people say he's on the left, he only knows one thing: he must think of a way to rescue his friends who were arrested . . . Chao T'ien-k'ai goes on talking without stopping. I lie on the bed looking at his stubble of beard my arm neck and part of my chest stick out from the covers. I tell him to calm down rest awhile. When the nurse comes in Chao T'ien-k'ai is lying under the covers beside me.

A large scar covers half of Lao-shih's face one eye stares blankly at me.

*All that happened so long ago I've completely forgotten I hope I won't
see those things before my eyes again.*

Fifty, sixty, seventy mph. The car goes faster and faster. Red lights,
yellow lights, black mud, red barns, white centre line, green trees, blue
cars, brown turkeys rush past. A summer breeze sweeps in the window.
I feel renewed.

Snow floats in the little crystal paperweight, floating above the Great
Wall. Keeping one hand on the steering wheel, Teng picks up the glass
paperweight from the dashboard and shakes it vigorously a few times.

The snow floats up in the paperweight, drifts over the Great Wall
again.

'Where to?' I ask Teng.

'Don't know.'

He picks up the paperweight again and shakes it vigorously.

I laugh. 'Looks like you're mad at that paperweight.'

'I'm mad at myself. I've been thinking. It took me the strength of
nine bulls and two tigers to escape from the mainland to Taiwan, and
the strength of nine more bulls and two more tigers to escape from
there to America. Once in America, I scrubbed toilets as a janitor,
waited on tables. I have only a few more months until I get my Ph.D.
But once I get it, then what? Go back to Taiwan? I couldn't stand it!
Go back to the mainland? I can't do that, either. Stay here? I'm
nobody! Today I went to work at the university library. I was five
minutes late. John Chang that son of a bitch bawled me out in English,
yelling at me that I couldn't show up late, couldn't leave early, Chinese
in America didn't come to pan for gold, everyone, no matter who, had
to work hard. I said to him, "Hey, Chang, are you a Chinese? Speak in
Chinese!" He pointed at me and said, "Just what are you? *You are
fired*!" I walked out of there with my head held high, only saw him turn
around and show the book of colour photos that just arrived,
Magnificent China, to an American professor in the history department. "*It's a wonderful country, isn't it?*" As soon as I left the library I
picked up an American girl.'

'And then what?'

Teng laughs. 'Mulberry, you don't need to ask what happened next.
Then, well, you know. Really coarse skin. Just to have somebody to do
it with. She even started to cry in bed, saying she'd never been so
happy.' Teng steps on the gas as he says 'happy'.

Ninety miles an hour.

172

'Good!' I look at the headlights in front of us, like two eyes staring at us. Behind us are two more eyes staring at us. I'm not afraid of bright lights anymore.

'Help! My car had a breakdown. Could you please help me?' A head suddenly pokes out of a car at the side of the road, looks at us desperately and yells.

We zoom by. The car behind us catches up and is about to cross the yellow line. Teng steps on the gas again: one hundred miles an hour.

The two cars race side by side down the highway.

'You crossed the yellow line!' Teng sticks his head out the window and yells.

'You're speeding!'

'So are you!'

'You didn't stop to help!'

'You didn't either!'

'I couldn't stop!'

'I couldn't either!'

'You're crazy!'

'You're the one who's crazy!'

'No, you're the one who's crazy!'

'I'll kill you!' Teng picks up the paperweight, and is about to throw it at that car. Suddenly he withdraws his hand. 'Mother-fuckers, it's not worth it to throw the Great Wall at those white devils!'

The paperweight rolls on the seat.

The snow floats in the paperweight.

The other car falls back, about to turn at the intersection. Teng pulls a sailor's knife out of his pocket, snaps the blade in position, points it at the people in that car and yells:

'Good luck!'

Teng folds the knife and puts it back in his pocket, his two hands firmly holding the steering wheel, his eyes blankly staring at the road ahead, his short chunky body sitting up tall.

'Teng, you've suddenly become a man!'

'You've suddenly become a young girl!'

'You thought I was too old before!' I eye him and laugh, as I light up a cigarette.

'I didn't mean that. I only meant, you're so radiant today, and seem suddenly younger!'

I blow smoke in his face.

'You smoke?'

'Uh.'

'Since when?'

'Today.' I blow more smoke in his face.

'You're making me itch all over, Mulberry! Damn! We've gone the wrong way!' He looks at the sign at the side of the road, slows the car down. 'Highway 5! I've never heard of a Highway 5! I'm muddled because of that smoke!'

'Just keep on going down the highway, we're sure to come across the right road.'

'That's true. Let's just keep going.'

The car follows the curving highway awhile. Highway 7. Highway 12. No more highway. No more road signs. The car races along the gravel road. Speeds through a little town with no sign.

'This is just like a labyrinth!' Before Teng even finishes speaking, the car makes a strange whine, and suddenly stops.

Out of gas.

We are stopped by an auto graveyard. Junked Fords, Dodges, Chevrolets, and Pontiacs are piled in the yard. Most are twisted, empty shells, smashed up in wrecks. Beyond the graveyard is a street lined with grey houses with black windows. An empty gas station on the corner. No sign of anyone. It's a ghost town. It was once a booming town, then the young people left to make their way in the world and the old people all died off.

'What'll we do?'

'Wait.'

'For what?'

'Wait till someone drives through and we can ask for some gas.'

'Who'd come to this creepy place?'

'What else can we do except wait? It's too quiet! Let's have a little noise!' Teng turns around and switches on the tape recorder in the back seat.

'. . . To tell the truth, our Action Committee still has not taken a position. We're only a bunch of free Chinese who have banded together. We not only have freedom of thought, we also have freedom of action. But the desire for freedom is like smoking pot, the more you smoke, the more you want it. Once you're addicted the trouble begins. What the Action Committee advocates is "action". Some people say we're people without roots in a world without faith, worth or purpose. But it's better this way! Then we can have true freedom to create by our action a life of worth and purpose, even create a God. What kind of action? How to take action? I*

174

hope everyone will think about that when he's finished work for the day, finished writing his thesis or finished helping his wife with the dishes . . .

'I propose organising a "Committee to Defend Human Rights" to protest against incidents which threaten human rights!

'We must first get to know ourselves. Get to know each other, be frank with each other. How to act as Chinese, this is the most important thing. So . . . I suggest that we first take action, to understand through our actions, so . . . What you said is not right. I think . . .'

I laugh. 'We're stranded here in this ghost town listening to Chinese debate how to take action.'

'OK, here's concrete action! Listen to a recording of hog butchering in a packinghouse. "Killing" should be a course of action!' Teng turns around and presses a button on the tape recorder in the back seat, adjusts the tape, then presses the button again. He turns around, picks up the little glass paperweight and shakes it.

The snow floats up in the paperweight. All around is pitch black. The snow on the Great Wall is white.

The sound of machines, people – deafening clatter from the tape recorder.

The clatter stops.

'Our slaughterhouse slaughters 450 hogs an hour. The method we use is highly effective, the result of a combination of man working with machines.

'But we also strive to make it as humane as possible.

'Now, all of you who have come for hog butchering, please come with me. I'll explain every step in the slaughtering process. Over there is a small gate. Those hogs over there in front of the gate, raising up their snouts and looking at us, it's really funny, isn't it? They're ready to enter the slaughterhouse. First a number has to be stamped on the hog's body. That little gate only allows one hog to enter at a time. Beside the gate is a board which blocks from sight the man who wields the club. On the head of the club are many tiny needles; those tiny needles, when dipped in ink, make up the numbers. When each hog goes by, the man behind the board stamps him with the club with needles on it, a number is thus stamped on the hog's body. That number is stamped on its skin beneath the bristles. When the bristles are removed, by hot water, the number remains imprinted on the hog's body. This is what we consider our most efficient point.'

The sound of machines, people – deafening clatter.

The clatter stops.

'Now, these little fellas are going to take a hot bath. There's a pool with

hot water. The hogs soak in it, the bristles soften up and then are pulled out. Then the preparation before entering the slaughterhouse has been completed.'

The sound of machines, people – deafening clatter.

The clatter stops.

'Now these little fellas are ready to enter the slaughterhouse. The method we use lessens the animals' pain as much as possible. The hog is on that slope. We use a pair of electric tongs like the curling irons women used to use to curl their hair a long time ago. You poke them in the hog's body. The hog is given an electric shock and it immediately blacks out and collapses. Someone above it lowers a hook, catches one of the hog's feet on the hook and lifts the hog up.'

The sound of machines, people – deafening clatter.

The clatter stops.

'Then a butcher raises a butcher's knife and skillfully pierces the hog's throat. He cuts right into the hog's heart. The hog's heart is very close to its throat. You could say the hog's an animal without a throat. (Laughter.) That one stroke, you could say, is quick of sight, quick of hand, beautiful and solemn, just like a religious ceremony.'

The sound of machines, people – deafening clatter.

The clatter stops.

'Now, the hog is hanging high in the air. The blood gushes down on the steel-ribbed, cement floor. The blood's bright red; it's very beautiful. That man standing on the high counter, wearing rubber boots, uses that thing in his hand, it looks like a broom, to sweep the blood into a gutter. He stands in the blood all day long doing that. He's been doing it for twenty-six years. When the blood flows out the gutter, it coagulates. Man can use coagulated blood to make all kinds of food products. The Scots like to eat pudding made from hog's blood. The Chinese eat bean curd simmered with hog's blood.' The sound of machines and people combine into a deafening din, as if it will never stop . . .

'Look! Teng!' I point to the fields in front of us. After our car stops, the headlights have remained on, shining into the field. 'There are many dots of light like lanterns in the distance. Do you see them? There, over there, they're moving! They're coming toward us! One, two, three, four, five, six, more than ten! There, there're some more!'

We get out of the car and run toward the moving lights. They disperse, scatter in all directions.

'Deer! The light's from their eyes!' I call out.

The deer race back into the trees on the hillside.

Teng and I walk into the graveyard. A statue of a black angel, wings outstretched, bends over protecting a grave. Teng strikes a match to light up the inscription on the tombstone:

'Nicholai Vandefield 1805–1861'

The grass on the grave is tall, a little red flower has been placed on the grave.

The black silhouette of a barn looms on the horizon.

Teng and I lie down on the grass of the grave. I undress him.

How could I have done such a shameless thing with that nice young man, Teng? I probably was insane I don't even recognise myself!

I hear my brain talking again, it seems like there's another brain inside my brain. The two brains are separate, one talks the other listens. I'm very frightened I sing loudly to suppress the voice in my brain but it still goes on talking I don't know what it's saying. The voice is unclear, it's as if it's ridiculing me now I can hear it. It says: 'You raped another man! You can't get an abortion!'

I-po didn't come. I called him over and over but no answer. Once it was Betty who answered I hung up. I want to tell him I don't want to get an abortion. I must not sin again.

> *'From the first to the fifteenth when the moon is full,*
> *Spring breezes sway the willow, the willow turns green . . .'*

I hear again our family servant singing a folksong in his soft voice. I ride on his shoulders to watch the monkey circus. We walk in wide-open fields. A beggar carrying a broken basket searches for burnt coal in the garbage. The field in front of us is crowded with people Li suddenly stops singing, points saying Little Mulberry let's go see the execution. I ask are they executing good people or bad people Li says they're executing Communists. I ask are Communists good or bad, Li says whoever gives the common people food to eat is a good person whoever lets the common people starve is a bad person. A volley of gunfire. Li runs over carrying me on his back. The people who have been shot are lying on the ground in a pool of blood a thin stream of blood trickles down the hill. A skinny old woman kneels by the side crying and burning paper money scattering water and rice over the ashes. A scrawny yellow dog is sniffing at the trickling blood . . .

When I see the blood my whole body turns to ice, I curl up into a ball. I want to talk with someone I call Teng I want to tell him that I'm a bad woman, when he and I were together I was already pregnant with I-po's child. But I can only utter one word to him: 'blood!'

The train is rushing over the Pearl River Bridge in Canton refugees cling to the roof of the train many heads are sticking out the windows. A telephone wire scrapes along the roof of the train. One two three people drop with a splash into the river. Someone standing on the roof of the last car is pissing in the river as he sees the people falling into the river. The people at the window say that on such a sunny day it's raining but the rain smells a little strange. People at another window say the Communists have already crossed the Yangtze River and will take over China. The heads of the people in the river come up several times then vanish.

One instrument that establishes contact between people is the body, another is the telephone. My Friday night pastime is making telephone calls.

351–7789. 'Hello!'

'Helen!'

'How did you know it was Helen?'

'You have a foreign accent.'

'I haven't used the name Helen for a long time.'

'I'm sorry. I can't pronounce foreign names. I can't even pronounce my own husband's name, I-po. I call him *Bill*. What does Mulberry mean in Chinese?'

'Mulberry is a holy tree, Chinese people consider it the chief of the tree family, it can feed silkworms, silkworms can produce silk, silk can be woven into silk and satin material. The mulberry tree is green, the colour of spring . . .'

'Helen, don't stop, go on talking, go on, it's coming, that magical feeling is coming, crawling all over my body! Crawling all over my eyes! Crawling into my brain! I can see the silkworms, silver, twisting, curling, spitting out silk, wrapping it all around their bodies, the multi-coloured silk, delicate and luminous, wrapped around the bodies of the silkworms, their heads emerging from the strands of silk, no they're human heads . . .'

'Betty! You're hallucinating again, you've been smoking dope again . . .'

'The water of the Nile is flowing, flowing, look, it's flowing right there, do you see it? Helen, believe what I say, it's all true. I've even seen many, many people, many different worlds, they're all surging forth! They're all real people, real worlds . . .'

178

'I don't understand anything you're saying! Betty! The thing that's most real to me is the child in my womb, it's I-po's and my child.'

I hang up.

353–1876. No answer.

351–9466. The telephone buzzes. Busy.

338–2457. No answer.

338–0060. 'This is a recording. The number you have dialled is no longer in service.'

351–9063. 'Hello.'

'Hello. I want to speak with Teng.'

'You've got the wrong number!'

'What's your number?'

'I won't tell you. What number do you want?'

'351–9063.'

'I'll say it again: You've got the wrong number!'

I hang up.

351–9063. 'Hello.'

'It's you again! Wrong number! Please don't bother me, I want to sleep!'

'Good night.' I hang up again.

351–9063. 'Hello.'

'It's you again – it's that woman! What's the matter with you anyway?'

'You listen, lady. Just what's your problem? You . . .' The woman at the other end hasn't finished speaking when the man takes the phone and yells: 'We're just having a hell of a good time in bed! If you bother us again I'll kill you!'

'Are you committing adultery?'

'None of your business!' Slams the phone down.

351–9063. 'Hello.'

I laugh loudly. 'I'm sorry. I've interrupted again.'

'I WILL KILL YOU!' Slams the phone down.

351–9063. 'Hi!'

'Hi! Teng! You've finally wiggled your way out from under the bed!'

'What are you talking about? I just wiggled my way out of the lab. I killed another cat.'

'Killing a cat in the middle of the night!'

'I have to finish my experiment. It was a pregnant cat. I raised her awhile, waiting until she bore the kittens before killing her. When I slit open the cat's stomach, guess what I was thinking about?'

'Thinking about the new-born animals.'

179

'Thinking about you!'

'My stomach has to be cut open, too. I'll have to have a Caesarean.'

'What? I don't understand what you're saying!'

'I'm pregnant.'

'We'll get married immediately.'

'It's I-po's child.'

'Oh. Well, then he should take the responsibility.'

'I'm through with him. I'll take the responsibility myself.'

'You want the child?'

'Eh. It's a life, too.'

'I agree with you. We kill too many living things. In the beginning it was only people killing other people; now people use machines to kill. I had a strange feeling: when I was killing the cat, for a while it seemed as if I were that cat, one stroke, another stroke cutting the cat's body, was cutting into my own body as well. Do you really want the child?'

'No doubt about it!'

'I admire your nerve. But, but, in your situation perhaps it isn't wise for you to have an illegitimate child. I still haven't told you: The man from the Immigration Service came to see me and ask about you. I said in my whole life I've admired only two women, one is my mother, the other is you. In my eyes you two represent all the good womanly virtues.'

'What did he say?'

'He didn't say anything, only copied down what I said. That reminds me. About your child, I have a plan. My sister's been married twice and has never gotten pregnant. You know, my sister's husband is a second generation overseas Chinese, working in New York as a stock broker, quite well off. All my sister does is go to concerts, travel in Europe, vacation by the ocean, buy works of art, buy designer clothes – several hundred dresses, twenty or thirty pairs of shoes. She also writes poetry, but it's only a pastime. She's been to Taiwan once, but her life style didn't change when she returned. There's no purpose at all. If she had a child, perhaps her life would change. Before school starts I want to go to New York, in order to apply for jobs and meet the people in the firms, also for the "Action Committee", you know. We can drive there together and talk to my sister about this. You're old schoolmates, you can talk easily about anything. You can have a good time in New York. You . . .'

'You don't need to go on. I decided a long time ago to go to New York, not to talk to your sister about the child, but to see the Empire State Building.'

180

'Can I go over to see you now?'

'There's no Empire State Building here!'

'The hell with the Empire State Building!'

We hang up. The phone rings immediately.

'Hello.'

'Hi! Mulberry . . .'

'Professor, Mulberry's already dead.'

'Don't joke with me! Betty's dead!'

'You're kidding! I just talked to her on the phone!'

'When I came back, the room was really dark; there was a strange odour. Like the smell of drugs. I turned on the light, Betty was lying on the living room floor, an empty wine bottle beside her. Her mouth was open, fluid trickling from her mouth. I called to her, shook her, but no response. I was terrified. It's a sudden heart attack and she's dead! I felt her forehead, it was icy cold! I felt her nostrils, no air being exhaled. She died just like that!'

'Hurry up and call the police!'

'First I have to find something.'

'Find what?'

'Find the letters you sent me. What about your going to New York?'

'I've decided to go next week.'

'In fact, you needn't . . .'

'I have to go open my door. Teng's here!'

'What's he doing going to your apartment in the middle of the night?'

'Didn't you come in the middle of the night, too?'

'Is the child in your belly his?'

'No. It's yours. Sorry. He's knocking!' I hang up.

I open the door the man in dark glasses stands in the doorway behind him is a long narrow corridor. He wants me to go to the Police Station at one o'clock to have a talk. I invite him inside to talk he says he wants to use the facilities at the Police Station. Is he going to use the lie detector? Is he going to torture me? Is he going to put me in prison?

I want to escape I don't dare meet the man in dark glasses. Since last time when he questioned me, he's certainly found out about a lot more of my crimes: my relationship with I-po my pregnancy my relationship with Teng Betty's death. Perhaps my being pregnant provoked her to commit suicide or perhaps she died of a stroke, perhaps I-po murdered his wife in order to keep his child. Although I didn't kill her I'm to blame. I call I-po on the phone no answer. Perhaps he went to the funeral parlour perhaps he was taken for questioning by the police. I call Teng on the phone no answer. I'm the only one left in the whole wide world I walk in circles around the room walking walking walking walking.

The police take me into a room shut the door and leave me there. The fluorescent lights in the room are all lit up the man in dark glasses sits behind a grey steel desk like the one at the Immigration Service. On the desk is a folder on the top is my alien registration number (Alien) 89–785–462 and an electric typewriter. He stands up and shakes my hand asks me to sit down. He says he came to this area to investigate a lot of aliens who are applying for permanent residency he'll take advantage of this opportunity to once again ask me some important questions. They are this careful with every case.

He suddenly asks me if I did or did not commit adultery with Chiang I-po I say we don't see each other anymore. He pulls a pile of papers from the file words crawl over the page, he says that is the information he found out since my first interrogation, all evidence in regard to my behaviour, some are the result of his questioning people some are the result of people reporting to him. He leafs through to a page that says according to the Landlady's report on the evening of 20 July, the very evening that the astronauts landed on the moon, Chiang I-po entered my apartment by way of the fire escape. He stares at me asks on the evening of July 20th did he or did he not have sexual intercourse with me I say yes, he asks how long did it last I say I can't say for sure, we weren't in bed we were in the bathtub, the small mustache below the two large dark lenses twitches he asks how do you have sexual intercourse in a bathtub? I say first it was I who got in, after a while he also got in after a while he got out after a while he got in again, after a while I got out again after a while the astronauts landed on the moon. He says he doesn't understand a thing I'm talking about but he must record every word I say. He taps out each word on the electric typewriter.

He says he still must continue investigating my case if they decide I am an undesirable alien they must deport me, where do I want to go? I say I don't know. He says he doesn't know what's the matter with Chinese all the Chinese people he's investigated answer the same way, the Chinese are foreigners who haven't any place to be deported to, this is a difficulty he's never encountered in investigating other aliens. I ask when they will decide he says he doesn't know. He tells me to wait wait wait wait . . .

My finger tips hurt suddenly I realise that the cigarette I'm holding is burning my fingers my shoes are splattered with mud on the table beside

182

*the bed there's a half-drunk Bloody Mary. What's happened to me. I
never touched alcohol cigarettes or mud. The calendar on the wall reads
2 September I only remember 30 August when the man in dark glasses
questioned me at the Police Station everything after that where I was and
what I did I don't remember at all.*

*My god there's a huge penis drawn in red in the mirror and there
are some words scrawled. Mulberry is dead. I have bloomed. I hate
Mulberry.*

I wipe out the obscene picture and the words whose joke is this.

It was my joke. You're dead, Mulberry. I have come to life. I've been
alive all along. But now I have broken free. You don't know me, but I
know you. I'm completely different from you. We are temporarily
inhabiting the same body. How unfortunate. We often do the opposite
things. And if we do the same thing, our reasons are different. For
instance. You want to keep the child because you want to redeem
yourself. I want to keep the child because I want to preserve a new life.
You don't see Chiang I-po anymore because you are scared of the
Immigration Service agent; I ignore him because I despise him. When
you're with Teng you feel guilty, when I'm with him I feel happy. You
and I threaten each other like the world's two superpowers. Sometimes
you are stronger; sometimes I am. When I'm stronger I can make you
do things you don't want to do, for example the evening the astronauts
landed on the moon, you teased and tormented I-po, when you acted
like a slut with Teng in the ghost town graveyard. After those things
happened you felt you were even more guilty – I like to do mischief
with you like that. Because you limit my freedom. Now, you're dead, I
hope you won't come back, then I'll be completely free! Do you know
what happened after you died? I thought Betty was dead. I walked up
to the Chiang house. Betty opened the door!

'I'm really happy that you're alive again! Betty!' I said to her.

She motioned to me to go around the yard and come in the back
door. She was waiting for me at the back door. We went down to the
basement. All I could hear was I-po and several people in the front
living room competing to call out the names of old alleys in Peking.

'Goldfish Alley!'

'Emerald Flower Alley!'

'Lilac Alley!'

'Rouge Alley!'

'Sesame Wang Alley!'

'Master Ma Alley!'

'Pocket Alley!'

'Magpie Alley!'

'Fresh Alley!'

'Slender Reed Alley!'

'Ladder Alley!'

'Candlewick Alley!'

'Bean Sprout Alley!'

'White Temple Alley!'

'Cotton Alley!'

'Pa-ta Alley!' I-po was shouting.

'The professor isn't thinking of Pa-ta Alley. He's thinking of the courtesans who lived there.'

I-po laughed. 'That's right.'

> The east is red
> The morning sun rises
> In China Mao Tse-tung appears
> He works for the happiness of the people . . .

'Communist spy! You're playing a Communist record!' A girl's voice.

'Revolution, revolution!' Chiang I-po's voice. 'This young lady is going to turn in her old friend. Hsiao-Chuan, do you believe it? I even went to Taiwan last year and Chiang Kai-Shek's own son shook my hand.'

'You're putting me on. I don't believe it!'

The basement was one long room. Clothes, newspapers, magazines, cigarette boxes, and empty liquor bottles were strewn everywhere. There was a kitchenette in the corner, all sorts of things piled on the filthy stove. The only furniture in the room was a large colour TV and a box spring mattress studded with cigarette burns. The room smelled of marijuana. A boy with long hair was lying on the mattress watching television. He was wearing only jockey shorts. When he saw Betty and me he gave an unfriendly grunt. The news announcer looked out into the emptiness and began speaking in a monotonous voice: '. . . *A bomb from the Second World War was discovered today by a cleaning lady in Carpenterville, Illinois. The police have warned the residents in the vicinity to be on guard for an explosion, and they de-activated the bomb. But a young professor maintained that the bomb would not explode, it was only a new toy left over from the war, he had picked it up in a junk yard in Chicago to use for a room decoration . . .*'

184

'This is my territory! I feel at ease here. And have everything: booze, sex, entertainment, dope, even violence!' Betty laughed, pointed to the confrontation of the police and rioters on the TV screen.

'. . . *A federal grand jury charged five political activists with inciting a riot. The five have been charged with planning and inciting the bloody riot at the August 1968 Democratic National Convention in Chicago . . .*'

Upstairs, I-po roared with laughter. The Golden Voice was singing a love song.

> He closed the door I had to go,
> Their two hearts entwine as one,
> Madame, if you can leave them alone, then do,
> Why pursue the matter any further?

'*Bill's* never been down here in the basement. I call him the upstairs Chinese; he calls me the underground American,' Betty said.

'I call him the empty man,' I said.

Betty smiled darkly and drew closer. 'That is why he can't leave me: I give him freedom to live his vacuum life. If he were willing to leave me, he would have left a long time ago. When I met him, he was working hard on his Ph.D. At that time he wasn't interested in anything Chinese, he didn't even have Chinese friends. But now, it's just the opposite! Anything Chinese is good! Chinese culture, Chinese literature, Chinese food, Chinese style clothes, Chinese women! He especially likes young Chinese women.' Betty got up to open a cupboard, took out a pile of letters and threw them in my lap. 'These are all love letters Chinese girls have written him! I won't mention anything before, but when he went to Taiwan to visit he added quite a few more! You know, you yourself wrote him a lot of letters, when the man from the Immigration Service came to ask about you, he asked if I had any material to give them, so I gave him your letters.'

'I couldn't care less!' I picked up that bunch of the girls' letters and weighed them in my hand, then threw them back at Betty. 'Are you jealous?'

She shrugged. 'We're very fair, he has his life and I have mine.' She pointed to the half-naked man lying on the mattress watching television.

'All these letters, and yours, he gave to me, to show his faithfulness to me.' Betty laughed. 'Last night, he thought I was dead; I was lying on the floor, in a daze. I thought I saw him walk in, I kept on thinking: I want to die once, I want to die once, I want to die once to scare him. I was thinking and thinking and didn't know where I was. I was floating in the clouds. The wind was blowing, the clouds floating, the flowers were swaying. I swayed along with those white round flowers, swaying, swaying. I suddenly understood why the wind blows in such a way, why clouds float along like they do, why the flowers sway like they do, that's the dance style of the wind, clouds, and flowers. I have my own dance style, too. We're each an independent life, and when we're together we dance differently to the same rhythms. I got up off the floor and went down to the basement, I came across *Bill* down there, that's the only time he's ever come down to my basement. He was holding a bunch of letters and looking through them, probably looking for the letters you wrote to him. "I've already given the letters you're looking for to the Immigration Service. I also know Helen's going to have a child, your child," I said standing in the doorway. He jumped. I laughed and said, "I'm not dead." He started laughing too. He said that bunch of letters was meaningless, he wanted to burn them. I said I still hadn't finished looking at them, I don't know Chinese, but those different characters look like different pictures. He said, well, then, save them for you as a pastime. *Bill* and I have been together for more than twenty years, our children are already married, and I still don't understand Chinese people. But I can communicate with you. We're very frank with each other. Now, I want to ask you a question. Do you want to keep the child?'

'And if I don't?'

'I can raise your child. I need a little something in my life.'

'Thanks, Betty. I want my child for myself.'

The people upstairs began singing Peking Opera. It seemed they were competing to remember opera verses – a line here, a line there, everyone scrambled to sing it first, intermixed with the singing was a girl's laughter.

'. . . Who was your first love?'

'At sixteen I slept with that King . . .'

'The feudal lords do not cooperate, with sword and lance they contend. Day and night I dream a thousand plots. I want to sweep the wolf out with the smoke, so peace will reign within the four seas like in the time of T'ang Yao . . .'

'Yo ya ya ya. But wait! On all sides are the songs of Ch'u. Can it be that Liu Pang – he, he, he's already captured the land of Ch'u?'

'Ah, great king, do not be alarmed. Send someone out to investigate, then you can make your plans.'

'Can it be my son is insane?' We switch operas.

'When I hear it said I'm mad I get so happy I just play along with it. I lie down in the dust and babble nonsense.'

'My son. Are you really mad?'

'What do you call it?'

'Mad.'

'Ha ha ha . . .' Chiang I-po laughed in a woman's voice then suddenly stopped.

I was standing in the doorway to the upstairs living room.

Who is that? I don't recognise her. She must be a ghost attaching itself to my body she frightens me she embarrasses me. How can I explain to people how can I make people understand that she isn't me? Since I barged into I-po's house since Betty and I criticised him I haven't the nerve to see I-po again, no matter how close we used to be I still need him with all my life the child in my womb is his. I call him and tell him I'm thinking of giving the child to Teng's sister, Tan-hung. That would solve two problems: Tan-hung will have a child and my child will be safe. He says that's a good idea he tells me to go to New York immediately to talk it over with Tan-hung. He wants to buy my plane ticket I say that's not necessary Teng and I are driving there together we'll stay at Tan-hung's place. As soon as I mention Teng he stops talking. I tell him Teng's sister, Tan-hung, and I are old classmates he's always treated me like an elder sister, he's almost finished with his Ph.D. and already got a job at a New York hospital, he wants to marry a very attractive girl, Chin, as soon as possible. I-po hangs up. I don't know why I wanted to lie to him.

New York. The Ford Building. I'm on Forty-Third Street.

The Ford Building is a huge glass tank, divided into smaller glass tanks. There's a person in every tank. Each person has a telephone by his side. There's a courtyard in the middle of the tank where flowers of all seasons bloom.

A blind man walks past the tank, led by a large fat dog.

Suddenly the blind man begins running and yelling in a frightened voice: 'The Ford Building is falling. The Ford Building is falling! My dog, where's my dog?'

I'm the only one who looks at him. I laugh.

It's drizzling, a good day for a funeral. There's a long long procession of anti-war protestors on Fifth Avenue. White, black, yellow, one by one, streaming from Greenwich Village, past Washington Square, the Empire State Building, Rockefeller Center, St. Patrick's Cathedral (a sign hangs on the door: please come in and rest and pray), the Metropolitan Museum of Art, streaming toward Central Park.

Not a single pedestrian turns to look at them. The pedestrians are pushed along in the mob, pushed into the entrances to the iron ribbed, concrete buildings.

Only one person follows the demonstrators. His body jerks up and down, his head rolls backwards, he stretches out a crippled hand and waves at the protestors, laughing, 'Hello, hello, can you hear me? Hello! I have something to tell you: a monster from outer space has invaded New York. It's taken over the Empire State Building. Hello . . . Did you hear me? A monster from outer space has taken over the Empire State Building. Did you hear me?'

The demonstrators don't listen to him. The pedestrians don't listen either.

I approach him. I'm listening, I tell him. He invites me to the Red Onion for a Bloody Mary.

Mulberry, I'm glad I'm the one who came to New York, not you. I'm having a wonderful time. I'll be certain to write down everything interesting that happens. If you show up by chance, you will know what's been happening. Look, I'll cooperate with you if you won't spoil all the fun.

I don't know how long I disappeared or what happened then. I'm really scared. Where am I? There's a black wall with a large water colour scroll. The furniture is so black it makes me panic. The people? Where is everyone?

Tan-hung walks in led by a Pekinese dog on a leash the Pekinese runs right toward me. From the sofa I climb onto the table and stand there as the Pekinese leaps up at the table. Tan-hung laughs and says she knows I don't like dogs but she didn't know I was that scared of dogs my face has turned green. She calls the dog A-king, A-king. The dog races over and buries itself in her breast she sits on the sofa with the dog in her lap and rubs her face against his fur, its tongue licks her arm slowly, methodically, relentlessly, licking, licking.

I get down from the table and sit in a chair in the far corner. I don't know how to begin talking with Tan-hung I can't remember anything I ask what day is it where did Teng go? Tan-hung laughs and says I look like someone who just fell down here from the moon I don't know anything at all, today is 9 September, Saturday Teng and I went out together in the morning, I came back alone in the afternoon. She says he came to New York to apply for jobs but he doesn't seem to care a bit about that, every day he's holding 'Action Meetings' with a bunch of people those people are radicals, her father was killed by the Communists she and her brother must never side with the people who killed their father. Perhaps one day she'll go to Taiwan again. She wrote some poems just for fun and to her surprise they got published in Taiwan. Finally, after a pause, she laughs and says she can tell I'm really close to her brother. I say I'm a jinx whoever comes in contact with me is in for trouble, that's not fair to Teng, I've decided not to see him anymore after we go back. Tan-hung asks whether I still want to keep the child? (She seems to know everything, how does she know? Did I tell her?) I say I want to give the child to her. Her eyes light up. She says the other day I firmly stated that I wouldn't give the child to anyone. She hopes it's a boy she even talks about how she will decorate the child's room she wants to hang pictures of the holy child all over the room, but, but . . . She suddenly stops.

It's getting dark I turn on the lamp on the coffee table. The Pekinese dog has disappeared. Tan-hung walks over to her bedroom door, looks inside and grins then waves at me to come over. I walk over and see the dog sprawled on her bed asleep. She whispers in my ear that A-king is her son.

I absolutely refuse to let you give the child to Tan-hung.

Teng and I go out sightseeing all day in New York. We go out at night. We go see a Broadway play. The people in the audience go up on stage, strip off their clothes and dance; the cast goes down and sits in the audience. They throw fruit peels at the people on stage. Teng explains that in that kind of play every person in the audience takes part. We don't tell Tan-hung about the play. She's too genteel to understand.

Suddenly I find myself lying in the bathtub and the bathroom door is open. Tan-hung's husband Jerry is standing in the doorway. His face is red.

I don't know what has happened. How did I get into the tub I must be insane. I wish I were dead.

I'll tell you what happened.

Jerry and I were in the living room with the black walls. Tan-hung and her Chinese friends had gone to the Chinese-American Friendship

Association to sing Peking Opera. Teng was at a meeting. Jerry's face was the colour of steel. Even when Tan-hung calls him Jerry darling his face remains the colour of steel. He was sitting at the table playing with his cameras. All in all he has fourteen different cameras, varying in size from a large box camera to a tiny match box. Recently he bought the latest German model, the one that fits into a match box, so the unlucky number thirteen became fourteen.

I sat on the sofa watching television: a girl in a long blond wig, blinked her long false eyelashes, thrust out her pointed breasts (perhaps, they're false, too!) and held up a Cralow electric mirror, her lips kept turning from pale white to pink to purple: '. . . All the mirrors of today reflect your face from only one source of light. In fact, there are many different light sources in the world. For this reason, Cralow Company has invented the Cralow True Light Mirror, all you need to do is press a button on the mirror and you can see your face in the various lights of sunlight, lamplight, and fluorescent light . . .'

'Pretty soon they'll be creating electric children,' Jerry said in English. 'Electric children would have one merit: they'd never grow up; they'd forever be in the state of infancy, then the world wouldn't have any more wars. Now we can use test tubes to make babies; the baby's sex and personality can all be decided beforehand, scientifically.' He was still playing with the cameras on the table.

I looked at his wristwatch: under the round glass shell were small cog wheels – the most recently invented toy. The knees of his tight pants were zipped closed with zippers. 'Tan-hung likes kids, you can make a baby in a test tube.' I was speaking in Chinese. I can't speak English to yellow faces.

'I don't like kids. I'd rather let Mary keep a dog.' He's never called her Tan-hung.

'Why?'

'People are more dangerous than dogs. If the world only had one-tenth the population it has now, it wouldn't be so chaotic. People create the chaos. Machines create order. It's best to interact with machines.'

The telephone rang. He went over to answer it, he listened a while, then said one sentence: 'Yao-hua, you must get hold of yourself.' Then he hung up, returned to the table and dusted the cameras with a soft cloth.

A-king ran over and tried to crawl up his legs, pawing at the zipper on his knees.

'Pete, don't move!'

'Pete?' I begin to laugh. 'Tan-hung calls him A-king; you call him Pete! Now which one is his name?'

'Both of them. Anyone can give him a name. You can call him John, too. This is the good point of keeping a dog: he doesn't protest. Mary calls him A-king. She says that name sounds like Peking, I can't pronounce Chinese names, so I call him Pete.'

The telephone rang again. He walked over to answer it, listened a while then again said only one sentence, 'Yao-hua, what you need is a good night's sleep.' Then he hung up. A-king leaped up at him. He picked him up, put him in the bedroom, closed the door. A-king scraped at the door.

The telephone rang again. He went over to answer, listened a while: 'OK, Mary, I'll bring Pete to the phone.' He opened the bedroom door, carried the dog over to the phone. It barked into the phone. He said into the phone receiver: 'Mary, hurry back. If you don't come back, Pete won't behave.' He hung up.

The telephone immediately rang. He picked up the phone and said: 'Hello. It's you again. Yao-hua.' He listened a while. 'You're not going to kill yourself. Get a good night's sleep and you'll be alright.' He hung up, walked back and sat down by the table.

The telephone rang again.

He shook his head and said: 'I can't stand it. Crazy.'

I laughed. 'Now you know machines can also be crazy.'

'I mean that person who's calling. That's Mary's cousin Yao-hua. He came from Taiwan several years ago. Mary doesn't like him. Dirty and muddle-headed. He studied philosophy at the University of Philadelphia. His English isn't any good. He hired someone to write his thesis. When the professor saw it, he asked him if he had hired someone to write it. He said yes. He was expelled. He worked as a waiter in a restaurant for three days then the boss fired him. Now, he calls several times a day, yelling that he's going to kill himself. Every Chinese has something wrong with him.'

The telephone started ringing.

He continued, 'Now they can use a scientific method to freeze people, you know that? Like freezing beef, freeze them for as long as you want, say a hundred years. For those one hundred years, he'd automatically defrost and he'd start living again from the age he was when he was frozen.'

'Then the present can be cancelled?'

'Right, cancelled; just live for the future.'

'After one hundred years, when you're defrosted, if there weren't people anymore, only mechanical people on all the planets, who would you make love with?'

Jerry laughed. 'The mechanical people can take care of that, too.'

The telephone stopped ringing.

I wanted to play a joke on Jerry. I went into the bathroom and filled the tub. I stripped off my clothes. I lay in the bath water. I didn't close the door. I watched my pubic hair reflect off black light in the water.

Mulberry, just at that time you reappeared. You saw his face turn red. You had to take over just at that moment, didn't you? I'll get even with you.

Teng and I are in the living room with black walls (Tan-hung's interior decorating is certainly unique!). Jerry went to Wall Street. Tan-hung took A-king to Fifth Avenue.

The telephone rings. Teng answers it. 'Hello ... Yao-hua? ... Please speak louder, I can't hear you ... Yao-hua, you mustn't think about killing yourself, you're a man, you can take action, do anything you want as long as it's meaningful to you. The only way out is to die? OK! Then go find a way to do it. Go back to Taiwan! Use your actions to kill yourself; but for heaven's sake don't kill yourself with your own hand ... hello, hello, Yao-hua, say something ...'

The telephone rings. Teng answers it. 'Hello ... Wang? If Yao-hua's locked the door then you must pry it open! He could try to kill himself ... Ah, the police are coming ... Yao-hua is coming up by the stairs! ... What! He ran when he saw the police! ... Do you think he's been smoking dope? ... Please find him by all means. I'll wait for word from you. I can't come. If I were to drive it'd take at least two hours. Please keep me informed about Yao-hua. Thanks.'

The telephone rings. I answer the phone. 'Hello.'

'This is Yao-hua. I didn't die. I just came from the apartment of a Puerto Rican girl. I was having a little fun there. You could say she's an old "flame". I saw her once before. The first time I met her in a bar on 86th Street. We went to her apartment. I said I was hungry. She said all she had were some eggs. I said let's eat fried eggs then! After we ate the fried eggs we went to bed, slept a while, were hungry again, ate some more fried eggs, went to bed again, slept a while, were hungry again! Ate some more fried eggs. By that time it was already getting light outside. We had just finished eating a dozen eggs. Today I ran into her on 42nd Street. I didn't even have any money to buy peanuts. I said her fried eggs were really good. She said then eat some more. I just ate two fried eggs; when I left she said she liked me. Tan-hung, don't you think that's wonderful? Tan-hung . . . can you lend me a little more money . . . I know, I've borrowed too much already, and haven't paid back a cent. But I'll pay you back someday. If I don't pay you back I would never forgive myself. Tan-hung, why don't you say anything? Are you Tan-hung? You won't lend me money, right? The hell with you! I'll show you! Goodbye!'

I hang up. The telephone rings again. Teng answers. 'Hello . . . Wang! Yao-hua just called. Wants to borrow some money, probably trying to get a fix, doesn't seem like he's going to kill himself . . . Luckily he still has friends like you; everyone's busy, no one has time to look after anyone else – OK, goodbye.'

Two hours later, the phone rings. I answer it. 'Hello!'

'A Chinese jumped to his death from the 35th floor of Rockefeller Center. We've found out the dead person's name is Jim Chang. We don't know if it's Chang Yao-hua or not.'

'I don't know either,' I say.

They're in the living room talking about Yao-hua's death I'm thinking about the child in my womb. Tan-hung still can't decide if she wants to raise the child as she talks she feeds A-king milk. When I think of the child's fate after birth – an illegitimate child with no roots I don't have the courage to keep it. If Tan-hung raises the child I won't ever worry about it.

The train roars past I suddenly discover I am standing in the subway tunnel from behind me shoes pounding the cement. It's probably the man in the dark glasses who's coming! I begin to run in the tunnel the tunnel so black, so dark I can't see the end in front of me appears a policeman. There's no way out! He's coming toward me! The shoes on the cement behind me stop I also stop the policeman also stops. Three people stand far apart from each other no one can grab anyone, no one can escape – there's no exit in the tunnel. I don't dare look around only hear the man behind me yell: 'Hello! Have you heard? A monster from outer space has invaded New York! It's taken over the Empire State Building! Did you hear about it? Did you hear?'

When Tan-hung goes out, Teng and I put the dog in a picnic basket and take him away. Teng says Tan-hung doesn't know what to do with her life, if she doesn't have the dog then she will want to raise a child, so we'll simply get rid of the dog. But I don't want her to raise my child, I only think killing the dog is something new to do.

193

We go by subway to the hospital, and we're going to give the dog to the hospital for their experimental research.

I like to travel back and forth in the subway network. I've never taken the wrong train. I know which train goes where. Some people jump into a car and ask in a foreign accent: 'Is this train going uptown or downtown?' I reply, 'This is the shuttle, it runs from Grand Central Station to Times Square and connects with the eastbound and westbound trains.' In New York, giving such definite answers to passengers is one of the happiest things in the world.

The subway is very colourful: skin colour, clothes, the advertisements. Miss Subway shows her white teeth as she smiles down from the blown-up photograph, her name, address and resumé are printed under her picture. 'College graduate, stenographer, likes to eat steak and pickles, hopes to find an ideal man and have five children. Sports: swimming, dancing. Her older brother died in Vietnam. Her younger brother is there now.'

That's what the colours are like.

On the subway Teng tells me how to kill a dog: first anaesthetise it and put it to sleep, give it an electrical shock in the cerebral cortex to keep it alive for a few days, then anaesthetise it again, slit open the chest, stain the cerebral cortex with a special dye and slice it into pieces. Then you can observe changes in the brain cells. When he finishes explaining the process, he changes his mind: we'll go throw the dog off the Washington Bridge into the Hudson River. Of course I agree.

We squeeze our way out of the subway, buy some strong rope, put a few rocks in the basket and seal the lid with some sticks. The dog desperately paws inside the basket, just like he pawed at Tan-hung's bedroom door.

We ride a bus past Central Park, riding along the river, we can see from the distance the high arch of lights on Washington Bridge. The dog thrusts himself against the basket. The basket is propped up against my legs. I can feel the dog's strength and warmth on my legs. The little body in my womb begins moving. Only three months now.

Teng and I are standing on Washington Bridge. The dark waters of the Hudson flow on below. I pick up the basket and weigh it in my hand; it's very heavy. 'Good-bye, little Peking,' I say. We let the rope out a little at a time and lower the basket to the water. The rope jerks in my hand, as it reaches the water it jerks more violently, then slowly grows lax and then is quiet.

Tan-hung has discovered that the dog is missing. She sits silently on the

194

sofa. Occasional noises outside make her sit up and she calls, 'A-king? You've come back. A-king, A-king.'

Her husband says he'll buy her another dog. She says, 'Don't bother.'

Does this face in the mirror belong to me? I want to cry but the face in the mirror is smiling. I'm grinning ear to ear just like a clown.

I write a note to Tan-hung, I killed your A-king, I don't know why I did such a thing I wish I were dead. Mulberry. I tape the note to her bedroom door.

The note is gone she probably read it and tore it up. I can't face her again, but I need her to raise my child.

I tore up the note, Mulberry. You mind your own business. I killed the dog. Tan-hung is not going to raise your child, so don't think about it.

I really have gone crazy. I'm afraid of that other self, her only purpose is to destroy me.

Suddenly I find myself walking between two rows of grey buildings on Wall Street. A strip of sky above. I don't know how I got here and I don't know where I'm going. Wall Street is crowded with men, most of them dressed in dark blue suits and carrying attaché cases. The man in dark glasses is hidden among them as soon as I see him I run away.

The man in dark glasses is walking toward me on the sidewalk I run into the stock exchange and squeeze into an elevator. The man in dark glasses is in the elevator. I can't escape! But he doesn't see me he's only looking at the buttons in the elevator. As soon as the elevator stops I dash out. He is there in the corridor. The man in dark glasses is everywhere. The only way I can get away is to find the women's restroom. I run through the stock exchange but I can't find the women's restroom upstairs I barge into a corridor, from that corridor you can see the world of stocks separated from you by glass: There in that enormous room people wave their hands some look like they are shouting some look like they are making speeches others move their lips some stand face to face opening and closing their mouths, someone else paces studying things he is writing in a notebook some throw scraps of paper on the floor and stamp on them. People run wildly around the room, they all seem drunk and they all look at the wall where an automated sign flashes countless symbols and numbers, right and left, flashing, changing continuously.

There's the man in the dark glasses. I run down to the basement. A

*policeman walks over and asks blandly what am I doing. I stammer that I
have to go to the bathroom. I'm sorry there are no women's toilets, he
says and takes the bunch of keys dangling from his waist, selects a key
and unlocks a door for me. He tells me this isn't a public toilet but he will
let me use it. With another key he opens another door to let a man in a
grey suit go inside.*

*I am safe in the toilet I don't want to leave. The policeman knocks on
the door saying I've been in here an hour and now I must come out I don't
answer. Then there's a click and the door opens the policeman is standing
there in the doorway of the toilet. I thought you went bankrupt playing
the market and killed yourself he says.*

I was the one who went to Wall Street, but you were the one who
returned.

Tan-hung and I left together. She went to Wall Street to see her
husband. I went to explore Wall Street. We took the bus.

'He killed A-king,' Tan-hung said suddenly.

'Who?' I asked.

'Jerry.'

'How do you know?'

'He's jealous. But he's so cold he won't even show jealousy. But I
know he did something to A-king. Jerry is just the opposite of Lu, my
first husband. Lu was very loving and sensitive when he was young.
When the Communists took over he came to America. I followed him
from the mainland to America.' Tan-hung smiled wanly. 'We were
married. When the Communists took over the mainland, he panicked.
His source of income was cut off. He didn't work and didn't study
hard, just loafed around; he wanted to organise some kind of a third
power. After I got my Master's, I found work in New York. He refused
to come to New York; he didn't want me to support him. We were
separated more than a year. When I saw him again, his features had
completely changed; his face distorted by bitterness. He cursed
the world, cursed the times, cursed the Communists, cursed the
Nationalists, cursed everybody. Of course he also cursed me. He
suspected that I'd slept with every man – my boss, my colleagues, even
the doorman! He threatened that he'd destroy me. I almost lost my life.
After that I've been afraid of men who get emotional. I married Jerry
only because he was so cold. He's a second generation overseas
Chinese, you know. He seems to have transcended problems of the
Chinese. The first time we met was at La Guardia Airport. I was sitting
in the boarding lounge waiting for a plane. He walked over and asked

196

me if I wasn't Chinese. He pulled a pile of drafts out of his bag. He said they were articles his father had written. Because they were in Chinese, he didn't understand them. Before, he had opposed his father because he was too stubborn, too arbitrary, conservative. He couldn't stand it. But after his father died, he then discovered he himself had his father's character. He suddenly wanted to know what his father was like; he had been looking everywhere for someone to translate his father's articles into English; he could get to know his father from his writings. He hoped I could help. That was the only time in all these years I ever saw him get emotional. That's how we met and got married.' Tan-hung paused: 'I hadn't been able to decide about raising the child. Now, I've made a decision.'

I looked at her.

'I've decided I don't want the child.'

'I never thought to give the child to anyone.'

She looked at me strangely. 'I've decided to leave Jerry.'

'Because of A-king?'

'No. A-king's death only helped me decide. Jerry and I have always had problems. Right now I'm going to Wall Street to meet him for lunch and talk about it.'

The bus stopped at Wall Street.

I call more than twenty places from a list in a magazine of New York city doctors who perform abortions before finally getting ahold of a Dr Beasley. He says he has a long waiting list of people waiting to get an abortion, he can't see me for two weeks. I say getting an abortion is a matter of life or death for me I beg him to find a way to see me earlier he laughs and says women wanting abortions all say that. He suddenly asks me what nationality I am. I say Chinese. He pauses and says he'll do the best he can to see me within three days, he will first perform an examination at his clinic then perform the surgery the next day at a nearby hospital. He will reserve a hospital bed for me. The total cost will be four hundred dollars.

I call I-po he is very happy that everything has been arranged. He insists on paying all the costs he says he's never loved a woman like this before.

I tell Teng I have decided not to get an abortion. He says I should be completely free to make my own decision. No matter what I decide, he'll support it.

We talk about Tan-hung and her husband's separation. We decide not to tell her about killing the dog. That incident helped Tan-hung make a courageous decision. He says that sacrificing a dog's life to save a human life is very humane. He thinks that constant change keeps us alive. A person changes by his own choice. He also has a decision to make. After he tells me that he becomes silent. I tell him how I teased Jerry and made him blush. He laughs and says he didn't think that Jerry was capable of blushing. He says he has a good story to tell me.

The Action Committee still hadn't decided upon a course of action when they had an internal split. One evening, Teng left the meeting feeling depressed and went alone to the Red Onion bar to drink. He met an American girl there, a baby face with a woman's body. They drank together, danced and then went to her apartment. She lives in public housing on 110th Street. She stripped off her clothes the minute she walked into the room. He made love to her. He fondled her. She moaned. He suddenly thought about the wooden sign at the entrance to the park in the foreign concession in Hankow: CHINESE AND DOGS NOT ADMITTED. He remembered how the foreign policemen used to beat the rickshaw pullers with their batons. He was still fondling the woman. Her moans were coming to a climax. He told her this was their first time and their last time. He never saw the same woman twice. As he said that his caresses became more tender. The woman didn't seem to hear what he had said, she cried and laughed yelling that he was a son of a bitch and that she had never been so happy. She jerked violently, then was calm. But he started to get excited. He entered her. She kept on saying: the bed is a man's magnifying glass, where a man's egoism is magnified ten thousand times. Relax. She didn't want anything to do with Chinese. She went to bed with him because she was bored. He was still moving on top of her. She picked up the phone beside the bed and called another man to discuss male genitalia. She laughed into the phone. Teng yelled as he lay on top of her – what she was saying excited him. At last she said into the phone 'This little Chinaman on me has a huge prick.' Teng suddenly went limp, and rolled off her body. She threw down the phone, saying that this was the biggest insult in her life; she'd never had a man become impotent inside her. Little Chinaman! Little Chinaman! Little Chinaman! She kept yelling at him, who lay naked on the bed. He put on his clothes and left. If he hadn't left then he would have pulled out the sailor's knife to kill her – he always carries his sailor's knife.

I am suddenly standing by the doorway to Number 34 of a large building the sign by the door says 'OBSTETRICIAN – DR BEASLEY'. I push the door open and walk in, the waiting room is packed with women more than half are young women they happily talk about the birth of their child. In addition are several young girls sitting in a corner not saying anything looking very nervous very shy. They're probably only sixteen or seventeen years old just the age I was when I ran away from home and had the adventure in the Yangtze River Gorges. I fill out my medical history form at the nurse's desk and walk over to sit in the corner with those girls. A cat walks over to me.

I see Sang-wa again she is sitting on the ground in the courtyard holding the white cat with a black tail, a strong light shines on her body I can't even open my eyes . . .

I don't know what happened after that.

But I know!

I only went to see Dr Beasley out of curiosity. He looked at my medical history form; examined me; discovered I was already three months pregnant, he couldn't perform the regular method of scraping the womb, he must employ injection of a saline solution. He explained that the special saline solution was injected into the womb, after forty-eight hours the embryo would automatically miscarry. That's a dangerous operation, it's no light undertaking to perform it; not only that, the hospitals in New York City which performed that operation didn't have any empty beds, there were too many people waiting to get abortions, I have to wait another month. In the state of Pennsylvania alone every two hours an illegitimate child is born; he could give me a list of doctors in the suburbs, if I'm lucky, perhaps I could find a suburban doctor who would perform the saline solution injection for abortion.

'I'm sorry! I've already done my best to see you within three days, because you're Chinese. During the war . . .'

'Doctor, which war?' I asked.

'The Second World War. I was a doctor for the army in Burma. I served the Chinese army. With my own eyes I saw so many, so many Chinese die.'

'I want to keep the Chinese in my womb!' I said, smiling. 'I'm happy I'm already past the safety period for getting an abortion. I don't plan to look for another doctor.'

'*Hen hao* – very good.' He spoke in Chinese. 'You're the only person I've seen who is happy because you weren't able to get an abortion. Good luck to China!'

199

I make more than forty long distance phone calls to doctors on the list Dr Beasley gave me. I'm sorry the doctor is on vacation I'm sorry the doctor does not perform abortions by saline injection I'm sorry there are too many people waiting for an abortion I'm sorry the doctor is too busy I'm sorry I'm sorry I'm sorry . . .

I have to go back in three days. I came to New York to see a huge pile of steel, glass and people – my trip wasn't a waste.

Teng is going back with me. His job at the hospital is all set, salary at $15,000 per year. But he's become very silent, only saying 'his heart is in turmoil'.

I call I-po, tell him I couldn't get an abortion. He stammers and can't say anything, finally says, 'Please wait a minute. I want to go to the toilet.' I hang up, laughing.

Tan-hung and Jerry are sitting in the living room discussing hiring a lawyer to prepare the divorce papers. Next week Tan-hung will go to Taiwan for a vacation. Perhaps she won't come back, she says. Jerry gives her a going-away gift, looks like a tube of lipstick, it turns out to be a new kind of camera. Tan-hung can use it on her trip, he says. They even talk about scenery in Japan.

I again make innumerable phone calls. The Family Planning Information Center finally found me a doctor in Worchester, New York. Besides performing abortions in hospitals he also performs saline solution injection abortions at his own clinic every day there are more than ten people who go to his clinic, he doesn't know when he can fit me in he tells me to wait for his call.

I wait by the phone all day.

In the evening I call I-po he tells me not to worry about the cost one thousand two thousand he can pay . . . I cry over the phone he says:

Dear, I love you very very much.

I have only two days left in New York, I must get out and see the sights. I wander around between the steel and glass. Every time I come out of the subway I encounter a new surprise: Radio City, Times Square, Metropolitan Museum, Empire State Building, Greenwich Village, Broadway theatres . . . I've come back to Wall Street!

I come out of the exit of the subway and run into a man. There were bags around his eyes. When you look at him, he doesn't see you at all. Even if a pretty girl walks by, he doesn't see her, either. I smile at him, no response. He is coming out of the New York Stock Exchange and walking along Wall Street. His head lowered, he walks very slowly, amidst the hurrying people he appears very odd. I am curious about him, so I follow him to the end of Wall Street.

I follow him into a cemetery. He sits on a cracked tombstone. It's drizzling. I stroll between the tombs. The words carved on the tombstones are already faded. This is the only quiet place in New York. I circle around the cemetery. The man suddenly stands up. 'What about it!' He suddenly speaks, then looks up at the sky. He turns around, looks at me. I walk over. He says his name is Goldberg. I say he can call me anything. He laughs and invites me to dinner.

We drink in the Oak Room of the Fifth Avenue Plaza Hotel, a trio stops at our table to play the violin. He suddenly 'livens' up, calls me Miura Ayako. He says in his eyes all Oriental women are Miura Ayako. During the Korean War he was fighting in Korea, he went on leave in Tokyo, he had a Japanese woman called Miura Ayako. I say during the Korean War I was a waitress at the Imperial Hotel in Tokyo, my sole desire was to be a movie star. I fell in love with an American G.I.; his name was David. I go on making up stories. He raises his glass and calls me Miura Ayako. I raise my glass and call him David. We click glasses.

When we finish eating, he says I'm an interesting woman. He picks a rose from the vase on our table and gives it to me, kisses me on the cheek saying, 'I lost a million and a half dollars today.'

Dr Johnson in Worchester calls. He says I can go to his clinic tomorrow night at six o'clock, that's his supper time, he must charge double, altogether eight hundred dollars. I say, 'I'm sorry, dear doctor, I want to keep my child. I'm not coming.'

I call Dr Johnson and beg him to see me tomorrow night at six. I'm willing to pay triple the cost I'm an alien with no way out I must get an abortion, he coldly says all right but don't change your mind again.

I ask Teng to drive to Worchester, then drive back home. He agrees.

I call I-po. He is very happy, he says he's been thinking of the way I looked soaking in the tub.

All right, let's see what's happening in Worchester.

Teng and I drive there. All along the way, sunny skies, black clouds, rain, fog, the weather keeps changing. The water flows, the wind flows, the light flows. The leaves are all turning red.

The car races down a slope. On two sides are dense forests. I smell a whiff of smoke, mixed with the fragrance of blood, mud, and fresh-cut grass. I don't know where it's coming from. Teng also smells it. When the car gets closer to the bottom of the hill, the smell of the fragrant smoke gets thicker. We drive to the front of a run-down gate, the smoke is drifting over from the other side of the wooden gate.

Teng and I get out of the car.

The wooden gate is open. Hanging on it is a rusty padlock. Teng and I walk in. The smoke drifts along the path. Several leaves float down, they float down, brush my face, wet and cool. I take off my shoes and walk in the mud; I breathe in deeply the fragrant smoke. Teng says I look so striking. It's getting dark. The smoke gets thicker.

The path turns and reaches the bottom of the valley. Thick columns of smoke shoot upwards; beneath the columns of smoke are mounds of mud; beneath the mud are burning branches; beneath the branches are pigs being roasted. Shadows bob up and down. Are they people or smoke? We can't tell. We stand still, then see they are people; then we see it's a large clearing, to the side are several small wooden huts. A strong beam of light shines from the corner of the clearing, the people are enveloped in the light. The light revolves, light and darkness alternating on the people's bodies like a slithering snake entwining itself around them, twisting and turning, the people begin to gyrate, too. All bright, then plunged into darkness. The people and the shadows sing 'Nothing Is Real'. Teng and I begin to dance along.

Suddenly a gunshot. The people and the shadows are still dancing in the slithering light. The smoke covers the entire mountain valley.

Another gunshot.

Someone says the gunshot came from the other mountain valley. Some people walk up the mountain path. Teng and I follow them, cross the low mountain, and descend into another valley. There is a river in the valley. There is a dense mist over the river. Several policemen and a woman are standing by the river. A strong beam of light shines into the small wooden hut on the opposite shore.

The strong light blinds me I can't open my eyes I see again Sang-wa sitting on the ground and holding the white cat with a black tail. The half-bodied policeman says house check take out your identity cards!

Suddenly a gun fires the bullet whizzes and disappears into the mist. Again the gun fires blindly in the mist. There is no god there is no god there is no god! A desperate voice cries out from the mist. George George don't shoot! I'm here your wife is here! George I love you come home with me! The woman on the bank shouts across the river into the mist. George shouts I have no home I have no home! Gunshots again. George don't shoot anyone put the gun down come home with me! Don't shoot anyone! George! I won't kill anyone I just want to kill myself I can't go on living there's nothing worth living for! George put the gun down come outside the house! I can't see you the mist is too thick! George I love you! George . . . George . . . come on home . . . George . . .

Teng drives slowly and steadily. He gives the glass ball on the seat a few shakes. Snow in the glass ball begins to fall floating above the Great Wall the land near the Great Wall is my homeland. I suddenly think of the abortion. Did I go to the doctor's? Did I kill my child? I talk to myself. Teng pats me on the shoulder and tells me to calm down. He says I've suffered so much he didn't know what to do, but now he knows. I don't need to go to see the doctor anymore, when he says that he stops, then picks up the glass ball again and shakes it saying Mulberry, I want to marry you, we can return to the mainland together, we can work together for the country, we can raise our children there together, our children should be raised on their own land. I stammer and can't say a word we both look at the Great Wall in the snow at last I say: Teng, you're still young you can't marry a woman who's already dead you must not see me again.

When I get home I call I-po. I call all day long but there's no one home. I hope to tell him immediately that I didn't go through with the abortion, I will take all the responsibility.

I call him the next day at noon.

'Hello.' His voice is very soft.

'I'm back! I've kept the child.'

'. . .'

'Hello, are you there?'

'Betty's dead. I need you.'

'Did she really die this time?'

'She really died. Heart attack. Just like that – gone. Now at the funeral parlour. The funeral's tomorrow morning. I'll come over to see you.'

'That's not necessary.'

'Why not? Our problem is solved! I'm happy you kept the child.'

'The child has nothing to do with you.'

'I want my child!'

'Then make one in a test tube!' I hang up.

I call Teng. No answer.

I call Teng no answer. I want to tell him he is my only strength, my reason to go on living, but he shouldn't marry a woman like me. I already owe him so much so much. I try all night to call him but no answer. Where did he go suddenly I am afraid.

I go to Betty's funeral from the entrance to the cemetery I can see I-po standing there. Yellow leaves drift all over the graveyard . . .

I didn't enter the cemetery, but went to Teng's place. His room was locked. His name wasn't on the mailbox anymore. No matter where he goes, he will take it as it comes. In his heart he's found freedom. Because he has decided his own course of action.

I get a phone call from the man in dark glasses. He says next Monday he'll be passing by my area he must question me once again because he has discovered some new problems with my case, before they make the final decision. He must make sure everything is clear . . .

(LONE TREE, IOWA) LAST NIGHT A FREAK ACCIDENT OCCURRED ON A ONE WAY STREET IN LONE TREE. AN EMPTY CAR CRASHED INTO A TREE AND BURNED. A WOMAN WAS FOUND LYING BY THE ROADSIDE A THOUSAND YARDS AWAY. SHE WAS UNCONSCIOUS, BUT DID NOT SUFFER ANY SERIOUS INJURY. SHE IS NOW RECOVERING IN MERCY HOSPITAL. THE CAUSE OF THE ACCIDENT IS NOT KNOWN. THE WOMAN'S IDENTITY IS NOT KNOWN.

I find the news story at the newsstand, I buy a copy for a souvenir after I escape from Mercy Hospital.

EPILOGUE

Princess Bird and the Sea

One day Nu-wa, daughter of Yen-ti the sungod, sets sail to the East Sea in a small boat. There's a storm and the boat capsizes. Nu-wa drowns, but she refuses to die.

She turns into a bird with a blue head, white beak and red claws. She is called Princess Bird and goes to live on Ring Dove Mountain.

Princess Bird wants to fill in the sea and turn it into solid ground.

Carrying in her beak a tiny pebble from Ring Dove Mountain, she flies to the East Sea, then drops the pebble in the water. She flies back and forth, day and night; each trip she takes another pebble.

The Sea roars, 'Forget it, little bird. Don't think that you can fill me in even if you take thousands and millions of years.'

Princess Bird drops another pebble into the sea and says, 'I will do it if it takes me billions and trillions of years, until the end of the world. I will fill you in.'

The East Sea bursts out laughing. 'Go ahead, you silly bird!'

Princess Bird flies back to Ring Dove Mountain, takes another pebble, flies back to the East Sea, and drops it in the water.

To this day, Princess Bird is flying back and forth between the Sea and the Mountain.

Hualing Nieh was born in 1925 in Hubei, China. Professor of letters and cofounder and director of the International Writing Program at the University of Iowa, she is the author of several novels and numerous volumes of short stories and essays, and has received honorary degrees from the University of Colorado, Coe College, and the University of Dubuque. In 1982 she received the Award for Distinguished Service to the Arts from the Governors of the Fifty States. Nieh is currently at work on a two-volume fictionalized autobiography. Her best-known work, *Mulberry and Peach*, has been translated from the original Chinese into five languages.